Truth Stranger than Crucifixion

It was just before dawn, but the fog was so thick it might as well have been midnight. Rob was one curve ahead of me. "My God!" he said as he rounded it.

At first I couldn't see what had startled him. I could see the cross, and it was very impressive indeed. I hadn't realized it had a carved Jesus on it. The fog swirled then and I caught a glimpse of color—green spattered with red. "Jesus!" I said. But I was lying again. It wasn't Jesus, or an artist's depiction of Jesus, or even a prank. There was a man nailed to the cross—a man with white hair, wearing jeans and a cowboy shirt, satin, I thought, with blood all over it.

TOURIST TRAP

Also by Julie Smith

Death Turns a Trick (1982)
The Sourdough Wars (1984)
*True-Life Adventure (1985)
*Huckleberry Fiend (1987)

***Published by
THE MYSTERIOUS PRESS**

TOURIST TRAP

JULIE SMITH

A *Rebecca Schwartz* MYSTERY

THE MYSTERIOUS PRESS

New York • London

MYSTERIOUS PRESS EDITION

Copyright © 1986 by Julie Smith
All rights reserved.

Cover design by Leslie Carbarga

Mysterious Press books are published in association with
Warner Books, Inc.
666 Fifth Avenue
New York, N.Y. 10103
A Warner Communications Company

Printed in the United States of America

Originally published in hardcover by The Mysterious Press.
First Mysterious Press Paperback Printing: August, 1987

10 9 8 7 6 5 4 3 2 1

ACKNOWLEDGMENTS

Heartfelt thanks to Brian Rood for generous and valuable advice; to my editor Michael Seidman, whose good sense and sharp eyes are really very much appreciated; and to a blue-ribbon panel of expert witnesses: Diane Schneider, Cliff Sharp, Dr. Ronald Roberto, Dr. Steve Holtz, and Tom Wendt.

"I'll see your quarter and raise you another quarter."

"I'm out."

"Me, too."

That meant it was my turn to bet. I had two kings and a nine showing, a pair of sevens down. We were playing baseball, a kind of seven-card stud in which nines and threes are wild and fours entitle you to another card. I already had what the others called a full boat, and I had another card coming. That sounds good, but in a game like baseball, as I had already discovered, five of a kind isn't unusual.

Alan Kruzick, my secretary, had three aces showing, though two of them were really nines. To have Kruzick take my last quarter was too much like real life. He was not only my secretary but also my sister Mickey's boyfriend and the bane of my every working day. I was about to fold—true to my conservative nature—when I caught the blue and attractive eye of Rob Burns. He shook his head and pointed to the quarter. Since I'd never played poker before in my life, I thought I'd better take advice where I could get it. Reluctantly, I pushed the coin into the pot.

Alan and I were the only two left in the game, but Rob was dealing. He gave each of us our last card, down. Mine was a two. Excuse me, a deuce. No help, as the others would say. Kruzick put in another quarter.

"I'm out," I said. "Flat broke."

Chris Nicholson, my law partner, put in her two cents: "Why don't you go light?"

"I don't think so."

"That's my boss," said Alan. "The gutless wonder."

That settled it. I borrowed two cents from the pot. "Your quarter and another quarter."

"And another," he said, throwing one in.

There was a three-raise limit, so what could I do but continue to bluff? I took another quarter out of the pot. And Alan turned over a pair of sixes.

"You're fired," I said.

"You can't fire me, I'm pregnant."

Mickey said, "Alan!"

And then there was dead silence.

Our friend Bob Tosi—who was Chris's current flame—got up to get some more wine. Finally, I asked Alan what he meant.

Mickey spoke. "He means I'm pregnant."

"Hey, I'm no sexist. We're pregnant."

"Mickey, honey," said Chris. "Congratulations. I mean, if they're in order."

Mickey squirmed in her chair. "I'm not sure yet." She looked at me as if pleading for mercy. "I mean I'm sure I'm pregnant. I'm just not sure what—Rebecca, I didn't mean to tell you this way."

I could only think of one thing to say and it was the wrong thing: "How could this happen to a counselor at Planned Parenthood?"

Mickey burst into tears. Instantly, Chris put her arms around her. "You poor peach." She looked at me as if I'd hit my own sister. Rob, bless him, put his arms around me. I needed comfort as much as the next person.

"So that's why you aren't drinking," I said, still putting things together. "Mickey, listen, baby, I'm sorry. If it's what you want—"

She broke away from Chris. "I don't know what I want. Yes, I do. I want to go home."

In about thirty seconds, she and Kruzick were out of there. And then Chris and Bob were gone.

"It's midnight," said Rob. "Happy Easter."

For some reason, that broke me up. Things didn't seem so bad all of a sudden. Mickey would have an abortion and everything would be fine. Lots of women did—she should know; she spent her life advising them.

Rob found some brandy and gave me some. "You okay?" he said.

"I think so. I'm a horrible sister, I guess. But for a minute here, I thought we might all be stuck with Kruzick for life."

Mickey phoned then. "Congratulations. I've made up my mind. You're going to be an aunt."

"Listen, Mickey, I'm really sorry—"

"Oh, that's okay. I know it was a shock."

"I'm glad you're not mad. I'll dance at your wedding to make it up to you."

"Who said anything about a wedding?"

"But I thought—"

"Oh, I'm going to have the baby, all right. But I'm not sure want to be tied down."

Alan took the phone from her. He said, "She'll come round," and hung up.

Rob poured me another brandy. "Mom Schwartz is going to ve this."

I nodded. "Thank God she's in Israel."

"How do you feel?"

"Woozy. I think I need a Coke."

He got me one and sat on the white couch across from the one I was sitting on, looking as if he'd be glad to speak if only someone hadn't cut his tongue out. "This is awful," I said. "If I fire him, I'm taking bread out of the mouth of my own niece."

"Or nephew."

"Nephew, yes. At least she can't name him Alan."

"Why not?"

"You don't know?" Rob is half Jewish, but doesn't know the first thing about Jewish tradition. He shook his head.

"You shouldn't name a kid after a living relative."

"It doesn't matter. Auntie Chris'll call it Diddley-bop whatever its name is."

It was true. Chris could never remember names—or common household words—and substituted whatever nonsense syllables came into her head. Somehow, remembering that homely fact made me laugh again.

Rob put a hand on my thigh. "You want to have an adventure?"

"Sure," I said, and got up. Having an adventure was our plan for the next few hours—an odd kind of adventure for a Bay Area native who thought she'd done everything San Francisco had to offer. I'd certainly done most of it in my nearly thirty years—I'd even once played the piano in one of our better bordellos, the dumbest prank of my life. But one thing I'd never done, partly because I'm Jewish and partly because I hate to get up in the morning, was go to the Easter sunrise service on Mount Davidson. This year, Rob, reporter for the *San Francisco Chronicle*, had the honor of covering it—a punishment, he said, for insubordination. He'd enlisted me for company and dreamed up the idea of an all-night poker game so we wouldn't have to wake up. Everyone had accepted, but no one wanted to stay all night. So he came up with a new plan—we'd play poker *almost* all night, the borrow Bob Tosi's van, drive it to the foot of Mount Davidson, and nap for a couple of hours before sunrise.

The van was parked downstairs now, equipped with a blown-up air mattress and sleeping bags. I fed the finny fellows in my hundred-gallon saltwater aquarium, and Rob and I were off.

It was about 2:00 A.M. when we got to Mount Davidson, and very quiet. I, for one, was exhausted, faint even, heavy with alternating thoughts of Kruzick as a brother-in-law and breaking the news to Mom that her baby daughter was going to be an unmarried mother.

Rob set his wristwatch alarm and we snuggled down in each other's arms on the air mattress, still wearing our jeans—this I'd insisted on. If a cop knocked on the window, I wanted a layer of dignity between myself and him.

"Rebecca," said Rob, "if you were pregnant, would you marry me?"

"Maybe—if you were responsible."

I don't know what made me say a jerky thing like that—the strain, I guess—but it made him turn away from me. That was disconcerting enough, but then a dog started howling somewhere in the west. I couldn't sleep at all.

"Rebecca, will you be still?" was all the sympathy I got.

And then, Mickey *was* getting married. I got the invitation in the mail and ripped it open. But it wasn't Mickey after all. It was someone with a French name, and *she* was marrying Alan. Or Alan was her father. Or something. "Mr. and Mrs. Alan DuPis," said the card, "announce the marriage of their daughter, Ani." Ani DuPis. I'd had two years of high school French and I knew how to pronounce it—*Ahnee Dupee*. But who could it be?

The effort of puzzling it out woke me up. That meant I'd been asleep after all. But how could that be? Because I hadn't. But I must have because now I was awake and the dream was right—I did indeed need to pee. I'd heard that people dreamed in puns and now I'd caught my own subconscious at it. There wasn't a public bathroom around, but there was certainly a wooded area—I could simply get out and pretend I was camping.

It was just before dawn, but the fog was so thick it might as well have been midnight; a cop would have to have X-ray vision to catch me in the act. I went behind a clump of bushes, dropped my drawers, and found myself quite unable to answer nature's call. I've been camping all my life, but the art of urination alfresco is something I've never quite mastered. Normally, I scoffed at the patriarchal notion of penis envy, but at times like this I thought the good Viennese doctor may have had a point. I breathed deeply and tried to relax the relevant muscle group. And then there was a crash, followed by a loud "Oof." Rob was out of the van in about half a second. "Rebecca? Rebecca!"

"I'm over here. Peeing." Lying, actually. By then I was standing up and tugging on my zipper; my bikini briefs were caught in it. No time to straighten it out then; I pulled my sweater down as far as it would go and nipped out in the open. Rob was already running up the hill. I caught up with him and we kept running. There was more noise up ahead, some sort of scrapings, so we figured we were headed in the right direction. We could see about two inches in front of us.

We ran for about a week and a half—why, I'm not sure. The "oof," I guess. Perhaps someone was being attacked under the giant cross at the top of the mountain. On the other hand running, even uphill, just before dawn in an eerie fog, with the smell of eucalyptus pungent in our nostrils, wasn't the worst way to spend Easter morning. But I was getting tired. Rob was one curve ahead of me. "My God!" he said as he rounded it.

At first I couldn't see what had startled him. I could see the cross, and it was very impressive indeed. I hadn't realized had a carved Jesus on it. The fog swirled then and I caught a glimpse of color—green spattered with red. "Jesus!" I said. But I was lying again. It wasn't Jesus, or an artist's depiction of Jesus, or even a prank. There was a man nailed to the cross—a man with white hair, wearing jeans and a green cowboy shirt, satin, I thought, with blood all over it.

2

A ladder was lying at the base of the cross, along with a rope. Somewhere quite near, a large animal scuffled in the brush and began to run, off to our left. Rob's head swiveled toward the noise, then back to the cross. "He might not be dead," I said, meaning the man on the cross. But his chin was on his chest and his eyes were staring open. And the running animal was, by now, clearly a two-footed one—no dog or deer ever crashed through brush quite so clumsily. Rob followed the noise, leaving me staring at a corpse.

But how could I be sure it really was a corpse? To my regret, I had some experience in these matters, but no expertise. If he wasn't dead, I couldn't just let him hang there. That was my first thought, I guess, but it was more or less subconscious. Consciously, all I could think of was how mad I was at Rob for leaving me alone.

The fog had lifted suddenly and I felt very naked. Maybe the person Rob was chasing wasn't the killer. Maybe it was just some derelict, or even a solid citizen who'd come early for the sunrise service, like us. Maybe the real murderer was lurking about, and now I was all alone. I was terrified.

It was all I could do not to turn around and go running right back down the hill, but I still wasn't sure the man was dead. I had to do something; or so my pathetic excuse for reasoning went. With quite a lot of effort, I lifted the ladder and leaned it against the cross. Then I started climbing up, about as distasteful an activity as I've ever undertaken. Not only was I frightened of any long-legged beast that might be in the neighborhood, I wasn't too keen on ladders at the best of times. I took it slow and easy, breathing deeply on each rung, not courting hysteria by looking down. "Hold it right there!" said a female voice. I slipped off the ladder, knocking it over as I fell.

"Oof!" I said as I landed and rolled to the right, so as not to end up under the ladder. I realized as I did it that what I'd surely heard a few minutes ago was someone making precisely the same sort of wrong move.

I raised my hands over my head, outlaw fashion, and turned, sitting up, to see who'd captured me. I was expecting a policewoman, maybe; I hadn't really thought about it. But my nemesis was a scrawny woman in her thirties with straggly brown hair and no makeup. If she'd paid $2.50 for her outfit at the local Goodwill, she'd been robbed. One hand was in the pocket of a tattered ski jacket, and there was a bulge in the pocket large enough to be a gun. Or a beer bottle. I was betting on the latter. She took a step closer. "Are you hurt?"

I shook my head, too stunned to speak.

"Stand up."

I did, and took a step toward her, still holding my hands up. She moved back, but not before I caught the reek of alcohol. "That's not really a gun, is it?"

"Stand back!"

I moved forward again. "If that's a gun, let me see it." I can't really explain why I wasn't terrified, except that the woman seemed so frail. Even if she had a gun, she didn't look as if she'd have enough strength in her trigger finger to use it. Or maybe I could smell fear, like an animal. They say you revert to a primitive state under extreme stress. And this was extreme stress. I'd just discovered a body on a quiet Easter morning, been deserted by my own true love, fallen off a ladder, and was now being threatened by a ragamuffin who was either drunk or had recently been drunk. But that wasn't the worst of it. I was in very real danger of wetting my pants. I was not about to brook any nonsense.

"This is a citizen's arrest," said the ragamuffin. Only it came out something like, "Thish ish a shitizen's arresht."

I giggled. Disrespectful, perhaps, in the presence of a corpse, but I couldn't help it. Thish was ridiculous.

The woman waggled the thing in her pocket. Somewhere not far away, I heard a car start up.

"Come on," I said, and put my hands down by my side. "Let's talk it over." I reached out my right hand, palm up, like cops do on TV when they've cowed the bad guy and he's ready to release his hostages. The woman should have put her beer bottle or gun or whatever it was peacefully in my paw, but instead she whapped my hand with her weighted pocket. Maybe it really was a gun. It certainly hurt enough.

Without thinking, I drew back the injured member and used it to bash her. It *is* true about those primitive instincts. I bashed her and then I got her in a sort of half bear hug with the other arm. And then I found out how frail she was. She grabbed me with her free hand, kneed me in the stomach, and jerked me down to the ground.

I pulled her hair. That gave her the idea of pulling mine. My face was very close to hers and she positively stank of booze. If I didn't wet my pants, I was certainly going to throw up. And that made me mad.

I started kicking, not really aiming, just flailing out. She started kicking, too, and we were banging up each other's shins pretty well. My right arm was under her body, which felt a lot heavier than it looked. I tugged, trying to get it out, thinking I could use it to push her away. But she wasn't budging. All of a sudden her grubby hand slammed down over my face, grinding hard.

"Ladies! Ladies, please!" said a gentle, rather cultured male voice. Through the ragamuffin's fingers, I saw another hand cover hers, a black one, and suddenly she was off me, standing up, writhing to get away, but firmly held by an elderly gent in a cream-colored suit.

"Thanks," I said, and sat up, getting my breath back.

"Easy. Easy now," said the black man, and the woman relaxed. I didn't blame her. He was a very reassuring sort of chap.

"Her pocket," I gasped. "She may have a gun."

"I don't have no gun." The woman's voice was sulky. She pulled out a beer can. (I'd been partly right, anyhow.)

Heavy steps pounded toward us. "Rebecca—what's going on?" yelled Rob. I got up and fell into his arms.

"Did you catch him?"

He shook his head. "He had a car. I heard him leave, but didn't get a glimpse of him or the car."

"People, people, will someone help me get to that poor man?"

The well-dressed black man, apparently undaunted at coming upon three maniacs and a probable corpse, was trying to jockey the ladder back into place. The minute his back was turned, the ragamuffin started to run. I tripped her. Not a civilized act, but I was still in my primitive state. She hit the ground cursing. I tried to help her up, but she flailed out at me.

"Rebecca!" Rob was shocked.

"She claimed she had a gun—"

I stopped in midexplanation, the sound of sirens drowning me out. I looked up again at the man on the cross. The sun wasn't up yet, but the fog had lifted enough so that the corpse must now be visible—perhaps some newspaper carrier or other early riser had called the police.

"Young woman," said the black man, "your fly is open."

"Who are you?" asked Rob, as I pulled my sweater back down.

"I am the Reverend Ovid Robinson of the Third Baptist Church. I am to give the sermon this morning. Who might you be, sir?" He didn't extend his hand and I didn't blame him.

But the opening was all Rob needed. He took over immediately, suddenly the reporter on a story, the self-appointed authority in charge. Quickly, he introduced himself and me, explained our presence, ran down the discovery of what was almost certainly a body, and was about to turn to the ragamuffin when the Reverend Mr. Robinson interrupted. "Very well, Mr. Burns. Now will you please help me do something for that poor man?" He pointed up at the cross. He practically had to yell to be heard above the approaching sirens.

"He's dead," said the ragamuffin. "Look at him."

The sirens stopped suddenly and we could hear running. Mr. Robinson must have realized the belated rescue was better left to the cops. He stepped away, relinquishing authority to the resident newshawk.

"What's your name?" Rob asked the ragamuffin.

"Miranda."

"Miranda what?"

"Miranda Warning." She cackled as if she'd just delivered the punch line of a knock-knock joke.

Rob let it go. I knew what he was thinking. He could get her name from the cops, but maybe not her story. He had to work fast. He went for shock tactics, nodding, hard-boiled fashion, toward the cross: "Did you kill him?"

"Hell, no. I hid in the car; on the floor in the back seat. You know where that two-timing sucker went? The Yellow Parrot. You know it?"

Rob nodded. "Gay bar."

"The sucker was a faggot, all this time. I should have known, the way he treated me."

"He went to the Yellow Parrot and then what?"

"I don't know."

"You don't know? What do you mean you don't know?"

She shrugged. "I fell asleep. I brought a six-pack along, just in case. I drank it up, waiting for him, and then got another one. When I woke up, I was still in the car, parked down the hill. I heard a noise and came up here. I thought she killed him"—pointing at me—"so I tried to make a citizen's arrest."

"What's his name?"

She didn't answer.

"Come on, the cops are going to know in a few minutes, anyway."

He was being too hard on her, I thought. I put a hand on his arm, but he shook it off. He walked down the path a little way, trying to get a glimpse of the first cops, hoping to figure out how much time he had, I guess, and then he walked back toward us. "Miss Warning. Why not tell us his name?" He was staring straight at her, trying to fix her with what passed for a steely gaze, but was really sort of a cobalt one, and he was paying no attention to where he was going. Which was how he came to twist his ankle and fall flat on his face.

I took a step to help him, but caught movement out of the corner of my eye. Miranda was off—off to the side, crashing through the brush. I forgot about Rob and went after her.

She was better at it than I was and seemed to know a few paths hidden in the bushes. But I was aided by a fall on my tuchas that resulted in a prolonged slide of twenty feet or more. Back on my feet, I dusted myself off and went after her again. I could just see her now. I was definitely gaining.

"Freeze!" The voice came over a megaphone. "Police! Freeze or we'll blow your head off!"

Heads. They should have said heads, I thought. Or could they see only me? Miranda didn't freeze and neither did I.

And then there was an awful noise. A noise like a hundred-cannon volley.

I hit the dirt so fast I got a mouthful of it.

I heard Rob yelling, "Don't shoot! Don't shoot—it's Rebecca! Martinez, you jackass—that's Rebecca down there!"

Martinez. Oh, no. My least favorite cop. And now Rob had called him a jackass. Martinez would probably take him in for assaulting an officer—good thing he had his lawyer with him.

"If you're down there, Miss Schwartz, stand up and put your hands over your head."

Put my hands over my head! Martinez *was* a jackass. Why did he have to treat someone he knew to be an officer of the court like a common criminal? But this was no time to give him a lesson in manners. I stood up and put my hands over my head.

"Now walk back up the hill."

He was doing it just to be a jerk. He could plainly see who I was and now he was making me walk back up the hill with my hands over my head. I wasn't going to do it, that was all. I lowered my hands.

"Hands *up,* dammit!"

It's a national disgrace that our criminal justice system can't attract a better class of public servant. I take that back—it does, of course—I have every idea there are literally thousands of fine, dedicated, very intelligent police officers abroad in this great country of ours. I don't know why I have the bad luck to keep running into Martinez and his lackluster sidekick, Inspector Curry. I put my hands back up and shouted, "She's getting away!"

"Who, Miss Schwartz?" Martinez yelled in a tired voice. "Exactly who is getting away?"

What was I going to say? Miranda Warning? Did I want the entire San Francisco Police Department laughing in my face? I kept my mouth shut and marched; at least I did for about ten steps and, as I marched, a meditative state came over me.

That and something else. And then a third thing—a really foolproof idea for getting the best of Martinez.

I dropped back down in the bushes.

"Miss Schwartz, what are you doing?"

"I'll be along in a minute, Inspector."

"What are you *doing*, Miss Schwartz? Answer me!"

Good. He couldn't see what I was doing, which was fiddling with my zipper.

I answered in my sweetest voice: "Relieving my bladder, Inspector."

I took my time about it, too. And then I sauntered up the hill, arms swinging casually by my sides. Martinez seemed to have lost his train of thought about my keeping my hands up. Short attention span, I suppose.

3

Martinez and Curry took us to the Hall of Justice, of course, or rather, they let us go in our borrowed van, which meant that we had a few minutes alone, of which Rob took full advantage to rib me about resorting to bathroom jokes. I was the least bit sheepish about it, but the truth was, it had worked. I'd nonplussed that creep Martinez, and I could tell Rob was proud of me, whatever my tactics.

I had another great moment after I got up the hill, too. Martinez said again, "Who is getting away, Miss Schwartz?"

Since I'd turned the advantage to myself, when I answered, "Miranda Warning," he was the one everyone laughed at, not me.

He got me back at the Hall, though. He made me wait hours while he interviewed the Reverend Mr. Robinson and Rob. (Miranda, of course, had gotten clean away.)

The man on the cross was definitely dead. He had no identification on him, we learned, and he had been shot in the chest, probably fatally, before he was hoisted up by the rope and nailed to the cross. Martinez deduced the part about the timing because a live person would hardly have stood still for it.

Martinez managed to keep us around, what with one thing and another, until about the time church was letting out for most Easter worshipers. I was all for falling asleep in the car on the way home, but Rob wanted to talk. What did I make of Miranda Warning? he wanted to know.

I summoned my meager resources. "From her outfit, I'd guess she lives in the Tenderloin. She was about half drunk—slurring her words some of the time, but not always, which probably meant she could control her speech when she thought about it. Which argues she's had a lot of practice at it. Which, along with her emaciated appearance and, once again, style of dress, indicates she's probably an alcoholic and pretty much of a derelict. If I had to look for her, I think I might try a Tenderloin doorway."

"Your basic bag lady?"

I reconsidered. "One step up from that, I think. Maybe not a doorway. A flophouse, perhaps. But here's something funny—the dead man didn't look at all like a derelict."

"And she said he was her lover."

"She didn't actually say that, but she certainly implied it. Maybe he was a john. Maybe she's a prostitute."

"She wasn't dressed like one."

"No, and the way she talked, the guy didn't really sound like a john. So scratch that. And me. I'm dead." I yawned.

Rob stopped the van in front of my house.

"I'm setting my alarm for Tuesday," I said. "Give me a call about then."

I went in and fed my fish, silently thanking the God of my people, whom I sometimes invoked when it was really necessary, that Mom and Dad were in Israel. Otherwise, my phone would ring the instant Mom heard about the murder on the radio.

Instead it rang three hours later, about a day and a half

before I felt up to answering it. I reached for it and got a dial tone. The door. It didn't even sound like the telephone—I must have been in a coma. I staggered to the intercom: "This better be good."

"My name is Michael Anthony and I have a check for you— for one million dollars."

I sighed and pressed the downstairs buzzer. It was Rob's voice. "I lied," he said, as he came in. "Really I represent the William Morris Agency. I'm on a nationwide talent hunt and . . ."

"Don't tell me. They're remaking *Gone with the Wind* and want me to play Scarlett."

"*Inherit the Wind*, actually. We thought, what with the feminist movement and all, we'd get a woman to play Clarence Darrow. One of our people caught your act in court."

"Oh? What did he see? My opening statement? Perhaps my final summation?"

"He didn't say."

"What *did* he say?"

"Said you had great tits."

"Oh, hell. I'm tired." I plopped down on one of my white sofas, hoping Rob would join me. Instead, he went in the kitchen and put on water for coffee. "Listen, I need help."

"Mmf." My eyes were closing.

"The cops found a wallet in a wastebasket near the edge of the park, and it belonged to the man on the cross. Driver's license identifies him as Jack Sanchez. A tourist from Gallup, New Mexico."

"Tourist! He didn't live here?" My eyes opened.

"Tourist: a person who makes a tour. Not a person who lives here."

"Miranda made it sound like she lived with him."

"Maybe she's a tourist, too. Sanchez arrived day before yesterday."

"She's not a tourist. She must have lied."

"I think we should check her story out. Drink this." He curled my fingers around the handle of a coffee cup.

Resigned, I sat up and took a swig. "You think *we* should check her story out. You've been a reporter for ten years, right?"

"Eleven."

"And suddenly you need me to help you. Now which of my many talents is suddenly indispensable?"

"Like I said, you've got great tits."

"Tits." I was mystified. "You need something to stare at while you type? A little inspiration, maybe?"

"I need a date for the Yellow Parrot."

I burst out laughing. "Wait till I tell Chris. Intrepid reporter for metropolitan daily won't go to a gay bar without an escort. Forget Chris—I'm telling your boss."

"I thought you might want to come, that's all."

He looked so hurt I laughed again. "Okay, pussycat. Let me get dressed."

He followed me into the bedroom. Emboldened by recent flattery, I pulled off the football jersey in which I'd been napping and gave him a kiss. But he just looked at his watch. "Come on, kid. I've got to make the first edition."

I should have known. A reporter on a story is like a teenage boy on a date: after Only One Thing; except it's not the same thing. So much for my alleged attributes—some guys will say anything to get what they want.

But as I dressed, he nuzzled my neck a little. "I shouldn't have waked you up."

"It's okay."

"You wouldn't have been up all night if it hadn't been for me."

"Really, it's fine."

"And wouldn't have gotten into a fight, and wouldn't have found a body, and wouldn't have ended up spending the morning at the Hall with your least favorite cop."

"To tell the truth, the worst part was finding out about Mickey."

"You need a little relaxation. How about a mud bath?"

"I beg your pardon?"

"Let's go up to Calistoga and have a mud bath. Or maybe a mineral bath and a massage."

"I don't get it—I thought you were on deadline."

"Not now. Next Saturday—we can even spend most of the day there and go wine-tasting on the way back."

"Really?" It sounded like the best idea since portable hair dryers. Maybe it would cleanse the psyche as well as the pores.

"Really. We'll leave first thing Saturday morning."

I gave him another kiss, then slipped on a purple sweater and a pair of black leather pants—if the Yellow Parrot was a leather bar, I wanted to look right.

It wasn't, though. It was just a dark, sad-sack sort of place where a few guys were having a few beers. The bartender had short brown hair with one long curl in the back, punk style. It would have been cute on a twenty-year-old; he was forty-odd. You folks tourists? There's something I've got to tell you about this place . . ." He looked as if he were trying to find a way to break it gently.

"We're from the _Chronicle_," said Rob, and explained our mission. I hadn't been sure exactly how he'd do it—whether he'd pretend he was somebody else or what. As well as I knew him, I'd never thought to ask exactly how reporters worked. As it turned out, it was simple—he just laid it all out for the guy: A tourist had been murdered, found nailed to the cross on top of Mount Davidson, and a witness had said he'd been to the Yellow Parrot the night before.

The reaction was similar to what you'd get if you turned a TV camera on a bunch of kids; people practically jumped up and down trying to get in the act. And we were in luck—the bartender (Jake Nestor—"with an _o_, not an _e_") had been on duty the night before.

"He was wearing a green cowboy shirt," said Rob.

"Older guy? Gray hair?"

Rob nodded.

"Yeah, sure. I saw him. He was here for a couple of hours. Amaretto artist."

"Beg pardon?"

"That was his drink. Amaretto and cream."

"Oh. Did you notice—"

"Man, what an outfit. Strictly Gallup, New Mexico."

"He said where he was from, then?"

"Yeah. Said he was a rancher. They have ranches in Gallup?"

Rob shrugged. "I'm not sure. Did he—"

"Said he owned half the state of New Mexico. Tell me about it, man! He got that satin shirt at the local J. C. Penney's; in the basement, probably. Synthetic City, know what I mean?"

Rob laughed. "Rhinestone cowboy?"

"Didn't even have boots. He was wearing Adidas."

Rob got serious. "Well, he's naked now. Lying on a slab."

That sobered Jake up. He shivered. "Dead. You don' think . . . ?"

"I think he met someone here who killed him."

"Sweet Jesus," said Jake.

"Did he leave with anyone?"

"Omigod. Yeah. He did. There was this other cowbo type . . ."

"Someone you knew?"

"No. He was weird, though. I should have known he wa weird. Terry liked him."

"Terry?"

"Yeah. Terry Yannarelli. Lives around the corner—you ca talk to him if you want."

"Terry liked him," said Rob, "but he didn't leave with him?

"No. That's the weird part. There's guys in this neighbo hood who'd kill to go home with Terry. I don't go in for th clean-cut type myself, but he's Mr. Star Boarder—I give him free drinks every night just to keep him here."

"A drawing card, is he?"

"Regular little belle of the ball."

"But Rhinestone's friend didn't like him."

Jake said, "It's coming back to me now. Terry sent him a drink and he came over and talked. But only for about five minutes. Never seen it happen before."

"Maybe the guy didn't go in for the clean-cut type. What'd he look like?"

Jake got a faraway look, as if trying very hard to remember. Rob prompted: "Good-looking?"

"Damned if I know. He had on shades and a cowboy hat, pulled down."

"Anything else?"

"Beard. Couldn't tell much, really Mystery man Jesus, he must be the murderer."

Rob nodded.

"Come to think of it, he wasn't dressed right either. For the hat. Jeans; that was okay. But he had on this kind of ordinary shirt."

"Synthetic City?"

"I don't know. Just ordinary. Jeez. A murderer. You know what?" said Jake. "Nobody else was interested in that poor dude."

"The murderer?"

"No. Rhinestone. He couldn't attract flies, you know? I should have given him a free beer. You know what about that guy?"

"Rhinestone?" Rob sounded confused.

"No. The murderer."

"What?"

"His beard looked kind of fake."

I almost said, "Synthetic City?" but stopped myself in the nick of time.

We'd drawn quite a little crowd by now, and a buzzing had

started. The regulars had caught on that a man had come into the bar last night and picked up someone and killed him. It was now occurring to them that it could have happened to anyone; that this sort of thing had happened before—and when it happened once, it usually happened twice, and three times. The gay version of Jack the Ripper.

Rob got Terry's address from Jake and nodded, as we left, to the little group of bar buzzers. "Fear stalks," he said.

"Huh?"

"That's my follow story. 'Fear Stalks the Streets; Lunatic on the Loose.'"

"We don't know that. It sounds as if the killer went straight for Rhinestone—I mean Sanchez; he must have known him."

"Yeah, but it'll still make a pretty decent follow."

I bit my tongue to avoid a fight.

If Terry Yannarelli was really Italian, he must have had a nose job—either that or his mother's name was McGillicuddy. He was a regular-featured redhead, but not the freckled kind; he had kind of gold skin that looked as if it had more than a passing acquaintance with a sun lamp. I could see what the guys saw in him. He was wearing only a towel when he opened the door, so I could see pretty well. He had excellent muscle definition, the kind guys get from working out three times a week. He was definitely eager to talk.

"I knew there was something funny about that guy. I told Jake—did he tell you? I knew it. He said it was sour grapes."

"You talked to him for a while?"

"Hell, no—I tried, but he didn't want to talk. Plain wasn't interested. Asked me where I was from and that was about it. I said, 'I live around the corner,' and gave him a wink, you know. That usually gets 'em. Jake thinks they like me because I'm cute, but, really, it's because I'm geographically desirable. The straight ones especially like that."

"The straight ones?"

"You know. The ones with a wife and kids at home—that come to Castro Street once a month or so. They like to g around the corner for a quickie. I'll tell you something—that's my weakness."

"Quickies?"

"Straight ones. I can always spot 'em."

"And this guy was straight?"

"Bet on it. He killed that old guy, didn't he? That's the kind that gets weird. They hate themselves because they're gay, so they want to beat up on gay guys."

"They beat up on you?"

"Sometimes. That's not the part I like. I like the danger."

I spoke for the first time, unable to keep quiet: "But you could have been killed—doesn't that frighten you?"

He shrugged. "I can take care of myself. That's probably what it was, come to think of it—he didn't think he could take me. I knew there was something funny about him."

"One more question," said Rob. "Did he tell you his name?"

"Yeah, now that you mention it, he did. Now, what the hell was it?"

We kept quiet, trying not to interrupt his train of thought.

"Lee, maybe," he said at last.

"You sure?"

"No, but something like that."

"Last name?"

"He didn't say. Listen, you want to take my picture or anything?"

4

And that was how Terry Yannarelli got the fifteen minutes of fame Andy Warhol assures us we will all achieve. Rob sent a photographer over and Terry made page one. Needless to say, so did I, though not my picture—only an account of my having accompanied intrepid reporter Rob Burns on his latest body-discovering expedition.

There were no plane crashes that day, no presidential surgery, and no uncovered civic corruption—indeed no other news of interest except an announcement of an early mussel quarantine. So the body on the cross was the lead story. Neither the Reverend Ovid Robinson nor Miranda Warning was mentioned—omissions I found oddly disappointing, but rereading the story, I didn't see how Rob could have worked them in without digressing. It was a tight, well-told tale, and I wished I weren't in it.

I was greeted at the office by my mother's voice—or at least a first-rate facsimile: "Rebecca. Your father is lying down. The doctor says he may possibly be all right, though no thanks to you."

"Alan, I am now going to count to five—"

"I just don't see why you can't find some nice boy like Mickey and stop tripping over bodies."

"Very good, Alan—you get an Academy Award. Just shut up!"

"You're almost thirty, you know, and your thighs are already getting kind of mushy."

"There is nothing wrong with my goddamn thighs!"

"Nothing three miles a day wouldn't fix." He dropped the falsetto and went back to his normal voice. "You can run with Mickey on her prenatal exercise program. You gotta look good at the wedding."

"I'll accept you as a brother-in-law the day Charlie Manson gets out of jail—that is, if Charlie isn't available."

"Some aunt. Don't you want your nephew to have a name?"

"Sure. Schwartz would be great. Or Yannarelli, maybe. Just so long as it isn't Kruzick."

I stomped past him into my office. I was definitely going to have to work on my attitude. Whether I liked it or not, I figured there was about a fifty-fifty chance I was really going to have Mr. Wonderful for a brother-in-law. Mickey'd shown poor judgment so far; it was too much to hope she was really smartening up.

"Why do I always have to read everything in the paper? You find a body nailed to a cross and you don't even tell your nearest and dearest?" It was Mom's voice again, but now it was coming out of Chris's mouth. She was standing in my office doorway.

"I get the strangest feeling there's an echo in here."

"An echo?"

"We've got to fire Kruzick; you're already sounding like him. What if you start to look alike?"

"My nose is getting longer already." I laughed. Kruzick had a healthy schnoz, but Chris was six feet tall and her nose was proportion; on her it looked elegant. "Who killed that poor man?"

"In the Castro, they seem to think it was a freak who hates gays."

"But you're not convinced."

I shook my head. "I'm not even sure either one of them was gay. The killer—Lee or whoever he is—dumped the beauteous Terry Yannarelli for poor old Sanchez. I think maybe he already knew him. If Lee wasn't gay and had simply arranged to meet Sanchez at the Yellow Parrot—maybe not even knowing it was a gay bar—that would explain it, wouldn't it?"

"You mean they had a date and Terry horned in? But wouldn't that have happened if they were both gay?"

"Yes, but Terry thinks Lee was straight. It could just be ego, but there was a woman on the hill who said Sanchez was her man."

I explained about Miranda, and then Chris left me to a pile of messages from various reporters in competition with the *Chronicle*. Out of loyalty to my true love, I declined to return their calls. Instead, I phoned Rob to brag about my faithfulness—and just happened to ask what was new.

"He was definitely gay. No question about it. Item one—he was staying at the Oscar Wilde Hotel. What does that tell you? Item two—I talked to his family in Gallup this morning. He had never once, not even in junior high, been known to have the slightest interest in females. Even a female horse. Item three—I had his sister poll the whole family and not one of them ever heard the name Miranda."

"So who is she?"

"That would seem to be the key question—but for one. Dinner tomorrow?"

"Sure."

And then I applied myself to my thriving practice. I'd been involved in a couple of murders before and noticed that they played hell with getting my work done. I thanked my stars I wasn't really in the middle of this one. But the next night over

Hunan food so hot I had to drink three beers, Miranda was still on my mind.

We were walking back to my place when I had my great idea: "Suppose she wasn't Sanchez's lover."

"I have been. Haven't you?"

"I mean, she has to fit in someplace. Maybe Lee was her man."

Rob quit walking and stared at me. "Miss Schwartz. You may have something there."

"So maybe she caught Lee with Sanchez and killed him out of jealousy."

"Unlikely. She was too drunk, don't you think? And not strong enough to get him on the cross."

"That's not the half of it. She'd have killed Lee, not Sanchez. At least I would. Kill you, I mean."

He kissed my ear. "Um. Would you? With the knife or the candlestick?"

"The knife. Naturally. But suppose she lied about the way it happened."

"You're brilliant tonight. Like I said, I've been so supposing, haven't you?"

"What if she were Lee's woman and for some reason Lee thought Sanchez was having an affair with her, which he wasn't, being gay. But anyhow, that's why Lee killed him."

"You're drunk."

"Chris says that, according to southern tradition, if you're drunk and get laid, it doesn't count. She says lots of southern women who've been to bed with half the men in the county still haven't lost their virginity."

"So if we make love it won't count?"

"Nope. We'll wake up as pure as Mormon missionaries."

"I just remembered a previous engagement." Sometimes Rob didn't like it when I acted silly.

On the other hand, he did like it when I'd had a few beers and felt like staying up making love far too late on a weeknight. Which was what we ended up doing and why we decided to spend the next couple of nights recuperating instead of seeing each other. So naturally when Rob phoned Friday morning, I assumed he was merely missing me and eager to confirm our mud-bath date. But then I realized he sounded far too excited. "I want to read you something."

"Okay."

"It just came in the mail. I think it's from the killer."

"Read."

He did. "'*Dear Mr. Burns: I'm glad you were the one who discovered the body. You have always been my favorite* Chronicle *reporter, so here is a tip. Look for action at Pier 39.*' It's signed, '*Tourist Trapper.*'"

"Tourist Trapper! Sanchez was a tourist."

"And Pier 39 is tourist heaven. I don't like to think about the implications."

"You really think it's real?"

"I'm afraid I do. You're always hearing about the police getting crank letters, but reporters don't. The last time I remember anything like this was back in the sixties."

"The Zodiac?"

"Yeah. Paul Avery was the reporter who covered the killings—the Zodiac decided Avery'd make a good pen pal."

"The letters ran in the paper. I remember them."

"Yes, but only after extensive conferences with the cops. It was decided that—"

"Don't tell me. The public had a right to know."

"Well? Don't you think that's right?"

"I don't know. Maybe it *is* some crank this time."

"Let's hope. Meanwhile, I've got to spend the day conferring with cops and editors. The last thing I want to do. You busy tonight?"

"Why, no, Rob—I'd just love to go to Pier 39. That's my idea of a dream date."

"Pick you up at seven. We'll make it an early evening since we're driving to Calistoga tomorrow."

Know-nothing easterners with an unreasonable prejudice against what they call "kooks and gays," as if the two groups are really one, should only know about Pier 39, a melanoma on the cheek of San Francisco. As late as 1976, it was indeed a pier; a scant thirteen months later, it was a municipal scandal of a shopping complex that looks vaguely like a misplaced New England fishing village, though some say it's meant to evoke the Victorian era as translated by the Old West. It's "weathered," at any rate, or perhaps it better deserves that term applied to ersatz antique furniture—"distressed." Distressed is certainly the way it makes the natives feel, those of us, at least, who do not operate shops or restaurants within its ticky-tacky confines.

One of us smart enough to know a lucrative thing when he saw it was our erstwhile city supervisor, Dan White, a kook who hated gays enough to gun down his fellow lawmaker, Harvey Milk, known as "the Mayor of Castro Street," along with George Moscone, who was then mayor of the whole city. White was one of the first entrepreneurs of Pier 39, the proprietor of a stand that dispensed baked potatoes to the hungry hordes from the Midwest.

I don't mean to sound bitter, but if you had a blight like Pier 39 in your city, no one would accuse you of sounding like that other Rebecca, either—the one from Sunnybrook Farm. We have other shopping complexes favored by our brothers and sisters from Paris, Tennessee, and Cairo, Illinois. We have, for instance, the Cannery, where canning was once performed, and Ghirardelli Square, where chocolate was once contrived, and I am wholly in support of both of these rehabilitated buck factories. To compare them with Pier 39 is to compare the Tivoli Gardens with Coney Island. The place makes my skin itch, as if it's turned to polyester.

When Rob and I got there, there were almost more cops than tourists—about 3 million of each, conservatively speaking.

"Chief Sullivan seems to have heard about your note."

Rob nodded. "I think he's taking it seriously."

"Are you going to run it?"

"Not now. Why scare people?"

That would normally have been my position, but I found myself arguing. "Why indeed? Wouldn't want to stem the flow of tourist bucks. Even if spending them is hazardous to health."

"But we don't know that. You think we should have gone ahead and run it?"

I thought about it. "No. But I'm beginning to see what kind of back-and-forth goes into these decisions."

"Aha. So you admit it's something more than cheap sensationalism."

"I'm reserving judgment. If something does happen, you can run it then and still have an exclusive."

"And you think it'd be wrong to run it then?"

"Oh, not really. I'm just being ornery."

"Which probably means you're hungry. Let's prowl around a little and then we'll find something to eat."

"Okay. Funtasia or Only in San Francisco Memorabilia?"

"I hate to say this, but—"

"Oh, no!"

"Right. Both."

He steered me into Only in San Francisco. Never, outside of a cattle car, have so many been packed so tightly. It was wall-to-wall with buck-bearers, plunking down for T-shirts adorned with the Golden Gate Bridge and misshapen mugs that said, "I Got Smashed in San Francisco." I took an elbow in the midsection and hollered, "Ouch!"

"What is it?"

I pointed to one of the mugs.

"Right," said Rob. "Let's go."

We did, retracing our ten or so steps in roughly three and a half hours, thereby satisfying ourselves the Trapper, if he existed, would strike there only at the risk of becoming the Trapped. Off to Funtasia.

Here you had your bumper cars, your video games, your skeeball, your video games, your boomball, and your video games. Mirrors everywhere to make the place look twice as big as it was; that funny kind of lighting like they have in casinos that resembles neither day nor night nor dusk nor dawn. And 93,000 kids. A rough estimate, but not entirely off, I think. A true nightmare, to think of the Trapper in here, but so far as we could tell, all was normal.

The Ship's Galley, where hundreds chowed down on Bayburgers, bagels, and Kabuki Yakitori, was dark, noisy, and normal. And so it went. The Trapper, so far as we could see, was not lurking at the Art Fair Outside Gallery (featuring framed San Francisco posters and cute animal pictures), nor at Chocolate Heaven, nor at the Music Box Store. Mostly, we were taking a cursory look wherever we went, not knowing whom or what to keep our eyes peeled for, but the Palace of Magic took Rob's fancy.

Here you could buy fascinating paraphernalia for the childish mind—bald wigs, fangs, frothing blood capsules, glow-in-the-dark face paint, thumb cuffs, switchblade combs, and smoke that came out of your fingers when you said "Abracadabra!" We got so engrossed the Trapper could have trapped us and held us for ransom. I may as well admit it—we bought one of each of the above. (At Rob's instigation, of course. I feel quite sure I could have resisted if I'd been alone.)

Somewhere near the middle of the complex is Center Stage, where a juggler was keeping three chain saws in the air. If anyone had given him the slightest little push, the carnage would have been horrific. But no one did. We walked past the crowd around him, past more stores. But all was serene.

We still had the second tier of the complex to explore—the one where restaurants with a close-up Bay view are crowded in among the souvenir shops. And by now I was so hungry I was as cross as two sticks (a southernism I learned from my Virginia-born law partner). So we went to the Eagle Café, the jewel of the pier and the one authentic Only in San Francisco bit of memorabilia in the whole place. It had green Formica tables with ketchup bottles on them, and the entire restaurant, dating from 1927, had been moved from its previous location to Pier 39 in 1978. We felt almost at home there.

As I demolished my burger, I mused. "Nothing's happening," I said at last. "Why don't we go home?"

"I'll send you in a cab if you like—I feel I ought to stay. It's sort of like a deathwatch."

I shivered.

"That's the news biz. Say the President comes to town to make a speech; theoretically that's the news, but what if he has a sudden heart attack or someone shoots him? Then that's the real news. So you've got to send someone to sit in the bar of his hotel and drink, just in case."

"How boring."

"Not really. The place is always full of other reporters on deathwatch."

"Trading sizzling repartee."

"And topping one another's war stories."

"But the Trapper, assuming he's real, didn't say he was going to strike tonight. It might be tonight, or tomorrow, or six months from now. You can't camp here permanently."

"Listen! What's that?"

I listened. I heard sirens, getting closer. Rob knocked over his chair running out the door.

5

Ambulances were drawing up to the Pier—one after another as if they'd been called to a disaster area. Feeling queasy, I realized I was about to learn firsthand why deathwatches were invented.

Rob was nowhere in sight, but I figured it was going to be no problem to find him. He'd be where the action was. And there was beginning to be quite a lot of action, as paramedics ran up the stairs and rubbernecks followed. If I didn't hurry, there was going to be such a traffic jam I'd get shut out—which was the only thing I could imagine worse than being at the center of the carnage. And carnage it had to be—I'd now counted six ambulances.

Following the crowd, I ended up at a fish restaurant called Full Fathom Five, mentally cursing the management for giving it such a bad-luck name in the first place. Cops had the entrance sealed off and had a path cleared for the paramedics, who were going in with empty stretchers and coming out with full ones. The people on the stretchers were strapped down, and some seemed to be gasping for breath; one young man was screaming. And an elderly man who looked dangerously white was very still.

After the first half dozen ambulances, another four or five came. I was beginning to lose count and not to feel very well myself. The crowd was buzzing, repeating two words over and over, high, low, soft, loud. "Food poisoning," they were saying. "Food poisoning, food poisoning. Food poisoning."

But I didn't for a second think it was. Even a restaurant dumb enough to name itself for a watery grave could hardly screw up this badly. Further, I imagined that food poisoning wouldn't really get into its nastier manifestations until a few hours after one had dined. Also, I knew something no one else in that crowd knew—someone who signed himself Tourist Trapper had written Rob to "look for action at Pier 39."

Not only had Jack Sanchez been a tourist, but San Francisco's Castro district—our gay ghetto—was certainly the hottest attraction in town for gay tourists. Pier 39 was frequented almost exclusively by tourists; as for Full Fathom Five, it was unlikely any native other than its employees and the random health inspector had even passed its swinging doors. If this was the Trapper's work—and I felt sure it was— there was certainly no doubting his intent; he was out to kill or hurt tourists in San Francisco. But why? I couldn't for the life of me figure out what he could possibly have against them.

I spotted Rob and waved him over to me. "Think it's the Trapper's work?"

"It has to be. But I can't get the cops to say so. In fact, I can hardly get a word out of them. All they'll say is that eleven people fell ill after dining at Full Fathom Five."

"Eleven!"

Rob nodded, his face unfamiliarly grave. "You'd think since I told them about the Trapper in the first place, they'd cooperate. But suddenly, it's 'Forget it, Charlie; who needs you?' Next time I'll keep it to myself."

"You had to tell them."

"Oh, I know. But you'd think—"

"You'd think there'd be justice in the world. Guess again, pussycat."

He grinned. "Fine thing for a lawyer to say. Come help me phone in my story."

Rob is one of those rare reporters who can dictate off the top of his head. He tells me all the hawks and hens of the Ben Hecht era could do it—it was just part of the job—but it's now a dying art, technology making it obsolete. He told me about a time when he left a trial to phone in the verdict, getting the booth next to the AP reporter. For some reason, his city desk had put him on hold for a minute or two; by the time he actually got through, the verdict had already come over the wire, phoned in, indirectly, by the guy in the next booth. Now there was no point in rushing to beat the competition—the machines did it for you. But my pal Rob took pride in his craftsmanship, he'd probably have been a lot happier back in the days of *The Front Page*.

I listened admiringly as he was transferred to a "rewrite man" named Kathy, and went into his act.

"Eleven persons were hospitalized last night after dining at Full Fathom Five, Pier 39. Police Captain Michael ('Slim') McGarrity characterized it as 'the worst disaster in the history of the pier.' McGarrity said diners began to fall ill shortly after 9:00 P.M., but he declined to comment on possible causes of the mysterious ailment. Asked whether poisoning was involved, he said, 'I can't say—forgot to renew my medical license . . .'"

That last, I knew, was going to end up on the cutting-room floor. Rob was always putting jokes into serious stories and complaining when editors took them out. He couldn't help it, he said—he was only quoting. But his city editor seemed to believe in certain kinds of censorship—on grounds of "good taste."

I tuned in on Rob again as he was switched back to the city desk. "Listen," he was saying. "You know what McGarrity said after he made that crack about his medical license? He said you didn't have to have one to know it was poisoning—but don't quote him on it. The thing is, it's got to be the Trapper's work. The cops will say so in the morning, just in time for the *Examiner* to get it first; if we don't go with it . . . oh, okay. I guess not."

He hung up. I said, "You guess not what?"

"I guess we'd look like fools if we ran the Trapper's note and it turned out the chef spilled soap powder in the soup or something. So I guess we can't."

"I see what you mean."

"Listen, the police have the place sealed off, but I'm going to wait and see if I can talk to people on their way out. Want to hang around, or will you be bored?"

"I need to move around a little. I think I'll take a walk; I'll meet you back here in a little while."

"Okay." He gave me a good-bye kiss.

I walked mindlessly toward Fisherman's Wharf—I say mindlessly because no one would choose that clogged and congested part of the Embarcadero for a late-night stroll if she were thinking. I had to nudge and elbow my way through clumps of possibly endangered tourists taking carefree ganders at the neon. Ordinarily I would have considered their presence annoying—who were they to get in the way of a genuine resident?—but now I was afraid for them. I found myself looking at their faces, at the way they looked at each other, at the pleasure they took in pointing out the sights to each other. Elderly couples especially; people who seemed to have spent most of their lives together and who now held on to each other for support. I thought of the old man I'd seen being carried out of Full Fathom Five, the one who'd been so white and so still. I wondered if he had a wife, and children and grandchildren.

For the first time in my smug little native San Franciscan's life (I'm from Marin County, but it's all the same), I found myself wondering about the tourists instead of considering them merely economically important nuisances. I wondered who they were and where they were from and what they did there and who wanted to kill them and why. Most of all, I wondered whether they'd be safe, these people who wandered so innocently, so unsuspecting, down the seemingly harmless Embarcadero, stopping to stare at kids in punk garb, listen to a drummer, absorb the exotica they wouldn't find back in Illinois. I was beginning to understand what Rob meant by "fear stalks." I was terrified for these people—and for myself, a little bit. How could the Trapper be absolutely sure of hitting tourists instead of natives?

"Easy," Rob would have said. "Test their clothes for polyester count."

Thinking of Rob made me smile, and turn around and head back toward him. I still had to slither my way through a slow-moving mass of bodies, but at least I had a goal. A well-marked goal at that—a line of police cars was still parked in front of Pier 39. I slithered past the Balclutha, the old square-rigger anchored in the bay, and past the punks and past the police cars; past the first one, past the second, and almost past the third. The cop inside the third was talking on the radio, quite audibly, and to my mind, quite interestingly. He was a macho kind of guy, I'd guess, who just couldn't keep his voice down if there was a chance to make himself sound important by raising it. He came in clear as a foghorn: "Nothing on Zimbardo yet."

I hesitated, hoping to hear more, but the cop lowered his voice, catching on, I guess, that he'd been indiscreet.

Back outside the restaurant, I found Rob winding up an interview with a couple from Oregon. He turned to me: "Nice walk?"

"Productive. How'd you do?"

He shuddered. "It must have been awful in there. What do you mean, 'productive'?"

"Does the name Zimbardo mean anything to you?"

"No. Why?"

"I think he or she might be a suspect."

I told him what I'd overheard.

"Let's find a phone book." His blue eyes were bright with the thrill of the chase. Sometimes I get upset with the newshawk side of Rob, but when he's infused with energy like that he's irresistible. I was getting drawn into his excitement against my better judgment—and not for the first time. Once we'd gotten involved in a high-speed car chase, caused an accident, and one of us had landed in jail by the end of the evening—not, I'm afraid, the one with the bright blue eyes.

"Zimbardo, Zimbardo—" Rob was tracing a finger up and down a page of the phone book. "Art Zimbardo; on Bush Street—let's go."

Zimbardo lived on the edge of the Tenderloin, not far from the Stockton Tunnel. A poor place for parking, normally, but Rob pulled up in front of a fire hydrant, put his Working Press Parking Permit in his windshield, and hopped out. I caught up with him as he was pressing the buzzer for a third-floor apartment. It was a long time before a sleepy voice answered. "Who is it?"

Rob drew a deep breath. I knew what he was thinking: The Trapper would know his name. "Rob," he said finally, and quite as heartily as if he were visiting his mother.

"Rob?" The voice sounded genuinely puzzled. "I think you've got the wrong apartment."

"No." Rob spoke urgently. "You're Art Zimbardo, aren't you? It's important."

"Important? It's not about Lou, is it?"

"I'm afraid it is."

Zimbardo buzzed us in without another word. The hallway was dim; the carpet on the wide, no-longer-grand stairs smelled of feet. As we started to climb, Rob said, "Listen, Rebecca, you'll see it'll be okay. I know I lied, but being from the *Chronicle* has a strange effect. Just withhold judgment a few minutes, okay?"

He knew me well enough to know I hadn't liked the lie, and I could see he was sheepish about it himself. But I thought he must know what he was doing if he said so; if I didn't withhold judgment, at least I held my tongue.

The kid who opened the door had on jockey shorts; his eyes widened, horrified, when he saw the two of us. "Excuse me. Just a minute. Oh, man." And he shut the door again.

I relaxed. I hadn't known exactly what we were getting into, and still didn't, but it didn't look as if we were about to enter the den of a mass poisoner.

The kid came back, dressed and shamefaced: "I didn't know you were bringing a lady." His eyes were nearly black, and they smoldered at Rob. The kid was resentful and angry, maybe about me, maybe something else.

He led us into his living room, obviously furnished by the management. The black plastic of the sectional sofa was torn, the beige carpet hopelessly stained. A tittics Danish-style blond-veneered end table held a dime-store plaster lamp, its paper shade still in cellophane.

"I'm from the *Chronicle*," said Rob, and told Zimbardo our names.

"The *Chronicle*?" Rob fired his first questions fast, not giving the kid time to think.

"Do you work at a restaurant at Pier 39?"

"Sure. Full Fathom Five—I'm a waiter."

"Were you there tonight?"

"No. It's my night off. Say, what is this? You said it was about Lou."

Rob told him what had happened. I watched Zimbardo as he took it in. He was very young, no more than nineteen or twenty, I thought, and would never have a weight problem. He was short, but well muscled, and lean as a fish. He had curly hair, lovely full lips, and those big, black, resentful eyes, coaster-sized, sad and pleading. They made him look deprived and rather desperate, like a child who's forgotten his lunch box. When Rob got to the words I'd overheard near the police car, the kid crumpled onto the sofa. "Oh, man." He held his face. "Oh, man. Lou was there, man. He was there."

"Is Lou your brother?" I asked.

The kid only nodded, didn't speak for a moment. Then: "I gotta get to him. You guys have a car?"

"Yes. But why don't you call?"

"He's got no phone. Just a room over on Jones Street. I offered to let him stay here, but he wouldn't—said he needed privacy after being in the joint."

"Your brother's been in prison?"

He nodded. "Rob, listen, he didn't do it, man. No way he'd do it. Can you put that in the *Chronicle*?"

Rob said, "Shouldn't we go find him?"

"I think he might need a lawyer. I think I better get him a lawyer." He was putting on a cheap vinyl jacket, made to look like leather but succeeding hardly more than the sofa had.

"Rebecca's a lawyer."

"Yeah? You a lawyer, Rebecca?"

"Uh-huh."

We went quickly down the stairs and out to the car. It was only a few blocks to the flophouse to which Art directed us, but this was no time to walk. "But why," I said when we were settled, "does Lou need a lawyer? It's you who works at the restaurant—why would Lou have been there?"

Art looked glum. "I got him a job in the kitchen. Tonight was his third night."

"Oh. Well, maybe he's still there. We should try to call him."

"No, man. He ain't there. There's cops around, Lou ain't." His voice shook a little and I thought his shoulders did, too, under the mock-tough jacket.

Seeing Lou's room, I thought he'd have done better to move in with Art, privacy or no. Surely his last cell couldn't have been much smaller. This one contained only a single metal bed with sloping mattress, nightstand, chest, and plain hard chair. Not a single personal possession in sight except a eat-up TV. I opened a drawer of the chest to assure myself he place was occupied, and was surprised to find socks. Lou adn't moved out, it appeared, but he wasn't home. Art was tarting to lose control of his face. He knew he couldn't cry in ront of us, but the effort of control was turning his pretty eatures into a strained-looking mask.

A car skidded and stopped outside. "This one," someone houted. A someone Rob and I knew. It was the all-too-amiliar voice of Martinez, the last person I wanted to see—or vanted Art to see—right then. Rob and I looked at each ther, to see if we were in agreement. We were.

Rob spoke quickly to Art: "The cops are outside. Is there a ack stairway?"

Art shook his head, pale.

I said, "Let's go up a floor."

It worked beautifully. We went up, listened till we heard Martinez and Curry go into Lou's room, then crept down and ut the door. Silently, we drove back to Art's.

"I've got to phone in," said Rob. "Can I use your phone?"

"You're not gonna put nothin' in about Lou, are you?"

"Of course not."

"The phone's in the bedroom." Art pointed, rather with ride, I thought. I saw what Rob meant about the *Chronicle* aving an odd effect on people. Even though his brother was a only slightly less trouble than Custer at Little Big Horn, ere was something in Art that felt important at being part of news story. He was treating Rob with a kind of proprietary espect, as if he had caught a Bigfoot and tamed it; as if he had his very own living room a kind of legendary monster which the moment was eating out of his hand and might roll over n command; or might rip him to shreds instead.

Bigfoot went into the bedroom. "If the cops come," I told rt, "you don't have to talk to them."

The big eyes took on plate proportions. "I don't?"

"Absolutely not. But call me if they give you any trouble." I ave him one of my cards. It was an odd thing to do—in a way it had an ambulance-chasing feel to it—but I knew Art didn't know enough about lawyer ethics to take it any other way than the way I meant it. I liked this kid; if you want to know the whole sordid truth, I was having almost uncontrollable maternal feelings for him. I didn't want Martinez and Curry taking advantage of him; I wanted Art to know he had a friend.

6

"**I**s Rob Burns there?"
Cheeky question to ask in an 8:00 A.M. phone call. It was
about a nine o'clock press conference at the Hall of Justice.
Martinez was working on Saturday, which meant Rob was,
too—but not all day, in his case. We could definitely still go to
Calistoga. He wouldn't have to write a story about the press
conference because there was no Sunday *Chronicle*. There
was only a hybrid *Chronicle-Examiner* to which each daily
contributed certain sections; the main news section belonged
to the *Examiner*. So Rob could read all about it there; he
needn't go to the press conference at all. But he was going
because he couldn't help himself.

"Come with me," he said. "We'll leave from there for
Calistoga."

I wanted to go like I wanted turnips for breakfast, but it
made sense—if enduring Martinez at any hour of any day
could be said to make sense. He spoke to the media—Rob, an
Examiner woman, and four sleepy-looking broadcast types—

in the second-floor pressroom. An informal setting, to say the least, cluttered and paper-littered.

"A toxic substance," he said, "apparently caused the illnesses of eleven persons who were rushed to San Francisco General last night from Pier 39. The substance . . ."

"What was the toxic substance?"

"The substance was apparently ingested by these persons at the Full Fathom Five restaurant as a result of . . ."

"Oh, come on, Inspector—how could eleven people . . . ?"

". . . as a result of eating contaminated food."

"What was *in* the food, Inspector?"

"That is not known at this time."

"But what does it *do* to you?"

"I do not have those details at this time."

"Hey, how is everybody, anyhow?"

"This morning six of the victims from Full Fathom Five are in satisfactory condition; four are still in serious condition and . . ."

"Wait a minute, that's only ten."

". . . and one man has died."

The dead man was Brewster Baskett, seventy-seven, of Winnemucca, Nevada. He and his wife, Hallie, had been visiting a son and daughter-in-law in the City. Brewster had caught the flu on their first weekend in town, had gone to bed for a few days, and had just gotten up the day before. The jaunt to Full Fathom Five was his first outing after his illness. Hallie hadn't been at all sure he was well enough to go, but he'd insisted. A doctor at San Francisco General thought the poison probably wouldn't have killed him if he hadn't already been weak from his recent illness.

"Inspector, how could such a serious accident have happened?"

"We are currently investigating the circumstances of the incident."

"Do the police think the poisonings were deliberate?"

"That matter is still under investigation."

I was glad I'd come. If ever I thought Rob pushy or impatient in his reporter mode, I was once again reminded that he was the soul of gentility compared with his fellows— particularly those of the electronic media. We'd met for the first time at a press conference—one I happened to be giving—and he was the only reporter there who didn't seem part of a swarm of ants at a picnic. Now he was quiet as his brothers and sisters wore out their vocal cords. Quiet as a mousetrap.

When everyone else had left, including Martinez, he sauntered out to the hallway, taking me along, and stood waiting for the elevator with the nice inspector. When the three of us were aboard, Rob said, "Caught up with Lou Zimbardo yet?"

Martinez was shocked into blurting, "What do you know about Zimbardo?"

"Think he's the Trapper?"

"I don't even know if the Trapper's for real."

"Yeah, but he might be. And if he is, you know about him because I told you. So how about giving *me* a break?"

"Okay, okay. When the first cops got there, he was gone. Out the back door, probably—who knows? Nobody saw him leave, just all of a sudden no Zimbardo. Anything else?"

"Um—humm. Anything new on Miranda Warning?"

"Who?" And Martinez stepped off the elevator.

Rob didn't follow. He was silent on the way back down to the first floor and the walk back to the car. When I'd fastened my seat belt and settled back contentedly, just beginning to contemplate the pleasure of the drive north, he said, "I think I'd better not go."

"To Calistoga? Why not? Aren't you feeling well?"

"It's not that. I just need some time to myself."

"Time to yourself!"

"What's wrong with that? You're always saying it."

"But I say it in advance—when declining an invitation; not when we're already on our way somewhere."

He shrugged. "Sorry. I didn't know in advance I was going to feel this way."

He was driving me home. We were turning onto Green Street now, which meant he'd most certainly made up his mind. I was so hurt I couldn't think of anything to say.

He touched my leg in a placating way. "Are you very upset?"

"I guess I am. I'm kind of numb, actually."

"Rebecca, you're not taking this personally, are you? Because it has nothing to do with you."

"It doesn't?"

"Of course not. I just can't make it this weekend, that's all. How about next week?" He stopped the car in front of my house.

I nodded and got out, not even kissing him good-bye. Upstairs, I sank into one of my white sofas, turned toward my aquarium, and watched, as if it were a movie. I had some truly spectacular fish at the moment—some fairy basslets that I hoped were going to make it. I watched them weaving in and out among plants and other fish, more graceful than any dancer in the Bolshoi. The hermit crabs scuttled comically, for once failing to amuse me. The anemones—my favorites—reached, as always, for something just outside their grasp, reminding me rather too vividly of the human condition. I was watching to stay numb, to get my mind off the way Rob had snubbed me; but it wasn't going to work. He'd said it had nothing to do with me—his sudden need for solitude—but the fact remained that I was the person he'd just said he didn't want to be with.

Of course it was true that we all had needs for solitude, but the perfunctory, sudden way he'd brushed me off, as if he'd just come to a decision, made me think this went a lot deeper. I figured he'd only mentioned next weekend to put off telling me the inevitable—that he was dumping me. I wondered what I'd done wrong. But that was no fun; feeling sorry for myself was more satisfying. While I was doing it, really wallowing quite luxuriously in it, I remembered something that made the wound even nastier—Rob and I had a date that night. We were going out with Chris and Bob and a friend of theirs from Los Angeles.

Rob must have forgotten it in his sudden need for his own company; but had he? Was he intending to go or not? Who cared? It was an excuse to call him. There was a new message on his machine: "This is Rob Burns. I'm away for the weekend, but I'll be back Sunday night if you'd like to leave a message when you hear the tone." I slammed down the receiver long before I heard the tone. Snatching up my gray suede jacket, I went out and got my old gray Volvo and drove to Loehmann's.

Shopping wouldn't mend a broken heart, but it could certainly take your mind off it. After a bittersweet forty-five minutes, I found a nice linen dress for summer, a steal at $125, marked down from $200. A very nice linen dress; gray, like my jacket, my car, and my mood.

Very well then; if shopping wouldn't work, maybe girl talk would. Actually not girl talk. Girl talk is for bawdy lunches with too many glasses of wine; I make a distinction between entertaining adolescent chitchat and having enough sense to seek support in moments of romantic stress from understanding females. Unfortunately, there was an irksome male between me and my understanding sister. Alan was on their tiny porch, having a cup of tea in the sun.

"Hiya, boss. Come to congratulate the groom?"

"You talked her into it?"

"She could never resist me."

"You're not kidding? She's really going to marry you?" I could feel the blood leaving my face.

"Hey, sister-in-law, what's wrong? You don't seem as happy as I thought you'd be."

"Sister-in-law! Oh, help." I leaned against the wall for support.

"Mickey! Mickey! Come out here—your sister's sick."

Oh, help indeed. Two seconds to compose myself and pretend to be happy. One day I was going to murder Kruzick.

"Rebecca!" Mickey came tearing out the door. "Rebecca, what is it?"

I stood up, leaving the safety of the wall, summoning what I hoped would look more like a delighted smile than a horrified grimace. "I was just surprised, that's all. But, sweetheart, I think it's wonderful. I couldn't be more delighted, really—"

She looked absolutely baffled. "Delighted about what?"

"I thought . . . I mean Alan said . . ."

"I've got to get some milk." Alan ran down the stairs and off around the corner.

"*What* did Alan say?" asked Mickey.

"He kind of implied that you two had gotten married."

"Oh. Well, we haven't—want to come in?"

I came in and had a seat on her sofa wicker so that Lulu the cat wouldn't claw it to shreds. Mickey made us some tea and sat at the other end. She was looking well, I thought. Always the leaner and slimmer of the Schwartz sisters—let's face it, the prettier—she was particularly rosy-cheeked and healthy. Pregnancy must be agreeing with her.

"I'm running three miles a day," she explained. "An unmarried mother has to be ready for anything."

"You're really not going to marry him?"

"I don't see why I should, do you? Our relationship is fine the way it is—why spoil it?"

"Because he might want some legal rights to his own child, for one thing. Also because Mom will open her veins if you don't."

"But what about me, Rebecca? What if I plain don't want to get married?"

"Mickey, frankly I don't get this. You're living with the guy

For reasons that I admit have always eluded me, you're in love with him—correct?"

"Yes."

"And you're going to have his baby. So why not marry him?"

"What's with you? You're the last person I'd expect to try to talk me into it—you nearly fainted when he teased you about it. I saw your face—you were as white as Lulu."

At that second, white and beautiful Lulu jumped into my lap. "I'm not trying to talk you into it. I'm trying to figure all this out."

"Okay. I guess I'm not entirely sure of him."

"Not sure you love him?"

"Oh, come on—no one could possibly live with him if she didn't love him. It's not that exactly."

Suddenly I got it. "You're not sure you love him enough."

"That's it. That's exactly it. I love him, but . . ."

Alan spoke, coming in the door: "But will you still love me when I'm sixty-four? Sure you will, babe. Look at this face—who wouldn't love it? Rebecca, don't answer." He walked past us, put the milk in the fridge, and walked out again. "I'm going to play basketball."

"He does have a certain boyish charm," I said, scratching Lulu's ears. "If you like six-year-olds."

Mickey nodded. "It might wear thin after twenty or thirty years."

"Make that twenty or thirty minutes. I figure if you can get past an hour, you might as well marry him."

Mickey smiled. "How are you and Rob doing?"

"Ouch. When you change the subject, you don't mess round."

"Uh-oh. You two are fighting?"

"I think he's dumped me, actually."

"Whoa. Tell all, starting at the beginning."

I did and it took a surprisingly long time—I had to explain out the Trapper and the poisonings and the press conference before I could even get to the good-bye scene. "Not good-bye," said Mickey. "No way."

Her theory was simple—Rob, though basically a prince of a fellow, simply turned into a sort of hairless werewolf when he was on a hot story, forgetting friends, loved ones, social conventions, obligations, and dates in his avid pursuit of the people's right to know. No doubt he hadn't dumped me at all, he'd be back soon, and wouldn't even notice he'd been missing. In short, she thought I was upset about nothing.

I felt better. "I suppose you're right," I said. "I should be glad he's not Alan."

"Oh, lay off Alan. He still might end up being your brother-in-law."

"You're still sure about the baby?"

"Absolutely."

"Funny world, isn't it? No wonder Mom has trouble adapting."

Mickey shook a finger at me. "She'd be a lot happier if you'd just dump that blue-eyed half-breed."

I left, laughing as I drove home. Poor Mom. She certainly did have trouble adapting. While it was certainly true that Rob was only half Jewish and that was only half good enough for her, she'd admit it in the same breath she endorsed the Ku Klux Klan. Even to herself. Mom was a compassionate, caring, politically correct liberal, with heart perennially bleeding—and eight or ten nasty prejudices she didn't even know she had. She was perfectly aware, though, that she didn't much like her older daughter going out with Rob; and remembering that made me feel protective toward him, brought him back into my good graces.

Until I got home, that is, and found the swine hadn't called Calling him, I got the same old message: He was gone for the weekend. I supposed I'd better believe it, and better resign myself to going to dinner alone.

7

I met Chris and Bob at the Hayes Street Grill, one of the very few of the myriad newish eateries specializing in "California Cuisine" that, to me, managed to pull off the old San Francisco style—friendly, unpretentious decor (dark wood, white tablecloths) and a nice piece of fish. At the old-style restaurants—joints with names like Jack's, Sam's, John's—your fish was simply grilled, and came, as likely as not, with thick, tempting fries. At the new joints, it had to be mesquite-grilled or, better yet, grilled over Nubian plumwood and garnished with an understated sprig of vitamin-packed cilantro. The fries were thinner, very crisp, very now, very today. Rarely were the customers grilled, but that night was an exception.

The others were bellied up to the bar, waiting for a table. When I came in alone, Chris raised her eyebrows. "Where's Rob, darlin'? Parking?"

"I'm afraid he couldn't make it."

"He's not ill, is he?"

"I don't think so. He just . . . we just . . ."

"You had a fight!"

"No, it's not that. He just wanted—I mean, he had to do something else."

"You're sure nothing's wrong?"

"Everything's fine. Really."

Bob cleared his throat: "Chris. Give her a break, okay?"

Bob's outspoken style had turned Chris off at first, but she'd learned to respect it—especially after he'd joined a men's consciousness group and done some serious work on his innate male chauvinism. He was now a budding feminist, but with a commanding way about him; Chris liked that a lot.

At the moment, I was grateful for it. I was still wearing the black velvet trench coat my mother had given me, and was beginning to perspire in it. I was aware, too, that my cheeks were flushed with the extreme discomfiture of having had to reveal a very shaky love life in front of a most attractive young man—Bob's friend from Los Angeles, who was tall, well dressed, and single, judging from his naked ring finger.

"Jeff Simon," said Bob.

Jewish. (If you cared about such things.)

"He's with Backus and Weir."

Another lawyer.

Cute—very cute. Both the situation and Jeff. He had brown crinkly hair, light brown eyes, and regular, not-quite-handsome features. He wore a dark gray suit that didn't hide the fact that he was a man who took regular exercise seriously. He was smiling—whether at me or my predicament I couldn't tell.

"Tosi," said the maître d', and showed us to our table.

Jeff was an entertainment lawyer, a job that entitles its holder to dine out anywhere in the country—but particularly in San Francisco—on riveting tales of the follies and foibles of the famous. I say particularly San Francisco because we San Franciscans do, in accordance with Angeleno myth, have a bit of a small-town complex. We care not a fig for emulating eastern sophistication, but desperately want to feel ourselves a part of what we Californians really think makes the world go around—The Industry, as they call it down south. We don't like to admit it, but we love nothing more than movie gossip. We thrive on rumors of who's gay and who's bisexual, who's stopped beating his wife, who's pinching whose bottom, who's burnt out on what drug. But with the snobbery bred of envy, we love best the stories that make Hollywood look silly and gauche and garish. Jeff had a million of them, and being a transplanted New Yorker, with his own geographic bigotry, told them with the same wicked delight that a native Californian might have. I was quiet for a while as he regaled us.

"So somebody at this studio got the idea to do *Catcher in the Rye*—not bad, huh? It spoke to the last generation, why not this one? Everybody thought it'd be a welcome relief from vampire demolition derby flicks—sort of a thinking kid's movie. My client was very timid and insisted I go with him for a meeting. This studio exec says, 'It's hot, like, it's the *E.T.* of the eighties, only the alien's a kid, see? But we gotta make it eighties, not sixties, you know?' I pointed out that we were really talking fifties, and the guy looks at me like I'm crazy. 'Fifties?' he says, like this is a new concept. The guy's head of the studio and only twenty-seven years old. So I let it go, and he says, 'Let's do it like *Miami Vice*, or better yet, *Repo Man*. It's gotta look like MTV, you know what I mean?' So we say we'll think about it and we leave, our heads kind of reeling.

"We don't know what to think, maybe the guy's burnt out on coke or something, but he says he'll set up another meeting. However, he doesn't and finally I call him. And guess what? The studio's already sitting on a proposal for *Catcher in the Rye*. Somebody else got the idea five years ago, only they never made the movie for certain reasons that I'll reveal in a minute. By now this baby mogul's completely turned around—convinced the five-year-old idea is the way to go. Here's what it is: an animated version in which all the characters are dogs."

Bob said: "Give me a break!"

Jeff held up a hand. "This is the verbatim truth. I am not making up one word."

"I suppose," said Chris, "they're going to call it *Fido*."

"*Dufus*. Can you guess what the hang-up is?"

"The S.P.C.A.," said Bob.

"The J. D. Salinger Anti-Defamation League," said Chris.

I said, "Salinger."

"Almost right. No one in the entire studio, located in fabulous Hollywood, the chutzpah capital of the world, has been able to work up the nerve to approach him."

He had me pretty well charmed. I could easily have listened all night, but eventually he started, as politeness demanded, to draw me out. I talked about what was on my mind—the Trapper's note.

It couldn't yet be published, but there was nothing wrong with four pals chewing it over along with the thresher shark. Jeff thought it was hokum—the work of an attention-seeking nut. He also thought the wine a little fruity, the fish a trifle overdone. On the last two points, he was right, perhaps—and yet both were delicious. If it had been left to me, I simply would have enjoyed my dinner rather than dwelt on it. He was a man with a very analytical mind.

"But something did happen at Pier 39," I insisted. "How do you explain that?"

"Simple. This Zimbardo character read about your Sanchez—the man on the cross—and cashed in on it."

"But why? What did he have to gain by writing the note? He had everything to lose, it seems to me—he put the cops on guard; they might have stopped him."

"I expect he just wanted a little attention. I can identify with that—can't you?" He looked straight at me with those light brown eyes, and I won't pretend I was entirely unmoved. I think perhaps I blushed, because suddenly he got very flustered, tripping all over himself with excuse-mes and I-didn't-mean-it-that-ways. Which naturally caused both

Chris and Bob practically to roll on the floor. Unnerved as much by their merriment as by Jeff's blatant flirting, I stayed a polite fifteen minutes after the coffee arrived, and beat a cowardly retreat. I wasn't used to being out on my own; it felt so good it made me nervous.

But if I thought I was getting away that easily, I was quite mistaken—Jeff insisted on walking me to my car, keeping up a running commentary on what a pleasure it was to meet another lawyer, and how very difficult it was to meet Jewish girls (why, I can't imagine—I could have introduced him to fifteen or twenty), and how very nice it would be to see me again. I stuck my hand out when we got to the Volvo, just in case; obediently he took it, kissing me gently even as he shook it, leaving me thinking Rob wasn't the only shrimp in the bay. And hating myself for thinking it. But dammit, Rob *had* deserted me.

The deserter phoned the next morning, about the time I'd finished reading my Sunday Exonicle (combined *Examiner* and *Chronicle*), learning that it was now official: The police were seeking kitchen worker Lou Zimbardo in connection with the Pier 39 poisonings. Rob's voice was the croak of a beaten man, but I managed to control my sympathy for a moment or two: "Oh, Rob, how are you? Did you have a nice time alone?"

"Not too good, to tell you the truth. Things didn't work out quite like I hoped."

"Oh?"

"I got mugged."

End of control: "Mugged! Are you hurt? Is anything broken? Oh, pussycat! Please say you're okay!"

"I'm okay." But he sounded so pathetic I had to fight back tears.

"You sound awful."

"My jaw's swollen. They hit me a little."

"Oh, Rob! I'll bring you some soup."

"Soup!" He whooped. "You sound like your mom."

"I didn't mean chicken soup," I said, very dignified. "I had in mind some thick and nourishing split pea. In the event of a concussion or broken leg, of course, I'd have offered to grill you a steak. But I thought with a bruised jaw you might not feel like chewing."

"I don't. But I don't feel like sipping either, thanks. I'm sorry I teased you."

"It's okay. Or will be if you tell me what happened."

"I guess I'd better. I sort of lied yesterday."

"Oh." Ouch.

"It wasn't that I had to be alone, exactly. I had some work to do."

"Is that all? Why didn't you tell me?"

"Because I knew you wouldn't approve. You see, I think Miranda Warning is the key to this whole Trapper thing; so I went to find her."

"How did you know where to look?"

"I didn't. I just went to the Tenderloin and asked around—remember, we thought she must live there?"

"Did you get anywhere?"

"Mugged."

"Poor baby."

"Stupid baby."

"No sign of Miranda?"

"Not a trace."

"You're sure I can't bring you something?"

"Positive. I'm about to break the world's indoor snoring record. How about lunch tomorrow?"

I didn't like it at all—I wanted to see him desperately, to make sure he wasn't maimed or disfigured, or if he was, to tell him I didn't care, I'd love him anyway. But I realized that this time he probably very much wanted to be alone; I could certainly sympathize. "Okay," I said. "Lunch by all means."

But it wasn't to be. I'd hardly gotten to the office on Monday when he phoned. "I got another note."

"From the Trapper?"

"Yes. He's real, Rebecca—I'm sure of it. Shall I read it to you?"

"Sure."

"*'Dear Mr. Burns: Ever since I came here I've had nothing but trouble and now the whole city is going to pay. What would this crummy joint be without tourists? Too bad a few of them have to suffer for the sins of Sodom and Gomorrah! But the more people who stay away, the better off they'll be in the long run. The ones that don't come here will thank me. Watch me close this hellhole down!'* It's signed *'The Trapper.'*"

"Ecch. Pretty awful—but he didn't actually say he did the poisonings."

"Listen to the P.S.: *'By the way, I hope the tourists liked the local mussels. I put the good ones in the cabinet in the men's room.'*"

"Mussels! They're quarantined!"

"Right. The cops were being cagey about the poison to see if the Trapper would 'fess up. They got the hospital and the victims' families to keep quiet, too. So now there's absolutely no doubt."

"The cops found good mussels in the men's room?"

"Uh-huh. When the local mussels are quarantined, all the restaurants use eastern ones. All the Trapper had to do was substitute a plastic bag of local ones for a bag of the eastern ones which he put in the men's room. That's why all the poisonings came at once. The restaurant opened the new bag and everyone who ate the first batch out of it got sick."

"My God!"

"Feel a cold wind blowing down your neck, babe? That's the start of a climate of fear. Listen, I've got to cancel lunch. Martinez and Curry are coming and someone from the mayor's office. We've got to hash things out."

"What things?"

"The cops don't want us to run the note. They're afraid it'll cause a panic."

"It will. I'm panicked and I'm not even a tourist."

"True; it will. But wouldn't you prefer to know there's a homicidal maniac on the loose so you could stay off the streets if you felt like it?"

"I think I would. I wish we could have warned people away from Pier 39 . . ."

"That's the way I feel. As it happened, though, he timed it so we couldn't. He substituted the mussels the same day we got the letter, so at least no one got hurt because we made the wrong decision."

My stomach contracted into a hard little knot. "I keep thinking about the poor old man who died. And his family. Rob, please don't . . ."

I stopped myself in midsentence.

"Don't what?"

"Nothing. Don't be a stranger. I'm sorry you can't make lunch. I'll miss you."

I hung up, thanking my stars I'd caught myself. I'd been about to tell Rob, don't get involved, don't expose yourself, stay out of this horrible thing; exactly—precisely—the way my mother had spoken to me on more than one occasion. Was it just habit—the habit of hearing it over and over—that made me want to say that? Fear was my mother's M.O.—was I catching it? I hoped not. I hoped this was an exception to the way I looked at life and not the start of a fear habit of my own, because I hated the way it felt. I was frightened for Rob and frightened for myself and frightened for all the poor souls from Cincinnati who wanted a look at the Golden Gate Bridge in spring, and frightened for anyone who might be mistaken for a tourist or who might be near a tourist attraction next time the Trapper struck. After all, plenty of our landmarks were part of our everyday life.

No doubt I could have worked myself up to a terrifying neurotic frenzy, but a distraction presented itself. Jeff Simon phoned and asked me to dinner. Of course I declined, but it did no good:

"Look, I just enjoy your company. That's all. I know you're

seeing someone—I even know his name and what he does, since you talked endlessly about him last night."

"I don't think I—"

"But I'm up here for a week on business. Taking a deposition—you're one of the few women I know who even understand the word—and I'm lonely, all right? I want to be with somebody intelligent and have a nice dinner. That's absolutely all, I promise."

"Rob might—" Rob might call. But then he might not. I had a right to do what I wanted with my evenings, without feeling I had to wait by the phone like some Valley Girl with styling mousse for brains. Things with Rob were definitely shaky; and I liked Jeff Simon. Maybe I owed it to myself to get to know him. "Okay," I said. "Eight o'clock."

"I'll pick you up at your place."

I looked at my watch. I had a deposition of my own to take in half an hour.

8

I didn't get home till seven, but that was still plenty of time to feed the fish, shower, and change clothes. With a little time left over to talk on the phone if anyone happened to call. But Rob didn't.

Very well then. I applied some unaccustomed violet eye shadow. But to what end I didn't know—in the hope, I guess, of getting a little male admiration from whatever quarter I could.

My attire for the evening was nouveau court jester—black pants that fit like tights, topped with a giant silver-gray sweater. In my case, the sweater had to be Godzilla-sized to cover telltale top-of-thigh bulge. In truth, being five feet five and a hundred twenty-five pounds, I was a bit on the short, rounded side for the medieval look, but I'd bought the outfit after seeing Chris in one like it. Being six feet tall and three-quarters leg, she pulled it off spectacularly. Oh, well. I'd gotten the entire costume, mohair sweater and all, at a January sale for eighty dollars. How could I go wrong?

Jeff didn't seem to think I had. He was quite mannerly

about it, sweeping his eyes face to foot most discreetly, but nonetheless sweeping them. He turned from my person to my pad. "Ah, a reader. Hardly anyone is anymore."

"All my friends read."

He shook his head. "I can't find anyone who does. I moved out from New York two years ago and I'm still suffering culture shock."

"Can't find anyone to read the Sunday *Times* with?"

"You understand!"

"I ought to—I've been out with enough New Yorkers."

"Oh. You seem like one of us. I mean—intelligent."

"I was born and raised in Marin County, California, hot-tub capital of the world."

"You must have gone East to school."

"Nope. Cal and then Boalt for law school. All I had to do was cross the bridge."

"But your apartment—" He made a sweeping gesture. "It's so spare—so Bauhaus."

In a way, I suppose he was right. It was all black and white, with here and there a little red, much like my wardrobe. I abominate brown, yellow, orange, and all warm colors. I had two deep white sofas, facing each other, with a chrome and glass coffee table in between, a chrome lamp, and a dark piano on a Flokati rug. Rather wintry and sparse indeed.

But I also had a seven-foot palm, two rife, lush asparagus ferns the size of medicine balls, and my hundred-gallon saltwater aquarium, teeming with marine life in every color on the planet. Was Jeff blind?

"How about the wildlife?" I asked.

"Nobody's perfect."

Sometimes I think there's something distinctly anhedonic in the ex–New Yorker. Still, Jeff had another side—he could tell a great story.

"So far," he said, "I've found the food in San Francisco fairly overrated. Do you know Khan Toke?"

"You didn't like the Hayes Street Grill?"

"It was okay." He looked crestfallen. "I just wanted to try something new. Don't you like Thai food?"

"Sure. Let's go there." I admit I was intimidated. Since he'd said he didn't like San Francisco restaurants I was afraid to suggest any place else—it mightn't pass muster with his eastern tastes. But I definitely had my doubts about Khan Toke, doubts that had a great deal more to do with the atmosphere than the very excellent food.

A waiter took our shoes and led us barefoot to our table, where we were invited to sit on the floor next to each other, not even across the table, but quite close, with shoes informally off and legs curled under us, as if we were longtime friends lounging together. It was a dark, elegant, sensual restaurant.

"Very romantic," said Jeff.

My hands started to sweat, but I said nothing. I was at odds with myself; it *was* romantic and on the one hand, I liked that quite well; on the other, I felt guilty and loyal to Rob and a bit bullied—after all, Jeff had made a particular point of not wanting romance. I ordered a glass of wine, knowing I would have to switch to beer when the fiery food came, but for the moment very much needing something smooth and grapy and likely to encourage the two disputatious Rebeccas to come to terms.

Jeff told his stories which, along with the wine, beer, fish balls, curries, and spicy, minty dainties, worked wonders to put me at ease. This time I learned that a certain sex bomb female singer liked to prowl lesbian bars in disguise, that three male heartthrobs were said to be suffering from AIDS, that two seemingly thriving studios were on the verge of bankruptcy, and that a cable TV station was doing a musical version of *Pride and Prejudice* set in the year 2100.

Once he was done entertaining me royally, Jeff apologized for hogging the floor and asked me once again about myself, whereupon I unleashed all my worries about Rob and the flapper, and all my unhappiness with Rob in what Mickey had called his werewolf-reporter role. Jeff clucked sympathetically until the bill came and then, suddenly horrified at what I'd done, I clammed up, too embarrassed to speak. "I've been awful company," I said finally. "I hope you'll forgive me."

"What?" Jeff spoke absently. "You've been great." We got up to leave. "You don't think we could catch something from this rug, do you?"

"Jeff, for heaven's sake—through your socks?"

His smile was a trifle rueful. "You never know. What did you think of the restaurant?"

"Delicious. Really terrific. Thanks for bringing me."

"You didn't think the duck was a little overdone?"

"It seemed fine to me."

"I thought the fish balls were a bit on the greasy side. Is this neighborhood safe to walk in?"

"Sure. One of the safest in the city." We headed toward his rented car.

"It doesn't look all that savory."

"You've got a nerve. Just about anywhere in New York makes me quail and quake."

"But New York's got so much *character*."

I was still feeling guilty about pouring out my troubles, and wanted to ask if I could buy Jeff dessert, but I was afraid he wouldn't like any place I suggested, so I let it go. I did scrape up the courage to ask him in for coffee and almost instantly regretted it. "It's Italian roast," I said.

"That's okay. I'll just have tea."

"Oh. Sorry, I haven't got any." I did, but it was only Lipton's, and I was damned if I was going to admit that.

Jeff took my hands in both of his. "I don't care what we drink, Rebecca. I just want to be with you."

I breathed a sigh of relief. "You mean the Italian roast'll be okay?"

Jeff made a face. "No. I meant I really don't need anything."

I made some for myself, anyway. I feel that when you ask someone in for a cup of coffee, he is obligated to drink one.

But if he declines to drink one, he is certainly obligated to leave when the time has elapsed that it would normally take him to drink one. I didn't want Jeff to lose track of time.

To tell the truth, I guess I was policing myself as well. When Jeff got started on my favorite subject—what a really sterling person I am and how lucky he was to have met me—he was at his most charming. I was learning that he was a little frightened of the world, a little picky—in short, a bit of a wimp, perhaps—but nonetheless I thought him a mensch.

So. Did I kiss him good night? Of course.

And I was glad I had when I saw the *Chronicle* the next morning—glad because it made me cross with Rob. The headlines screamed; the prose was pretty shrill, too. "Random Killer Targets S.F. Tourists," said the banner, and underneath was Rob's story, connecting the so-called gay murder of Jack Sanchez of Gallup, New Mexico, the man Rob and I had found nailed to the cross, with the poisonings of eleven people at Pier 39 that resulted in the death of Brewster Baskett of Winnemucca, Nevada. Photos of the Trapper's notes were reproduced, but the last sentence was blocked out of the second note—the part about the mussels in the men's room. That meant the *Chron* had made a deal with the cops to withhold it.

Along with the main story were four sidebars. One contained opinions of selected psychiatrists as to the sort of person who would do such a thing. "An angry, vindictive person," deduced one. "Someone with a grudge," another proclaimed. "A fruitcake with half a dozen screws loose" wasn't among the opinions. Maybe the shrinks thought it was self-evident, or maybe they were saving themselves to be expert witnesses.

The second sidebar was about PSP—paralytic shellfish poisoning—which you get from quarantined mussels. The next was a gory little walk down Memory Lane, detailing the fearsome activities of yesteryear's Zebra and Zodiac serial killers. And the fourth, headed, "S.F. Tourism Endangered," outlined the chilling truth about what the Trapper's work could actually do to the economy of the city. Explaining that tourism is San Francisco's largest industry, it noted that approximately 2.5 million tourists visit the city each year, dropping over a billion dollars, supporting some 60,000 jobs and bringing in almost $60 million in local taxes. If the hordes stayed away even for a few weeks—especially now, in the peak spring and summer months—if, as the Trapper predicted, he "closed this hellhole down," jobs would be lost, hotels and restaurants would get shaky, places like Pier 39 and companies like the one that gives boat rides on the bay would be history in no time at all. The story quoted the Trapper himself: "What would this crummy joint be without tourists?" Rob admitted in the story that no one really knew, but it wouldn't be completely off-base to say that parts of it— Fisherman's Wharf, for instance—would resemble a ghost town. And that the economic damage would be devastating.

I had to give Rob credit for doing his homework. If the Trapper really was a serial killer—someone as dangerous as Zebra or Zodiac—the impact on the city's economy was the real story, and the Trapper knew it. I certainly saw nothing to contradict the shrinks' opinions that he was a very angry, vindictive person with a grudge, and that the grudge apparently was against the city. "Ever since I came here," he had written, "I've had nothing but trouble and now the whole city is going to pay." He might be a fruitcake, but there was a clean, taut logic about his current project.

But I still wasn't convinced that the Trapper was the person who had killed Sanchez and done the poisonings; he (or she) might be a person who read the newspapers and liked to write notes. The person who did the poisonings probably had written the notes, I admitted, because he knew where the eastern mussels were. But how could we be sure he'd killed Sanchez? I thought Rob was making too much of the whole thing—terrifying people who could be going about their lives in blissful ignorance. And yet, I'd told him I myself would rather know than not know if there were a homicidal maniac about.

But all those screaming headlines were so needlessly fear-inducing. So *tacky*. And all the doomsaying could very well be creating a self-fulfilling prophecy. I knew Rob had considered all that. Had spent a horrible day in meetings with cops and editors and city officials who were all very seriously considering all that; who had arrived, probably, at a mutual decision to break the Trapper story. But knowing that didn't make me like it any better.

The phone rang. "Your boyfriend," said Jeff Simon, "went a little overboard, didn't he?"

My first impulse was to protect Rob. "Jeff, you've got to remember, San Francisco is different from New York. We don't have the good gray *Times*."

"Just the San Francisco Comicle."

I was starting to feel crummy for associating with someone on such a rag—an absolutely disloyal attitude. I wished I weren't so ambivalent; I could hardly defend Rob, feeling the way I did.

"Miss Schwartz, you need some fresh air. Let me take you out for a walk tonight."

"A walk?"

"Dinner and a walk. To clear your head." If I understood him correctly, he was saying that no one in her right mind would dream of going out with such a churl as Rob. It made me mad, but I had the nagging feeling he might be right. Really, what I needed to clear my head was an evening at home playing Scarlatti.

"Sorry, I'm booked," I said. "And you're going back to L.A. tomorrow, aren't you? Listen, I really had a terrific time last night. I'd love to see you again, but maybe next time you're here."

"I could stay over an extra day."

"You could?"

"Sure. I'll pick you up at seven tomorrow."

I had certainly outsmarted myself, but having dinner with Jeff Simon wasn't the worst way in the world to spend an evening—and it looked as if my evenings were all mine for the time being, anyway. I wished Rob had taken time for a hello call, at the very least.

Since I had a hearing at nine, I didn't get to the office until the noon recess. No calls from Rob. Being a modern woman who wouldn't dream of playing the passive role in a relationship—certainly not—I picked up the phone. And promptly put it down again. First, I'd have a sandwich.

When I got back form the deli, Kruzick was there, eating his own sandwich. "Hey, Rob's rockin' out, huh? Reeeeal tasteful. Did you love it the way they ran photos of the notes and everything? Mickey was so scared she almost lost the baby."

"What?"

"Hey. Little joke, you know? She's fine, honest. The baby's fine. But listen, I'll tell you one thing—that newshawk yellow-journalist boyfriend of yours really did scare the bejezus out of her."

I hadn't thought of being afraid for Mickey before. But she was as likely a target as anyone else. My stomach turned over as I stared out my office window, gnawing with no great interest at my sandwich. Was it my imagination or were there fewer people out than usual? An odd thing—I hadn't had to wait in line at the deli where I usually waited fifteen minutes. Was the Trapper already terrorizing the city? Or was Rob the one doing the terrorizing?

Okay, no more excuses; I called him. And ended up leaving a message, naturally, because naturally he wasn't there. Is anyone ever there when you have to work up the nerve to call?

I continued to call throughout the day and continued not getting him. "Night," Alan said as I left. "Don't get Trapped."

Driving home, I thought the streets looked a little empty, as if people expected to be picked off by snipers. That was the way the Zebra had worked; the Trapper, I thought, was a lot more subtle.

Scarlatti got me through the night and if I ever needed him, it was then. Because Rob didn't call.

His story Wednesday morning was a collage of interviews with members of the terrified public. The headline: "Fear Stalks the City's Streets!"

9

arling! Thank God you're all right."

"Mom—how was Israel? Aren't you back early?"

"Early! Of course I'm back early—how could I stay away knowing the kind of danger you and your sister were in?"

"Mom, I think you're exaggerating—how's Dad?"

"Exaggerating! You're a fine person to talk about exaggerating."

"I exaggerate?"

"No, not you, darling. Rob. That Rob of yours."

"Oh. You mean in the paper."

"Of course in the paper, darling. Haven't you read yours this morning?"

"But, Mom, if Rob's exaggerating, you could have stayed in Israel."

"I certainly couldn't have. It's just *because* he's exaggerating that your father and I had to come back. Because you're close to him, darling. Everyone who's close to him will be in the worst danger of all."

"Why would the Trapper want to hurt Rob? Rob's making him famous." The minute I said it I knew I shouldn't have.

Sure enough, Mom said: "Rebecca, do you really think you should be going out with that sort of person?"

That was far too tough a question at the moment, so I asked again, "How's Dad?"

"Tired. Very tired. And I'm not sure he's over the shock—"

Dad came on the line then. "I'm certainly not, Beck. The minute we leave town you start going to Christian services." He was teasing me, but he took me off-guard.

"You know about that?"

"Sure. You're famous in Tel Aviv."

"Oh, Dad, come on. You just went through your back *Chronicles* and found the Easter sunrise story." (It had to be. Because if I were famous in Tel Aviv for discovering bodies at Easter services, Mom would have mentioned it first.)

"It must have been pretty awful."

"The worst part was getting the usual VIP treatment from Martinez and Curry."

"I can't understand it. I always get along fine with the cops."

"Listen, Dad. I'm going to be late if I don't get going. Maybe I could come over this weekend and see your slides."

"Okay, Beck. You take care."

Dad was definitely jumpy. He had twice called me "Beck," which he knows I tolerate only from him and only at times of stress. Well, why shouldn't he be jumpy? After all, fear stalked the city's streets.

I could have walked to work, but I didn't. I certainly didn't want to be out there with fear rampaging. I wasn't the only one. Hardly anyone was jogging. A few people were walking, but they were mostly men. So far, of course, the Trapper had killed only men, but women were used to feeling vulnerable, I supposed. It was funny how odd the streets looked without the usual floods of women in jogging shoes and business suits. And traffic? Like a snarl of barbed wire.

"His nibs would like you to call," said my properly respectful secretary when I walked in.

"Surely you don't mean the mayor; you would have said her nibs."

"Very good, Ms. Boss. Maybe you should have been a detective."

"Alan. Who wants me to call?"

"Why, our town's man of the moment, unless you count Mr. Trapper himself. Mr. Rob Burns of the *Chronicle* actually dialed the humble number of drab, insignificant Rebecca Schwartz."

I drew back my right foot, thinking not of a simple toe-in-the-shin, but something along the lines of the moves you see in kung fu films. But then I noticed I was wearing my new red Joan and David shoes (purchased, needless to say, for half the usual $120); if they'd been black or gray, I would have gone ahead with it. But Kruzick wasn't worth wrecking a pair of red shoes over.

"Hardly drab," said Chris, breezing in. "Nice shoes."

"Thank you." I turned back to Kruzick. "I'd like to go on record as saying I don't care to be insulted first thing in the morning."

"Okay, okay. Maybe not drab. Just a shade on the unexciting side."

"Thanks a lot."

He shrugged. "Hey, boss, you gotta remember—the competition's a multiple murderer."

He had a point. I was certainly a bore compared to the Trapper. I was cross at the notion of having to compete with a psychotic killer; and annoyed with Rob for going overboard on the Trapper stories; and for ignoring me; and for putting me in the position of having to defend him when I didn't really feel I could support him. And I was annoyed at myself for being ambivalent. Thus, I may not have been in the best of moods when I called him back.

"Hi, babe," he said. "How'd you like the stories?"

"Frankly, I think they're a bit much."

"Rebecca, the guy's killing people."

"Maybe I spoke harshly. I'm sorry, but you asked for my opinion. I find them upsetting."

"Upsetting how?"

"Scary."

"The Trapper's scary."

"The stories were needlessly scary. Nightmarish."

"You've got to remember the guy poisoned eleven people at a restaurant. As it happened, only one person died, but he didn't care how many he killed. It *is* a nightmare."

"I just don't think the stories are in very good taste, that's all."

"Rebecca, sometimes you are the most amazing sushi-eating, Volvo-driving, *New York Times*–reading, Saks-shopping, foreign-movie-going Yuppie prig. Would it be good taste to report the antics of a maniac who wanted to wipe out every Jew in Germany and damn near did?"

"It's not the same thing."

"Okay, what's different about it?"

"It's not important to the whole world—it only matters in San Francisco."

"Sweetheart, have you noticed that the *Chronicle* is a local San Francisco paper?"

"Rob, I can't talk to you when you're in this mood."

"When *I'm* in this mood! Rebecca, do you have any idea how hard I've been working lately? How do you think it makes me feel when you of all people don't support me in my work? Instead, I haven't talked to you in days, and finally when I do you tell me I'm in bad taste."

"It was your choice not to talk to me for days."

"I couldn't, don't you understand? I literally didn't have a spare second."

"People always find time for what's important to them."

"Listen, it's no good trying to talk on the phone. Let's have dinner tonight, okay?"

"I have a date with someone else."

For a moment he didn't speak. Then he said, "Another man?"

"Yes." I wondered why my voice sounded like a croak. "Another man."

"I see."

I didn't say anything.

"How about tomorrow then? Or lunch—today or tomorrow; you name it."

"I think maybe we shouldn't see each other for a while."

I didn't realize I thought that before I said it, but as soon as it was out, I knew it was true. Jeff had helped to distract me, but actually talking with Rob, I realized how deeply hurt I felt about his temporary abandonment—and how very much my brain felt like scrambled eggs when I tried to sort out my feelings about the Trapper stories. I really did need some time away from him to try to figure things out.

Jeff brought flowers—purple irises that were perfect for my apartment. The first time Rob and I had gone out—gone to lunch, actually—he'd brought daisies. If Rob and I were really breaking up, I realized that similar scenes would be played out hundreds and thousands and tens of thousands of times in the next few months or maybe even the next couple of years. No matter what happened, no matter how insignificant or how seemingly happiness-producing, it would remind me of Rob and would sting. The thought was profoundly depressing.

I wanted to go someplace loud and cheerful, someplace with pasta, and Jeff had asked me to name the spot, so I picked Little Italy in Noe Valley.

Since I knew the city better, we took my old gray Volvo instead of Jeff's rented car. And practically had the streets to ourselves. If fear stalked, he was doing it in solitary splendor. And he was certainly stalking—or *it* was, I should say. Fear was nearly palpable on those not normally mean streets. The few people who were out walked close to the buildings, glancing around far too frequently.

Even Castro Street, the liveliest in the city, looked deserted. Funny, I thought, that was probably one of two safe places left in town—the other being Pier 39. I guess I was too quiet, because Jeff offered me a penny for my meager mental processes.

"I was thinking about the Trapper."

"Kind of depressing topic, isn't it?"

"Jeff, I know you can't really tell, since you don't live here, but the city just isn't itself."

"It does seem a little gloomy out."

"I was trying to think what he might do next—I think he'll go for something different every time. So the Castro's probably safe, and Pier 39, wouldn't you think?"

"You certainly think about funny things on a date."

"It doesn't interest you?"

He shrugged. "Not really. I don't go in much for mass murder."

I started to get nervous because it was time to look for a parking place, then realized I could have my pick. That gave me a frisson.

Jeff put a not entirely unwelcome arm around my shoulders. "What is it, Rebecca?"

"The town's so weird, that's all."

"Hey, look—aren't those Chicanos?"

"Mm-hmm. Why?"

"Are you sure this neighborhood's okay?"

"Pretty sure. It's not a tourist area."

"That's not what I meant."

I laughed, even tousled his hair. I was beginning to get a kick out of his big-city naïveté. "You're hopeless, you know that?"

He looked back at me in a puzzled way, as if I'd spoken in Venusian.

Not only was there no wait for a table at Little Italy, the place was less than half full. It's usually so noisy you have to shout, but that night it was unfamiliarly subdued. The atmosphere reminded me of something from my childhood, the year I was in fifth grade. Mom and Dad had strongly opposed the intrusion of Christmas into our Jewish lives, breaking the hearts of their two usually indulged daughters by absolutely declining to have a Christmas tree. This particular year a new family had moved in next door—the Walkers, whose three sons, in the most coltish high spirits, spent nearly the whole month of December bringing home trees and large evergreen branches and giant shopping bags; helping their parents make wreaths and cookies and fruitcakes; playing Christmas carols on their various musical instruments; and wrapping things. Mickey and I were driven mad with jealousy. Never did two children whine and beg and pout and plead more in a single month. And yet, we were not allowed to have a tree or to get in on the fun in any way. True, Mom went to special pains for Hanukkah that year, but our celebration seemed like thin gruel next to that overflowing feast of Christmas goodies.

On Christmas Eve, we were invited to the Walkers' for eggnog, along with all the other neighbors, and I didn't think I'd ever seen anything so splendid as the Walker Christmas tree or been a part of anything so magical. But when the next day came, and the celebration began in earnest, we had to watch wistfully as Mr. Walker carted loads of paper wrappings to the garbage, and the Walker boys spilled all over the street with their new bikes and games and toy trucks, eating cookies, eating fruitcake, eating candy from their stockings. We could smell their dinner cooking, and see all their relatives coming over with more presents, and hear Mrs. Walker calling the kids to dinner. Mom and Dad heard it, too, and, unable to bear the sight of their pitifully envious offspring a moment longer, they got the bright idea of taking us out to dinner. They said it would be an un-Christmas dinner, like the Mad Hatter's un-birthday party. Cheered and delighted, we ran to get our coats.

We went to our favorite restaurant, also an Italian one in downtown San Rafael, and no one else was there except an older woman eating alone. After a while, a man came in with two children dressed to the nines—the girl all got up in a dress and pink socks and the boy in a new red T-shirt. The boy was younger, was obviously trying to keep from crying. Instinctively, I knew their mother had died and their dad hadn't known how to cook Christmas dinner or hadn't had the heart.

Mom and Dad let us order anything we wanted, all our favorites, even found new things for us, special tidbits we weren't normally allowed to have—side orders and appetizers and dessert, absolutely everything we wanted. They made a big to-do of re-creating the Mad Hatter's party. But no amount of forced good cheer could penetrate the gloom of the place; it made the House of Usher look like a stately pleasure dome. And that's what Little Italy was like that night.

"Ah, spiedini. And every kind of pasta you could want. And risotto, and calamari, and spumoni. What can I tempt you with?"

Jeff's voice sounded so much like my father's had that Christmas nearly twenty years ago that I had to laugh—a desperate, rueful little laugh, I'm afraid. It seemed to hurt Jeff's feelings.

"Why do you laugh at everything I say?" He spoke with real pain, as if he'd been trying hard to get through to me and had found it about as rewarding as meaningful colloquy with *la belle dame sans merci*. And so of course I had to tell him the story of the un-Christmas party. He seemed to disapprove of our envying the Walker children. "But what happened the next year?" he asked. "Did your folks take you to Mexico?"

That's what we used to do at Christmas—except it was the Bahamas."

"Actually, no. We made the un-Christmas party a tradition, complete with an un-Christmas tree and un-Christmas gifts. Mom even used to make a roast beef—she was strict about not having a turkey—and we'd have Uncle Walter and Aunt Ellen for un-Christmas dinner."

"I'd want my children to grow up Jewish."

Not sure what he meant, I said, "We grew up Jewish. Mom and Dad just found a way to give us an extra holiday, that's all."

"But not a Jewish holiday."

"Labor day isn't a Jewish holiday and neither is the Fourth of July—do you think Jews shouldn't celebrate them?"

"It's not the same thing."

It's not the same thing. I heard myself saying that to Rob when we were talking about his Trapper stories. Jeff's train of thought, his argument, his conclusion seemed completely inane, indeed designed only to irritate and annoy—had mine been? I thought it might indeed have been; perhaps I'd been deliberately finding fault with Rob, blaming the Trapper on him, projecting like Mom loved to do, when what really upset me was the Trapper himself.

I said, "Jeff. Are you angry with me?"

"Angry? No. Not at all. Why?"

"Because you sound like it. You're arguing with me when there really isn't anything to argue about."

He looked down at his fettucini, as if expecting the noodles to form themselves into letters and words, spelling out the right answer. But he wasn't a noodle-mancer; he was just gathering his thoughts. And for that I gave him a lot of credit. Jeff seemed a very fair person; he sometimes spoke out in anger or jealousy, but he obviously had the ability to look at himself and what he'd said, reevaluate to determine whether it was what he really meant. It was one of the things I liked best about him.

"Rebecca, I do beg your pardon. You're right. All I want, really"—his face was the face of a very earnest small boy—"is to get to know you better—to get closer to you—and I do seem to be pushing you away. Honestly, I haven't the faintest idea why."

"I have. It's oppressive here. The whole city's oppressive." I spoke with heat. "In case you haven't noticed, fear stalks the streets."

"I guess it's even worse for you. You must feel partly responsible."

"Responsible? How so?"

He shrugged. "Because it's your friend who's done it."

And there we were. Back to my least favorite question in the world—was it Rob or the Trapper who was causing fear to stalk? I didn't want to think about it—I just wanted to have a good time with Jeff on his last night in town.

"Oh, Jeff, can't we just forget about all that? Let's have a good time in spite of it."

My hand was resting on the table and he took it very gently and diffidently. "I'd like that."

"Listen, I know what. Let's take in the view from Nob Hill."

"Meaning?"

"Drinks at the top of the Fairmont. My treat."

"I thought the Top of the Mark was the place to go."

"Uh-uh. At least not in my book—at the Fairmont you get to ride the outside elevator."

"I'm cheered up already."

So was I. We both felt good enough for a little bright chatter over our coffee, and for a while, the ugly pall lifted. Lifted, that is, till we had to go back and walk those lonesome streets again. But then, shortly after that, we were in the lobby of the Fairmont and that was good for both our moods. Like all my favorite hotel lobbies, it's a great bustling womb of a place that somehow manages to make you feel both at home and as if you're someplace terribly glamorous.

Funny, I thought, here was a place populated almost solely

by tourists—a perfect target—and yet they remained here. On the other hand, where else were they going to go? Out on the streets, where not even the natives ventured? To another hotel, where they'd still be sitting ducks? I began to realize for the first time that the Trapper's threat to close the place down was an idle one by no means. Little Italy was certainly already suffering and so were the bars in the Castro. The impact on the hotels probably hadn't yet been felt because the Trapper was relatively new—maybe word of him wasn't big national news yet; people probably hadn't had time to cancel their trips to San Francisco. But it would start soon if the murders continued. If the next one were in a hotel . . . and suddenly I was sure the next one would be. Perhaps it would be arson; perhaps the Trapper would find a way to set a hotel on fire and kill hundreds of people at once. Perhaps it would be the Fairmont, and perhaps while we were on our way up in the elevator made famous by *Ironside*. Jeff was pressing the button now. Perhaps we had only minutes to live. But wait, I told myself—all we had to do was walk out without boarding the damned elevator. I could say I suddenly felt ill . . .

The elevator came and Jeff whisked me inside. I could have spoken up, but the arrival of the elevator, into which nine other people pressed confidently, brought me to my senses. What was I, Chicken Little? Or Rebecca Schwartz, Jewish feminist lawyer? A Jewish feminist lawyer afraid to get on an ordinary elevator in a well-known hotel on a random Wednesday would suck eggs. I relaxed a little.

Instead of looking at the view, I watched Jeff watching it. And then people started screaming; people right in the elevator not six inches away. And yet we were still going up. If the elevator wasn't falling, what was happening? Jeff's face, changing from near rapture to horror, told me it was something outside. I turned and saw every San Franciscan's worst nightmare—a runaway cable car on Nob Hill.

It was hurtling down Powell like a roller coaster, nearly at the intersection, almost there, and the light was green on

California. People must be screaming, I thought—the people on the cable car—surely they must hear it on California Street. And they must be able to see the car traveling at what looked to me like the speed of light. But would they be able to get out of the way? A taxi, probably paying no attention, just trying to make good time, was right in its path, and there was a car very close in front of it. If the taxi even had time to get out of the cable car's way, it was going to hit the other car. However, that seemed the better choice to me. Suddenly, the taxi did speed up, the driver apparently just seeing the runaway. But it wasn't fast enough. The cable car hit the taxi in the rear, probably just about in the back seat area, where the passengers would be. But the cable car was going so fast it merely knocked the taxi aside, where it hit another car, and continued hurtling down the hill.

10

I read all about it in the
Chronicle the next morning. The cable car continued to Pine
Street, where it hit another car quite a bit harder than it had
apparently hit the taxi, and finally came to a stop. Four people
were killed, thirteen hospitalized, six of them in critical
condition. Reading it, I would have burst into tears, except
that I was already cried out. Someone had had hysterics in the
glass elevator, and I figured I was next if I didn't get home
soon. So Jeff took me—immediately. He wanted to stick
around and be comforting, but I simply wasn't up to it. If I
couldn't be with a San Franciscan, I didn't want to be with
anyone.

All I wanted to do was cry my eyes out and I'd be much
happier doing that alone, anyway. It was too much. First, the
Trapper, and then Rob and now this. It wasn't lost on me, of
course, that the cable car collision might be the Trapper's
work. But whether it was or it wasn't, he was bound to claim
credit for it and fear would continue to stalk and San

Francisco would remain slightly less habitable than Plovdiv, Bulgaria.

Having read the distinctly uncheering news in the *San Francisco Chronicle* and having forborne to break into tears yet again, I was contemplating a dispiriting morning of catching up on detail work, tying up loose ends, returning phone calls, and wishing I were in the Bahamas when Alan came in to announce a Mr. Mike Lewis. As he did so, the phone rang. And as Mr. Lewis had no appointment, I elected to answer it first. It is hardly rude to keep someone waiting who is lucky to find you in in the first place.

"Rebecca, listen, I've been thinking over what you said— about not seeing each other for a while."

"Rob?"

"Who else aren't you seeing for a while?"

"Rob. I can't talk to you now."

But he didn't hear me—he was listening to an assistant editor calling his name—I could hear him over the wire. "Oops, sorry. I've got another call. Call you right back, okay?"

Not okay. Absolutely not; a perfect example of why I wanted the trial separation—good God, I sounded as if we were married. Well, this was a perfect example of why we probably never would be—he couldn't even beg forgiveness without his stupid job interrupting. Of course, I probably wouldn't even have called him in the first place during my own office hours, but I had time for him afterward, and he didn't always have time for me. So what was I doing sittin waiting for the phone to ring again when I could be cleanin up details, tying up loose ends, returning my own calls, an seeing Mr. Mike Lewis? Certainly not making an importar feminist statement. The phone rang.

"It was him."

My stomach did a little flip-flop. "The Trapper?"

"Yes. He said he nobbled the runaway cable car."

"But of course he'd claim he did it. If he didn't do it, he ge a free one."

"He said it wasn't easy, but it was worth it."

"I don't feel well."

"He told me exactly how he did it, Rebecca. I've got to call the MUNI to make sure it was done the way he said it was, but it sounded all too plausible."

"Still. Anyone who knows anything about cable cars could probably figure out what has to happen to cause a runaway."

"I asked him a couple of control questions."

"Such as?"

"What did he say in the postscript to the second note?"

"And?"

"He knew about the mussels in the men's room."

"Oh." It sounded all too convincing. "What was the other question?"

"Miranda Warning's real name."

"And?"

"It's Waring. Miranda Waring—how do you like that?"

"He really does know her?"

"Seemed to. Though I admit he sounded pretty surprised when I sprung her on him."

"Oh, Rob." I couldn't keep the dismay out of my voice.

"What's wrong?"

"He probably didn't know she was in the car when he killed Sanchez. Now what choice does he have? He'll kill her."

"I never thought of that. He seemed to get awfully upset when I mentioned Miranda. Now that I think of it." He sounded properly sobered.

"Oh, Rob," I said again, afraid to say too much; I didn't want to lose my temper so early in the day.

Rob said, "Wait a minute! It's okay—she's safe."

"How so?"

"His motive for killing her would be to conceal his identity, right?"

"Yes, but he's killed for less a few times already."

"He told me his name."

"The Trapper told you his name?"

"Uh-huh."

"And you didn't tell me?"

"I just hadn't gotten to it yet."

"Well?"

"Lou Zimbardo."

I was disgusted. "Oh, for heaven's sake. The Trapper knows that's who the cops are looking for. Everybody who reads the paper does. Why *wouldn't* he say that's who he is?" I rang off without waiting for an answer and began searching my purse for tissues; I felt another good cry coming on. But I'd hardly tuned up when Alan came back in: "Mr. Lewis is getting impatient."

"Oh, screw him. He should have called for an appointment."

"He's with a guy says he knows you. They wanted me to give you his name."

"Oh, hell. Who is he?" I blew my nose and started rifling my purse again, this time for makeup to repair the damage. "Ow." I'd stuck my finger on one of the fangs Rob and I had bought at the Pier 39 magic shop. When would I remember to clean out my purse?

"Art Zimbardo, if that means anything." He turned and sauntered out. Even Kruzick had to know the cops were looking for Art's brother Lou; he was pretending to be cool.

When I felt reasonably presentable, I went out, made a big show of greeting Art, and quickly took him back into my office, making sure I didn't give him an opening to introduce Mr. Lewis first. Because I had a feeling Lewis might be Lou, and I figured Alan had the same feeling and I didn't want to give him the satisfaction of finding out for sure. Which just shows you how small-minded I was feeling that morning.

Safely inside, I extended a hand: "Mr. Lewis, how do you do?"

Art's moon-sized eyes smoldered at me, not resentful now, pleading instead. "Not Lewis," he said. "Lou. This is my brother, Rebecca."

"I thought it might be. Sit down, both of you."

"Remember I said Lou might need a lawyer?"

"You kept my card. I'm glad." I was glad because I still felt motherly toward the kid, dammit, but I wasn't ecstatic about having a suspect in a mass murder case in my office. The cops might come in and start blasting; knowing Martinez, that would be more likely than otherwise if he had any idea where Lou was. Oddly, I wasn't a bit nervous on Lou's account. Or not so oddly—he and Art were two people who couldn't possibly be the Trapper.

Even as that thought ran through my head, I realized I really didn't know if it were true. "Can I get you some coffee?" I said.

Lou nodded, Art just stared. I suspected that, having been in prison, Lou wasn't as susceptible to shock as his younger brother. Outside the office I spoke softly to Alan: "Make us some coffee, will you?"

"Need something to steady your nerves, do you? Being alone with the Trapper and all."

"Alan, was he with Art the whole time I was talking to Rob?"

"You mean the Trapper? Yep. Never took my eyes off him—that's how you'd want it, right?"

"He's not the Trapper."

"Oh, come on. He's gotta be the kid's brother—looks just like him."

"Just make the coffee, okay? I think he needs it."

"Me, too, boss. And by the way, I want a hazardous-duty raise."

I went back and joined the Zimbardos. "Lou, you look like your brother."

"Older and meaner."

A lot older, I'd say—the man was close to my age. He was as slender as Art and better looking if you preferred men to boys, but he had a tired look about him; in another man, it might have been a wised-up look. But Lou looked as if he wasn't ever going to wise up; he looked as if a lot of bad things had happened to him, and he knew for a fact that a lot more were due, but he was going to be surprised, hence infinitely more mournful, more hurt every time another came along. Definitely not a cockeyed optimist; where Art's eyes smoldered angrily, Lou's were resigned. Mean was a way he didn't look at all.

"I know the cops are still looking for you," I said. "Have you come for legal advice about what to do?"

"Art said you wouldn't give me any bum steers."

"I hope not. But there really isn't much choice about this situation. Any lawyer will tell you the same thing."

"Give myself up."

I nodded.

"Yeah, I know. You ain't the first lawyer I been to—went to my old one first."

"And he gave you the same advice?"

"Yeah. Also, he acted like I was going to pull a knife on him. Couldn't wait to get me out of his office."

I winced, thinking I might have acted much the same way if the Trapper hadn't been on the phone to Rob while Lou Zimbardo was sitting in my office.

"Art said you wouldn't be like that."

I smiled, feeling like a fraud. "I'll try not to be."

Kruzick came in with the coffee, rather spoiling the whole effect of safety I was working on by staring first at me, then at Lou, then back at me again, like a Doberman trying to decide whether its mistress is about to be raped and mutilated. would have been touched if the timing hadn't been so bad

"Before you call the cops—"

"I'm not going to call the cops unless you want me to."

"Okay, okay. Before you throw me out, then—could I te you something?"

"Of course."

"It ain't me that's doing all this."

"You know something? I believe you."

"You believe me?"

"I do, actually. But I want to hear your story before we talk about that."

He looked hunted and trapped, as if that were a worse idea than going back to prison. "I don't know where to start."

"How about the restaurant on the night of the poisonings. What did you see?"

He shrugged. "People getting sick."

"What did you do when you saw people start to get sick?"

"Panicked."

"Uh-huh. And then what?"

"I left."

"You left. How'd you do that?"

"There's a side door."

"Did you leave by the side door?"

"I said I did."

"Funny, I didn't hear you say that."

"It's what I meant."

I stopped and counted to ten, mentally, very fast. I was beginning not to like this guy at all—he seemed about as interested in telling his own story, keeping his own hide from coming to grief, as I am normally interested in the Super Bowl. In fact, he seemed to have about as much life to him as a dead battery. And I figured he had a lot in common with one. He'd used up all the juice in himself—or someone had used it up for him. The fact that he seemed rude and sullen might not have anything to do with what he was really like— the older brother Art had known as a child—and I was a spoiled brat if I couldn't remember that and do my job properly. I swallowed.

"Sorry," I said. "I didn't understand. It's important for you to be as clear as possible about your story. Okay, you left by the side door. And went where?"

"I walked."

"You walked. Back to your apartment?" I knew, of course, that he hadn't, as I'd been there with his brother and Rob that night; but I thought if I gave him some guidance—something to push against—it might help.

"Thought you were there that night."

Wrong approach. "Not all night. I thought maybe you were there before or after."

He shook his head. "Nope."

"Where did you go, then?"

He shrugged again. "I just walked."

"All night?"

"Almost."

"What did you do after you finished walking?"

"Slept for a while."

"Where?"

"I don't know. Doorway, I think."

"I see. And where have you been staying all week?" I was shocked saying it—the disaster at Full Fathom Five had happened on a Friday and this was Thursday. Fear had stalked for nearly a week now. It was getting to be a way of life.

"Doorways. Stuff like that. Around."

"Have you been in touch with Art at all?"

Art shook his head, clearly distressed and growing nearly as impatient as I was. Lou said: "No. Not till after I saw that other guy."

"What other guy?"

"Other lawyer."

He sounded at the end of his rope. Looking at Art, I saw the pain in his eyes. He knew Lou wouldn't have called him if he'd had any other options.

"All right, where are they?" It was a loud threatening voice from Alan's reception area.

Lou got up and ran to the window, looking for a way out. Alan buzzed me. "Miss Schwartz, a couple of—uh—chaps are here to see you."

Chaps, not gentlemen—as if I didn't know already who was out there. "Tell Inspectors Martinez and Curry I'll be right out."

But the door slammed open, knocking a hunk out of my nice paint. The chaps had their guns drawn. "You have no right to come in here," I said, but my words were drowned out by Martinez.

He was saying, "Lou Zimbardo, you're under arrest. You have the right to remain silent, you have the right to an attorney . . ."

When they'd dragged him away, Art let his eyes smolder at me. He said: "Please help me." Not even, "Rebecca, please help me," or "Please help my brother." Just the three simplest words that said what he wanted. I wanted to take him in my lap and rock him.

I sent him home. Then I phoned Martinez and left a message. After that, I phoned Rob and filled him in. He, of course, had just left a message for Martinez as well, intending to tell him about the Trapper's latest call, in which he claimed to have caused the cable car accident. The call had come through the switchboard and been transferred to the city desk before coming to Rob—all of Rob's callers who didn't use his extension were being treated this way now—just in case. And now the case had arisen. The time of the call had indeed been noted—and by someone other than Rob. That was good. What wasn't so good was that there was no way to prove that Rob's caller had been the Trapper.

Naturally, I got the bail machinery in motion right away, but the case against Lou looked awful. Which meant the D.A. must be rubbing his hands together in glee. What looked awful to me had to look terrific to him. It was this way:

The night of the poisonings at Full Fathom Five, when the cops searched Lou's flophouse room, they found the gun that had killed Sanchez. And, ominously, a book on bomb making. Martinez had also turned up another neat little circumstantial piece: It seemed that Lou Zimbardo, before taking up residence in San Quentin, had been a cable car gripman; in other words, one of the few people in the world who might know how to wreck a cable car. On learning that, I hopped into my gray Volvo and pointed it toward the Hall of Justice.

Lou seemed more sullen than ever, and my heart sank. But could I blame him? The man had just gotten out of the joint and now it looked as if he were almost certainly on his way back—for six or eight decades, maybe, if he lived that long. A most unfortunate situation if one were innocent—and I believed he was—but maybe it wasn't my problem.

I started out with the basics. "Lou, do you want me to represent you?"

He looked as if I'd whacked him with my briefcase. "Don't you want to? I thought you thought I was innocent."

"I do." I told him why, hoping it would make him open up. In a modest way, it worked. He closed his eyes and let his body sag back against the chair, as if the knowledge that one person in the world thought him innocent, and not because that person was his brother, but because there was actually some reason to believe him innocent, was all he'd ever wanted out of life. That gave me a lot of power; it also made me more vulnerable than anything else he could have done. I realized that I'd be his lawyer, not just till he could get another one, but all the way, if he really wanted me to. My parents had raised me to have a social conscience and I still had it; this man was getting a bum rap and I didn't want it to happen. I seized my temporary advantage.

"Lou, do you really want me to represent you?"

This time he nodded. "I don't want no other lawyer."

"Okay. I'll do the best I can. Let's shake on it." We did, and then I continued: "But you're going to have to help me. You might have learned to keep your mouth shut in the joint, but you're going back if you don't start learning to talk, okay?"

He nodded.

"Say it, please."

"Okay."

"How about, 'Okay, Rebecca'?"

"Okay, Rebecca." He smiled. He was pleased, as I thought he'd be, that I wanted to be called by my first name.

"Okay, Lou. You know the cops found the gun that killed Sanchez in your room?"

"They've mentioned it once or twice."

"How'd it get there?"

He shrugged.

"Cat got your tongue?"

He stared at me, and I was looking at a desperate man. "I don't know." It was almost a whine. "I don't have a gun. Never have."

"What were you in prison for?"

"Assault." He lowered his eyes, sullen again.

"Tell me about it."

"It wasn't like this. I did it."

"Lou, could you tell me about it, please?" I spoke a little sharply, just to get my point across.

And Mr. Leave-Me-Alone-Sister-I-Don't-Need-You-Or-Anybody-Else started sobbing. I didn't want to wait till it was over, knowing I'd lose some of the momentum I'd finally got going.

"Tell me," I said again, as gently as I could.

And finally, he did, as if he'd been dying to tell someone for the last few years. "My wife left me."

I nodded encouragement.

"It hit me hard; real hard, man. See, I didn't think I'd miss her. I guess I sort of took her for granted. But then, all of a sudden she wasn't there. She left me for another guy, see? Like . . . I don't know. It just hit me real hard.

"One night on the cable car there were all these drunks, singing and acting out of hand."

"Violent?"

"No. Just loud. They get like that sometimes—you just have to put up with it. But my nerves were raw, man. I couldn't take it worth a damn."

"So you told them to be quiet."

"Hell, no, you can't do that. I didn't do nothin'. I mean I didn't do nothin' till this other drunk starts getting abusive. See, he wasn't with the group that was singing. He was pissed off about the singing and feeling sorry for himself, so he tries to get me to make them stop."

"And you told him it was a free country."

"Yeah. So then he starts getting abusive."

"What did he say?"

Lou had more or less stopped crying, but now his eyes filled again. "He says, 'I lost my wife, man. I lost my wife, and it's your goddamn fault. It's your fault, man; if you guys would do something about this kind of crap like you're supposed to, do your goddamn jobs properly, I wouldna lost my goddamn wife.'"

"Sounds exactly like a drunk rambling."

"Yeah, it does now. But, man. At the time it pushed all my buttons. See, I'd lost my wife, and now here were these drunks driving me crazy when I felt so low and he's blaming me not only for the drunks, which are driving me out of my own fucking mind, but not only that, he says it's my fault he lost his goddamn wife. You know what I mean? It pushed all my goddamn buttons."

"So what happened?"

"I ordered him off the cable car."

"And then?"

"He wouldn't get off; just kept laying the same trip on me."

"So you hit him."

"Yeah, man, I hit him. I remember hitting him once, but I don't remember nothin' after that. Except things turned red."

"I beg your pardon?"

"You know that expression, right? Seeing red. Well, i happened to me. It's no joke, man. Everything turned red on me after I hit him and I don't remember another goddamn thing."

I was beginning to have a horrible feeling in the pit of m stomach.

"I kept hitting him, they told me later. Fractured his goddamn skull. The drunks had to sober up and pull me off of him or I guess I'd of killed him. They said I was beating his head against the concrete. But I don't remember a goddamn thing about it. Just everything went red and then some people were holding me, waiting for the cops. I went nuts for a while, you know? My buttons got pushed."

"Did the guy recover okay?"

"Oh, yeah. Testified against me. You know what? I didn't hardly recognize him. He looked like some guy I'd never seen before in my life. I didn't want to hurt him, man—we were just two guys on the wrong cable car at the wrong time. I've felt awful about it ever since. If there was anything I could do for him, I would."

"Who was he?"

"Guy named Les Mathison."

"I like the name."

"You like the name? You're my goddamn lawyer and all you can say is you like the name of the guy I beat up? What's so great about the guy's goddamn name?"

"It sounds like 'Lou.' And also 'Lee.'" I told him about Terry Yannarelli, who had been told the first name of the Trapper and had promptly forgotten it, just, I suspected, as he forgot the names of his sex partners.

I was ready to call it a day as soon as I checked a couple of other points. "Sanchez was killed on Saturday, the night before Easter. Were you doing anything special that night? Seeing Art or anything? Maybe seeing a girlfriend?"

"No. I don't have no girlfriend and Art works Saturdays. I don't know nobody else."

"Then what were you doing?"

He shrugged. "Same thing as always. Watching television."

"Do you remember what you saw?"

"Hell, no; it all runs together."

"Was that all you did that night? Watched television?"

He brightened. "Probably not. It was Saturday, man. Once

in a while on Saturday—I mean the few Saturdays since I been out—I treat myself to a few beers."

"Great. Where do you usually go?"

"Different places. I'm looking for a place to hang out."

"So where were you that night?"

"Hell, I don't know."

"Well, I want you to think about it, Lou. It might be extremely important." I was stern, like a schoolmarm. Extremely important wasn't the half of it. If I could find someone who saw him at the same time the Trapper was at the Yellow Parrot, I might have the beginnings of a defense.

"Rebecca, tell me something."

"Sure."

"When you went out to ask for the coffee, did you tell your guy to call the cops?"

"Of course not."

"Then how'd they know how to find me?"

It was a question I'd been dreading. "They had Art's phone tapped." He looked down at his lap. That had to be a hard thing to learn for a man who clearly hated to ask for help as much as this one did.

"Listen, Lou, I'm going to try to turn it to our advantage. You came to me because you wanted to turn yourself in, didn't you?"

I held my breath; I'd certainly been leading the witness— hoped he'd pick up the lead.

He gave me one of his shrugs. "Yeah. Why else?" Not only was it the right answer, I was pretty sure he meant it.

"That should help us in the bail hearing."

But it didn't. The city of San Francisco wanted blood, and Lou Zimbardo's would do as nicely as anyone else's. Bail was denied.

11

Chris and I kicked the thing around over a couple of glasses of wine. I had a very nasty little theory and I wanted to see how it hit her.

"Tell me the truth. Do you think he's guilty?"

"Rebecca, I know he's a loner who doesn't like to ask people for help. But he's bound to have at least one friend—someone he could have gotten to call Rob when he was in your office. Or Art could have gotten someone to do it."

"Neither of them seems to have the guile for it."

"If Pigball's the Trapper . . ."

"Lou."

". . . that's the least guileful stunt he's pulled—if you can call multiple murder a stunt."

"I just don't think he did it."

"A good thing, too. You're his lawyer."

"But do you really think he's guilty?"

"One thing—if the Trapper struck again, I'd think twice about it."

I shuddered. "Look. Suppose Lou isn't the Trapper and yet

the Trapper doesn't strike again. Doesn't it seem strange that he hasn't already? After all, the three incidents came within a few days of each other. It's been a week now and not a peep out of the Trapper. Which, of course, argues that Lou's the bad guy. But suppose he isn't. What would you think is going on? The Trapper seemed so proud of himself: Why wouldn't he at least let Rob know he's still out there?"

"I have a hard time stretching that far. After all, Lou has good reason to have a grudge against the city—at least I think a twisted mind could see it that way. Lou knows enough about cable cars to have caused the crash—and what could be better poetic justice for that same twisted mind? And it was Lou's restaurant where the poisonings took place."

"Yes, but how does the man on the cross fit in?"

She drained her glass and shrugged. "The D.A.'s not asking that question."

"Right. But that's because he doesn't have to, to satisfy a jury. Nonetheless, the logical mind must ask it."

"Okay. I'll ask it. How?"

"I've asked myself again and again, and I can't come up with anything—that is, if Lou's the Trapper. I've even put the question to Lou and he doesn't get it."

"Of course he'd say that."

"The point is, I can't get anywhere. But if the Trapper were someone else, it might fit in."

"But who?"

She just wouldn't bite—I'd thought the wine would loosen her mind up, but it hadn't. Chris being a Virginian, I would have been better off with bourbon, but it was too late to switch now. I hit her with my theory: "The person who's trying to frame Lou."

She put her wineglass down and rubbed the side of her long nose with one of her long fingers, a gesture that seems to help her think. "A frame-up. The only possible alternate solution. Yes, I see it. The only tricky part would be getting the mussel into the restaurant without Lou's seeing him—but it's not that tricky. He could have come before Lou's shift started."

"Right."

"Why would anyone want to frame Lou?"

"Think about it."

But she didn't need to. Her mind was now sufficiently loose to work without prodding. She answered her own question: "For beating his head in."

"Right again. Les Mathison."

"The Perry Mason solution! Partner, you're flat out colorful."

"But it does make sense, doesn't it?"

"Let's put it this way—I don't see what other defense you've got. You can put Rob and Alan and yourself on the stand to testify about the phone call—"

"And make laughingstocks of all of us."

"And you can have whachadoogy . . ."

"Lou."

". . . testify that he was watching TV that night—or maybe he was in a bar he can't remember the name of—"

"And make a laughingstock out of my client."

"Or you could try something else—and frankly, I can't think of a single other possibility."

"Except finding the real Trapper."

She sighed. "Okay, I'm game. Where do we start?"

"Let's call Terry Yannarelli."

But Terry wasn't in the phone book. This time I sighed. "I guess I'll have to go see him. Want to join me?"

"Can't. Bob and I are going out to dinner."

It was a bit unusual interviewing a potential witness without a witness of my own (in case he later changed his story), but I'd be taking only a preliminary statement, certainly not a formal one. He might be more relaxed if I went alone.

Terry wasn't at home, so there was nothing for it but to try the Yellow Parrot. He was there, talking to a kid who looked rather like a blond version of Art Zimbardo. Not Terry's type, I should have thought, but maybe there weren't any older married types in the place at the time.

He remembered me, greeting me with a hearty "Where's Rob?"

"Why? Want your picture in the paper again?"

"I got a lot of tricks out of that."

"I'm sure you do okay without benefit of press agent."

He shrugged. "My face is my fortune—at least it gets me a few free drinks."

"You know, Terry—you're the only person I know who's actually seen the Trapper."

"What do you mean? You haven't seen your own client?"

"I'm working on the theory that my client didn't do it. Did you see his picture in the paper?"

"Sure."

"What did you think?"

"Not bad. More or less my type, to tell you the truth." The blond kid made a face and walked away. I cocked an eyebrow. Terry shrugged. "No problem. There's plenty more where he came from."

"Could you get serious for a minute?"

"About what?" He looked genuinely surprised.

"My client. Was he the guy you talked to the night Sanchez was murdered?"

"Who's Sanchez?"

"Rhinestone, dammit. How many murderers have you talked to lately?"

He smiled. "Maybe lots. I like danger, remember?"

"Terry, can I buy you a drink?"

"I thought you'd never ask."

Jake the bartender set us up and I started over. "Now, about my client. Did he look familiar to you?"

"I couldn't really tell. He's clean-shaven and the trick had a beard."

"I thought he wasn't a trick."

"They're all tricks. He just didn't work out."

"If you actually saw my client, do you think you could tell? Maybe if he talked to you—could you recognize his voice?"

"Maybe."

"But you don't think so."

He shook his head. "I don't remember a damn thing about the guy except he didn't want to su—"

"Never mind. Listen—that name he gave you. Was it Les, by any chance?"

He thought for a minute. "Could have been."

"I'll bet you're a whiz at Trivial Pursuit."

"Huh?"

"Having total recall and all."

He laughed. "I do too many drugs."

"Les, Lee, or Lou?"

"Haven't a clue."

So much for my only possible witness.

The next day was Saturday and I had it all to myself. Rob and I had never finished our conversation about a "trial separation," but things were sort of working out that way. We were wary of each other. I was preoccupied with Lou's case and he, I think, had gotten his feelings hurt by my admission that I'd had a date with someone else. To tell the truth, I think he might have been dating someone else, freed to do it by my admission. I didn't know what I wanted from him right then and didn't have the energy to confront the thing at the moment.

I fed my fish, played a little Beethoven, and looked up two names in the phone book—Miranda Waring and Les Mathison. There wasn't even an M. Waring, but there was a Leslie Mathison on Twelfth Avenue.

For a while, I stared at the fish, trying to figure out what to do next. If this was my Les, he was a guy I suspected of being a lunatic who'd as soon murder me as put on his socks. I could hardly phone such a person—that would serve no purpose except to put him on his guard. But I couldn't see the point of confronting him either. At least not yet. The thing to do first was figure out if he was my pigeon.

I drove out to Twelfth Avenue and looked at his house. It was a duplex, his address being the second-floor apartment. A perfectly nice place, if slightly characterless—big enough for a family. I remembered Lou's telling me that Les had lost his wife—though whether she'd died or left him I didn't know; I wondered if he had children, too. It was hard to think of the Trapper as someone's dad.

I got out of the Volvo and stood on the sidewalk, staring rudely until I saw a curtain move in the downstairs apartment. Gathering my nerve, I rang the doorbell. Two scruffy children answered my ring in about two seconds, followed instantly by a tired-looking woman, overweight and lank of hair. "You look too old for a baby-sitter."

"I am, I think. Are you expecting one?"

She looked downcast. "She's half an hour late already."

"Oh. I'm actually looking for Les Mathison."

"Les moved out six months ago."

"I'm not sure I've got the right Les. Is this one married?"

"He was. You must have been out of touch for a long time if you don't know about all that."

"We sort of lost track of each other."

"Are you his friend or Darlene's?"

I hated it when Rob lied to get a story, but I could see how tempting it was. I paused a moment, trying to stem my mendacious urges, and finally blurted out, "I heard he had an accident on a cable car."

She looked terribly distressed. "Look, I'm afraid I don't know where to find him."

"Do you know anyone who would? I really need to talk to him."

"His mother, maybe, but I don't know her name. All I know is she's from Turlock. She came down to take care of him after he—I mean, I always just called her Mrs. Mathison." The distress suddenly left her face. "Oh, there she is. Thank God." I looked around, half expecting Mrs. Mathison herself, but the only human in sight was a teenage girl. The baby-sitter.

I left elated, pretty sure I was on the right track. Les's neighbor, I thought, had pegged me for an old friend and didn't want to be the one to tell me bad news—either about Darlene or about Les's assault on the cable car. At any rate, there was something she didn't want to tell me; if this was a different Les, he'd had his share of bad luck, too.

Now I had to figure out how to approach Mom Mathison. On practical grounds, I decided against driving to Turlock. I might have all day Saturday to myself, but that was ridiculous.

In the end, I phoned, using one of Rob's favorite tactics for getting people to talk. He claims experience has taught him it's what they really want to do, anyway—just give them a chance and they'll probably go at it full tilt. I wasn't sure what I'd do if Mrs. Mathison asked any difficult questions—like why did I want to find Les—but I felt that after berating Rob for lying to get information, I ought to try to avoid doing it myself.

There were four Mathisons in Turlock, and the third time I asked for Les a woman spoke up hopefully: "Les? He's not here right now—did he tell you he would be?"

"Is this Mrs. Mathison? His mother?"

"Yes, it is. Are you a friend of Les's?"

"I'm afraid not, Mrs. Mathison. But I need to talk to him, and his neighbor told me he might be there. My name is Rebecca Schwartz," I added, hoping she wouldn't recognize it.

"Oh." She sounded disappointed. "Well, I haven't heard from Les in—oh, maybe a year or more. Before that, only every once in a while. Ever since his accident he's stayed away. I so much wanted him to come home, too—he never had a worry in the world till he moved to San Francisco."

I was starting to get goose bumps. Controlling myself, I said, "You mean the accident on the cable car?"

"Yes. Unless—don't tell me there's been another! I couldn't stand it."

"Not that I know of. It's just that I don't know what he's been doing lately."

"Trying to find himself, I imagine. I pray to God every night that nothing else has happened to him and that he'll come home to us soon. And come home to Jesus, too."

The last sentence sounded so heartfelt I could almost feel Mrs. Mathison's pain myself. "I didn't know he was a religious man."

"Went to church every Sunday of his life until he left Turlock. Active in Sunday school, too. And the 4-H and the Boy Scouts and president of the Future Farmers of America. We brought him up to lead a good, healthy life and he did, too—a model boy. They still remember him over at the high school."

"So Les grew up on a farm."

"More like a ranch, really. I never saw a boy that cared so much for his animals. Hated it when he had to slaughter 'em—but he did have to, of course; they teach 'em that in 4-H; what's the point of raisin' 'em if you don't slaughter 'em? But he was always a sensitive boy. Said they hadn't done anything to anybody, so why should he hurt 'em? My husband had to whip him till he'd do it; hurt him more than it hurt Les but he had to—only way to teach him. We never believed in sparin' the rod, but there was a lot of love here and Les knew it. He'd never have left home if we hadn't lost the ranch. He said there was nothing for him in Turlock anymore—he had to go to San Francisco and try to make it on his own." She started to sob. "I've wished so many times he'd stayed here but I know it was God's will that he had to go. That's what ou pastor said when I went for counseling and I know he's right. I pray every night I'll learn to accept it someday."

"Did he move to the city with his wife?"

"Say, are you a girlfriend of his?"

"No. I'm a lawyer and I thought he might have some information about a case I'm working on."

"He's not in trouble, is he?"

Only the worst possible kind. I said, "Frankly, I'm a little worried that no one seems to know where he is."

"I don't understand. I thought you said his neighbor told you to call."

"She told me he's moved away."

"Oh, lordy, lordy, I knew I shouldn't have stopped writing him. My husband told me to, said Les would get in touch when he was ready; I think he thought he'd come home like the prodigal son one day."

"Maybe you should file a missing persons report."

"Oh, I couldn't do that. We aren't the kind of people who have dealings with the police."

"I see. I wonder if you could tell me something else. You said Les's trouble started when he moved to San Francisco. Did something happen besides the incident on the cable car?"

"Are you a Christian, dear?"

"I'm not, actually."

"Well, I'm not sure I should be talking to you. I think I ought to pray about it."

"I understand how you feel; but I feel I should tell you the truth. I think Less really might be in trouble."

"Are you trying to help him?"

There it was—the crunch of conscience. I took a deep breath, but before I could say anything, she spoke again: "I don't think you are. You're not a Christian and sometimes I don't think there is one in the whole city of San Francisco— just last Easter they crucified someone like they did Jesus."

"Why don't I give you my address and phone number, just in case?"

She cheered up. "I could send you some very interesting pamphlets."

"I'd like that."

"And if you hear anything about Les, you'll let me know, won't you?"

"I'll be glad to. But turnabout's fair play—if *you* hear something, will you let me know?"

"I don't know . . ." She sounded very doubtful indeed.

"I know you'll do what you can." I gave her my stats and hung up in a cold sweat.

I'd found the conversation chilling. Mom Mathison talked almost like the Trapper wrote—blaming all her son's problems on the city itself. I went straight to the piano and spent most of the rest of the day there. The next day I drove to Marin, squirmed through my parents' slides of Israel, and finally managed to get Dad to take a walk with me; I knew talking about the case in front of Mom would cause about the same reaction as announcing I'd just joined the Hare Krishnas.

When I'd laid the whole thing out, he said, "I'd been wondering how you were going to pull this one out, Rebecca." I breathed a sigh of relief—he hadn't called me Beck; that meant at least he wasn't about to have an aneurysm from worry. "The thing's plausible, all right. A kid from an upright all-American home—and yet abused."

"Abused?"

"They beat him, didn't they? Beat him to make him kill his pets?"

"Dad, they don't think of them as pets in 4-H."

"But he thought of them as pets—his mother said so. Can you imagine anything more horrifying to a child than being beaten by his own parents because he refused to heartlessly kill the helpless animals he'd raised and loved?"

"Dad, for heaven's sake—this is me, not a jury."

"I may be being a little dramatic, but think about it—can you?"

"It sounds pretty awful, all right. I wonder if any of them were lambs."

"I don't think things like that unbalance a person, exactly, but suppose someone with that kind of history actually does go off the deep end; he's bound to have a skewed sense of justice. And even as a youngster, this kid had justice on his mind—the mother said he thought it was unfair to kill animals that didn't hurt anyone, didn't she?"

"Something like that."

"Add the element of Christianity and you get another set of contradictions. You get Jesus saying to turn the other cheek, but the Old Testament God saying, 'Vengeance is mine.' You also get Jesus saying, 'Blessed are the meek,' and Christian parents beating up their kids for acting wimpy. Most kids work it out somehow or other, but in the case of one who's slightly unbalanced, all that stuff is still in the brain somewhere, mixing it up like a couple of street gangs."

Suddenly I had a mental image, not of thugs at a weekend rumble, but of tiny knights in heavy armor, flailing about with mouse-sized swords somewhere in Les's skull.

"I'll bet Mrs. Mathison wasn't lying when she said there was a lot of love in that home and that Les knew it. I'd be willing to believe he was a perfectly sincere, if somewhat confused, Boy Scout and Future Farmer. But suppose he became severely disillusioned, convinced God wasn't quite the benign shepherd He's cracked up to be."

"He might get cranky and nail someone to a cross on Easter Sunday."

Dad sighed. "He might if he were messhuge. But nothing Mrs. M. said really indicated that. I wonder about those animals."

"I beg your pardon?"

"Suppose I wanted you to kill Noah."

Noah had been my childhood cat. "And suppose I forced you to do it by beating you." I nodded, trying to take it in.

"Then when you actually killed Noah, do you think you might still be angry?"

I was beginning to get the hang of it. "Angry enough to kill, you mean? You mean in some weird way, I might be so mad at you I'd actually enjoy killing Noah?"

He nodded. "I'll have to talk to one of my shrink friends. It might possibly work that way."

"The only problem is, it's just a theory. The only way we'd ever find out is if Les told us."

"Hold your horses, babe. I'm just kicking it around, trying to figure out if I can believe in Les as the Trapper."

"And?"

"Well, let's put it this way—your client's going to the green room if you don't come up with some better defense than you've currently got."

"Dad!" It hurt, hearing it put so bluntly.

"Don't get upset, Beck. You've got to be practical about this. What if you do lose him? You have to be prepared for it. You can't get too emotionally involved."

"I like the way you said, 'lose him,' not 'lose the case.' That's keeping a healthy distance."

"You also have to remember that if you lose the case, he's a goner. And I've got to tell you, I think there's a good chance you'll lose."

"You don't like the Les Mathison theory."

"I think it's worth pursuing." He gave me one of his famous smiles, the kind that showed off all the cute crinkles around the blue eyes.

At least he didn't think I was completely off my nut. And he and Chris were in agreement—they both thought it was my only chance. That made three of us.

12

"You've got two choices," Chris said when I brought her up to date the next morning. "Hire an investigator or get Rob to help."

Without hesitation, I picked up the Yellow Pages and turned to Private Investigators. I knew who I wanted, a guy who'd done some good work for some people I knew. I'd even met him a couple of times—a big Italian guy—but try as I might I couldn't get his name to come to me. I ran my finger down the lists, turning the pages, but nothing jarred my memory. I'd have to call one of my friends who'd used him. I picked up the phone, held the receiver so long I lost the dial tone, punched the button to get it back, and dialed Rob's number. Deep down, I must have been looking for an excuse to call him.

I was sure of it later when I walked into John's Grill and saw him waiting for me on a barstool. When he saw me, he smiled, and his face looked as if somebody'd plugged him in and flipped a switch. If I'd been worried that I was wearing nothing nicer than a lawyerly black suit—and needless to say,

I was—I forgot about it. "You look terrific," he said, and I knew he'd have said it if I'd had a stocking over my face; he didn't really care how I looked at all, he just wanted to be with me, and I loved him for it. To my unmitigated horror, tears popped into my eyes.

"So do you."

"Well, don't cry about it."

"It's my party and I'll cry if I want to."

"Where does it hurt? I'll kiss it." For the next couple of minutes we must have looked like a standing tangle of black linen and tan corduroy. I couldn't imagine what had made me stay away.

"I must have been crazy," I said.

He looked alarmed. "To see me?"

"Not to see you."

Relief flooded his face. "Certifiable."

"I was hurt."

"I know. I'm sorry."

"*I'm* sorry."

The drunk at the next table leaned over. "You two belong on daytime TV."

"We are getting a little sudsy," said Rob.

"I'm enjoying it."

"Wallow in it, baby. Cry me a river."

"Oh, can it."

"Speaking of cans . . . and suds—"

"Beer's for journalists."

He hailed the bartender: "One beer and one insipid white wine."

"Please, no Yuppie jokes."

"I like Yup women. They have money."

"Same old Rob."

"Admit it. It's been hell without my acerbic wit."

"There's always Kruzick."

"That reminds me—how's the little mother?"

"Still determined to go through with it; I think she's working up the nerve to tell Mom and Dad."

"Marin General better double their emergency room staff."

"Let's don't talk about it." Mickey's pregnancy was an area of my life—along with Rob—that I'd managed to put out of my mind since taking Lou's case. Thinking about it—especially Mom's reaction to it—depressed me too much.

"Sorry," he said. "Let's talk business first."

"And then what?"

"How about a rousing game of gin?" He reached in his pocket and took out an envelope. "Look what I brought you."

"Clips!"

He nodded. "Clips indeed. Guaranteed to make you the happiest lawyer on Montgomery Street."

"You found something on Les Mathison." I'd asked him to look, realizing it was only an outside chance.

"Not just something, babycakes. I've got what you want."

I'm no good at coquettish looks, but I attempted one: "I'll bet you do." And then I fell upon the clippings like a bulimic in a box of doughnuts.

There were two, the first a routine crime story about a woman killed in a random incident of violence aboard a cable car. The woman's name was Darlene Mathison.

The second was an interview with the bereaved husband, Leslie Mathison, formerly of Turlock. The reporter, one Annie Ballard, had hit pay dirt, turning up a human interest story so good she'd written a long, moving feature about it—a story detailing the life of a simple man who grew up on a ranch, who knew only an innocent kind of life in which he'd been a churchgoer and a member of the 4-H Club; a man who, after moving to San Francisco with his wife and daughter, had found the same kind of hardships any city dweller might have. And then the hardships began to multiply. He had frustrations with banks, buses, and restaurants as anyone would—the sort of problems all city dwellers take for granted. But Les didn't take them for granted; he found himself frustrated everywhere he turned and had no armor to cope with his frustration. He took a job at a flooring company in South San Francisco.

His family suffered because banks wouldn't take out-of-town checks without a waiting period, because a decent apartment for a family of three was far beyond his means, because everything cost too much. He found himself horrified by the crowds on the bus, in restaurants, everywhere he went on business, everywhere he took his family for fun. He was a man who'd never before had to wait in line to see a movie. Because his rent was so high, he'd had to sell his car. Aside from the inconvenience of having to leave for work an hour before he had to punch in, aside from the vandals and druggies on the MUNI, there was a very real problem with that—the buses sometimes didn't run on time, sometimes broke down, and caused him to be late to work. He would have left earlier, he told Annie Ballard, but his wife worked a morning shift as a waitress, which meant he had to get their daughter, Kathi, ready for school. Even so, he had to leave Kathi alone for half an hour: "I'd see that kid sitting there, hardly able to hold her eyes open, looking so forlorn every morning when I left I just couldn't stand to think of making her get up at 6:30, and stay alone an hour in the house just so I could make sure I got to work on time for some bozo who didn't care about anything except the almighty dollar." Ms. Ballard noted that his voice shook as he spoke.

The inevitable happened: He was late to work once too often and lost his job. Before he found another, his daughter was killed in a motorcycle accident—hit by a kid on drugs. It was hardly a month after that that Darlene was stabbed to death on a cable car, having gotten in the middle of someone else's fight.

It was almost too much to believe. "Annie Ballard," said Rob, "must have thought she'd died and gone to heaven when ol' Les started letting down his hair."

"Oh, Rob."

"Sorry," he muttered, and had the grace to flush a bit. "Great quotes, though.".

I couldn't argue with him. For instance: "When I lost Kathi, I don't mind telling you, I about lost my faith in God. But I was raised to be a Christian and I kept on prayin', kept on going to church. Now that Darlene's dead, I don't feel that way. I feel like God's made a monkey out of me. Right now I feel like burning every church in this miserable hellhole."

Ms. Ballard closed with this one: "When I think about what's happened to me since I came here, I'd like to do to San Francisco what the God I used to believe in did to Sodom and Gomorrah."

I got goose bumps reading—worse ones than when I'd read the Trapper's notes to Rob, because those were just the maunderings of a sick mind; now I felt as if I knew the man behind the sickness. He was real to me, and scarier than the shadow man; there wasn't a shred of doubt in my mind that Les Mathison was the Trapper.

Rob said, "The Trapper's words are even in there. 'Hellhole'; 'Sodom and Gomorrah.'"

"Rob, do you realize the most horrifying thing about this? That wasn't even the end of it—after all that, he got beat up by Lou Zimbardo."

"Poor sucker. No wonder he went nuts."

"Excuse me, but did I hear Rob 'Hard Case' Burns call a multiple murderer a poor sucker?"

He shook his head unhappily. "I never heard of anything like this."

"You're just jealous because someone else got the story."

"I've got feelings, too, you know."

I patted his hand. "I forget sometimes."

"So now what? Do we go to the D.A. and lay it on him?"

"I don't think it's good enough. He's got physical evidence against Lou."

"What? The gun that killed Sanchez? All part of the frame-up."

"It reads like that if you don't think he's guilty, but what if you do? And he's got reason to prosecute Lou—he can get a conviction."

"But surely if you know about Mathison, there's a reasonable doubt."

"Yes, but there's no proof against him; there's proof against Lou."

"So let the cops get some."

"I don't think this will convince them; I think we have to have more."

"I thought you'd be thrilled."

"I'm beside myself."

"You know what he must have done? He must have been planning the thing all the time Lou was in prison, waiting for him to get out."

"My goose bumps have goose bumps." I shivered and reached for Rob, for comfort, just as the bartender shouted: "Phone for Rob Burns."

Rob answered the page and came back flushed. "A bomb went off at the Bonanza Inn. An elevator crashed with a load of conventioneers aboard." He was fumbling in his pocket for money to pay up so he could get out fast. "Want to come?"

I did not. Not in the least. But the Bonanza Inn on Union Square was one of the top five hotels in the city—enormous, nicely appointed but not fabulously expensive, maybe fifty years old (which made it historic without being a relic), newly redecorated, conveniently located near Union Square, and currently, due to the massive refurbishing, very much in vogue—in other words, a prime Trapper target. I remembered my premonition the night of the cable car crash that the Trapper would strike a hotel. I followed Rob out the door, though I knew I wouldn't catch him. He'd slammed down a couple of bills and charged out like a rhino; I was reminded rather sickeningly of the night the Trapper struck Full Fathom Five, when Rob left me in a cloud of dust at the Eagle Café. As I clacked after him this time, wishing ardently for

Nikes to replace my Joan and Davids, I was discomfited that I was now using the Trapper's shenanigans as mileposts, that I'd done it twice in the last five minutes. In a way, as I thought about what the city had been through and might be about to go through again, I wished Lou really were the Trapper.

The police hadn't yet cordoned off the building, and the emergency vehicles hadn't yet started to arrive; apparently, the second word came over the police radio the city desk had called Rob, who was known to hang out at John's Grill and could be at the scene in about three minutes, only half hurrying. But on a breaking story Rob wouldn't have dreamt of half hurrying and had no doubt kicked small children and helpless winos out of his way in his relentless protection of the people's right to know. I'd say I got there in about three minutes ten seconds, and already he was nowhere to be seen.

A phalanx of security guards blocked the doors. "Is something happening?" I said in a concerned voice.

"We can't let you in right now, ma'am."

"But I'm staying here."

"I'm sorry, ma'am. We can't let you in."

"What is it, a fire?" I let my voice rise. "My husband's in there."

"No, ma'am, it's not a fire."

"But my husband!" I wailed.

The guard didn't answer, just stood there impassively. That made me mad. In truth, there was no real reason I had to go in, but I was getting caught up in the excitement, so caught up I'd already compromised my principles by lying and hadn't even realized it, hadn't even stopped to consider the ethics of the situation. I tried to push past, still doing my imitation of a terrified wife. The guard grabbed my arm. "Ma'am, you can't go in there now."

"I've got to." I tried to jerk my arm away, but he held on. To my horror, I saw that I was beginning to draw a crowd, and I could also hear sirens getting close. If I didn't get in now, I probably wasn't going to. Should I retreat?

And then I heard a male voice say, "The lady's with me." It was Pete Brainard of the *Chronicle*, evidently the photographer they'd sent to meet Rob. He was flashing his press card.

"Let's see her press card."

"She's not a reporter. She's my assistant." Pete took his heavy camera bag off his shoulder and put it on mine. "Here, Rebecca, take this will you?"

"We can't let her in without a press card."

"Dammit, she's with me!" The guard had relaxed his grip on my arm, and now Pete grabbed me every bit as roughly, and whisked me past the rent-a-cop.

"Goddamn newshawks!" the guard said, giving up the fight. It made me giggle. "Newshawk" was what my mother called Rob when she wanted to be particularly insulting. There was no one quite so arrogant as a newshawk on a story, be he or she reporter or photographer. If I thought I had a right to be in that hotel, I was probably catching the disease myself; no doubt Mom would be disappointed in me, but it wouldn't be the first time.

The lobby was nearly deserted, the elevators being around a corner and down a corridor. We ran toward them, me weighed down by Pete's heavy camera case. In the distance, we could see a crowd. Up close it proved to be not a dense one, but a milling one, again kept at bay by the hotel's security staff. Rob was at the front.

He was pale. Looking past the line of guards, I could see why. More than a dozen men and women were lying on the floor, some moaning, some lying still, as maids, bellmen, and hotel executives raced back and forth with blankets and first-aid supplies. I started to feel as if I shouldn't have come.

As Pete and I reached Rob, we heard a commotion behind us, and the crowd parted, the line of guards parted, to let the first paramedics through. Pete went into frantic action, snapping the overall scene, the carnage on the floor, the faces of the paramedics, the faces of the victims. He couldn't yet get close enough to get to the fallen elevator itself, but I knew he'd stay there until he could, even though as the first photographer on the scene, he was bound to have the best pictures.

Rob was simply watching, scribbling on his notepad, not bothering anyone. I supposed he'd already talked to hotel personnel and witnesses, and he'd talk to more later, but at the moment he was a witness himself. I felt profoundly depressed; the breathless excitement had passed and I was watching something that resembled one of the more frenetic war-is-hell scenes from M*A*S*H. I wondered what the hell I was doing there.

"Rebecca, give me a long lens, dammit!"

I fumbled in Pete's bag, found the lens, and promptly dropped it. I thanked my stars the floor was carpeted, but when I bent down to pick it up, I bumped someone who was thrown off-balance and who accidentally kicked it just past one of the guards. I was going to ask him to hand it back, but Pete pushed past me, reaching for it. The guard grabbed him and pushed him back, hard. The crowd fell back in a shudder, but they were mostly well behaved. Which was more than I could say for Pete, who shouted, "Stupid asshole!"

"Who're you calling asshole?" The guard doubled up his fist.

"I'm from the *Chronicle*!"

"I don't care if you're from the *New York Times*, you're out of line."

"Goddamn jerks got no respect for the press." Pete was only mumbling now, having better sense than to provoke fisticuffs, but still obsessed with the one thing on his mind: "This is a news story and I am currently God."

I was starting to feel my old revulsion for my boyfriend's job, but something took my mind off it. Loud and clear, even in the midst of all that, I heard someone calling Rob's name— a bellman who'd come to tell him he had a phone call. I didn't think hotel employees would have gone to that much trouble for just anyone, but thanks to the Trapper, Rob was currently something of a VIP around town. He looked dismayed, torn between what was probably an instructional call from his office and the story itself.

Finally, he said, "Rebecca, could you take the call?" I wanted out of there, anyway, and jumped at the chance. As I turned around, Pete grabbed his bag, still on my shoulder, and pulled. I snapped: "Take it easy, will you?" But he didn't even bother to answer.

"This is Rebecca Schwartz," I said to the caller. "Rob can't get away right now. He asked me to relay the message."

The caller spoke in a calm, authoritative voice: *"This is the Trapper. I did it with plastic. Two charges—one for the hoists, one for the governor. There's only one way to stop this—pay me half a million dollars. I'll call back about the details. In the meantime, tell Burns he better put this in the paper tomorrow."*

The Trapper hung up; I wasn't so quick. I stared into space, still holding the receiver, until finally it occurred to me to jot the message down. All I had was the back of a check, but that would do. I was still writing, trying to get it exactly word for word, when I felt an arm around my waist. "Was it the city desk?"

"Oh, Rob. It was the Trapper."

"No!"

"I'm afraid so." I read him the message.

"You're sure that's exactly right?"

"Pretty sure. I might have a 'the' where there ought to be an 'a,' but believe me, that's basically what he said. I don't get the stuff about the plastic and the governor, but the hoists must be cables."

Rob said, "He never asked for money before."

"You think it wasn't Les?"

"What did his voice sound like?"

I tried to think. "A regular man's voice. Very calm. Sort of icy calm."

He shrugged. "My caller was calm, too, but I don't know where that gets us. Damn! What if it wasn't Les?"

"If it wasn't, there's another one out there, trying to cash in on his operation." My head was spinning. "Maybe it's starting all over again."

Rob said, "I wish I'd taken that call."

13

And that wasn't the fun part of the evening; it was just one laugh after another when I tried to do my duty as a citizen and tell the cops what I knew about their case. "Miss Schwartz," fumed Martinez, "you gotta be nuts, coming to me with a thing like this."

"A thing like what?"

"You're the defense lawyer in the Trapper case, right? Well, naturally you're gonna do anything you can to get your client off."

"What!" I was on my feet, no longer wishing for Nikes, grateful instead for any height I could muster.

"Look. So you trumped up the call. I'm not gonna arrest you for giving false evidence—I'm gonna forget the whole thing, okay? Maybe you're not nuts. Maybe you're still a little inexperienced; maybe you didn't know any better. But you gotta be nuts if you ever try anything like this again."

I deliberately put my purse and briefcase on the floor; if I continued to be tempted with a ready weapon I was most certainly going to commit assault on a police officer. I had once been to jail and I wasn't going back even if I had to deprive myself of the supreme pleasure of belting this android. I cleared my throat, but still my voice sounded husky. "Inspector Martinez, I came to you out of courtesy—because the Trapper case is your case. I answered a call for Rob Burns tonight—"

"Very convenient."

"—that I thought might have some bearing on this case. I could have gone to someone else in the department, and I will if you decline to take my information. Meanwhile, I'll ask you to apologize for your insulting implications."

"Apologize!" I believe the sound he made next could be accurately called a hoot. Even the colorless Curry seemed amused, though there wasn't a peep out of him; just a malicious set to his mouth.

"I believe," I said, not quite calmly, but not yet losing it, "I believe you accused me of giving false evidence."

"False evidence!" Martinez was beginning to guffaw; Curry joined in, but they still weren't satisfied. "Hey, Franklin! Hunt! Listen to this." A couple of bored-looking cops turned his way. "Schwartzy here's the lawyer for the Trapper so guess what she tries to pull?" Tears were starting to run down his cheeks. Apparently, he was just realizing he could dine out on my story for weeks. "She says the Trapper called her constant companion, Rob Burns—"

"Rob and I haven't even spoken—"

"And she just happened to intercept the call."

Franklin: "You gotta be kiddin'."

Hunt: "Some people'll do anything."

Curry: "I never yet met a lawyer told the truth twice in the same day."

There had to be ways around this. I could call Martinez's superior. I could repeat the whole preposterous conversation to Rob and let him write a story about it that would make Martinez sorry he ever tangled with the likes of Rebecca Schwartz. I could get my dad to— I stopped in midthought.

None of the above. I couldn't turn to Rob or Dad. I could call Martinez's superior, but not till tomorrow. I had to handle Martinez myself, and now. My hands itched for my purse or briefcase.

I said, "Inspector Martinez, I don't even understand what the message meant. I'm just telling you what I heard."

"You mean what your client told you to say."

"My client? My client's in jail—how could he have done this?"

"You ever heard of a timing device? Let me tell you something, Miss Schwartz. Elevators are serviced every week, but the servicemen go into the shaft only every two weeks. So he could have set it two weeks ago. And God knows how many more booby traps he's left around. Let me tell you something else. That crash was caused by two charges—one that severed the hoist cables and one that severed the governor cable that should have stopped the car. You know how an elevator works? If the hoists are severed, the governor pulls up wedges underneath it called safeties, and the safeties stop the fall. As it happens, I've spent the evening with elevator specialists, who tell me the one thing your client probably didn't know: It's practically impossible to kill somebody in a falling elevator. So maybe nobody's going to die as a result of this, but it won't be because your client didn't try. By the way, guess what explosive was used at the Bonanza Inn?"

"How should I know?"

"You seem to know quite a lot. Plastic explosive, Miss Schwartz. Just like your client told you. Remember that little book on explosives we found in Lou's room? There's a big fat chapter on how to make Plastique. Another thing—didn't you notice the Trapper doesn't ask for money? And he writes instead of phones? Next time get the M.O. right, okay?"

"He phoned about the cable car."

"I am just about at the end of my patience!" He was bellowing. "You try it once and it doesn't work and now you try it again. Do you think I'm a complete fool?"

I said, "What I think is quite beside the point, Inspector Martinez. The simple fact is that you have blown this case. You may get a conviction, but I'm telling you right now that Lou Zimbardo is an innocent man. Not only is my client not the Trapper, but I know who is."

"Yeah? Who?" Martinez was only too happy to play, probably thinking I'd say something like, "I'm not at liberty to disclose that information at this point in time."

Instead I said, "Les Mathison."

"Who?"

"Inspector Hunt, are you listening? Franklin? Curry? The Trapper is Les Mathison."

Martinez: "Who the hell is Les Mathison?"

Franklin: "What's she talking about?"

Hunt: "What the hell does she know, anyway?"

Curry: "Where is he?"

"Good night, gentlemen," I said, reaching, with perfect cool, for my two bags. Whether they'd taken me seriously or not, they were too bewildered to toss out any more insults. I'd gotten them off my back, but it was a complicated thing I'd done. It might actually start Martinez's pea-sized brain in motion; maybe he'd run some checks on Les, get interested, perhaps even find him.

Before it was too late, I got hold of myself. I was so flushed with victory I'd forgotten whom I was dealing with. Martinez would do something intelligent when the Bay Bridge started galloping like Gertie. In the meantime, he'd ignore the Les theory just because it was mine. I wondered if I'd hurt my client by baiting him. But surely not. The D.A., not Martinez, would decide whether or not to investigate Les— that is, he would if I ever got enough evidence to go to him.

Needless to say, the more tender moments of my reunion with Rob had to be postponed. So I perused the *Chronicle* alone the next morning, and could certainly have used a warm hug when I saw the headline: "Elevator Disaster—Police

Fear Trapper Booby Trap." Martinez had been careful not to libel my client, but he had told the press that the bombs had been set using a timing device, and that police were investigating the possibility that they were set by Lou Zimbardo, the Trapper suspect, before he was incarcerated; and he did say that police were checking other hotel elevators for bombs, thus renewing the famous climate of fear. It was also going to be a climate of vengeance—I figured Lou had about as much of a chance of getting a fair trial in San Francisco as Martinez had of getting into MENSA.

A sidebar by Charlie Fish, a young hot dog who was bucking to replace Rob as star reporter, explained how the bombs were set: Someone went into the machine room and lined the opening where the cables go through to the elevator with plastic explosives; he then put another charge in the case over the governor. Timing devices were found for both bombs, but the demolitions experts couldn't be sure when they'd been set.

The casualty count was twelve injured, three seriously; no one dead, thank God.

Nowhere in either story was the Trapper's phone call to me mentioned. I was thinking about bursting into unlawyerlike tears when the doorbell rang—Rob, with coffee and crois-sants. I wasn't hungry. Rob said, "I hope you're not mad; I did something I'm not sure about."

I had a feeling I knew what it was, but was prevented from asking by an urgently ringing phone. I picked it up, resigned: "Hi, Mom."

"Are you psychic, darling?"

"Just a good guess."

"Have you seen the *Chronicle*?"

"I'm afraid so."

"Whose side is that Rob on, anyway?"

"He's just doing his job, Mom."

"He didn't have to make it sound like your client set those bombs."

"I don't think he meant to, Mom. He was just quoting the cops."

"He could have left that stuff out."

"I wish, Mom, but reporters have to report."

"There's no such thing as objectivity."

"Well, they try for it."

"You'd think he could help you out a little."

"I've got to run, Mom. Call you back, okay?"

Rob had finished his croissant and was working on mine. I said, "Mom thinks you could have made my client look better. That was kind of an odd position I was in, just then. Defending modern journalism."

"Listen, I did something that might not be ethical; I'm all mixed up about it."

"I noticed you didn't mention the Trapper's call. Is that what you mean?"

He spoke softly, so that I had to strain to hear. "Yeah. I couldn't bring myself to do it. I mean, I know if the defense lawyer had been anyone else, I would have—and thereby made him or her a laughingstock. But I couldn't do it to you."

"You could have asked me how I felt about it." I was just trying that on for size—more or less playing the devil's advocate—because I didn't really know how I felt about it. In a way, I wanted it made public. It was true, dammit—the real Trapper had called and was still on the loose and I thought people should know. On the other hand, I knew they wouldn't believe it—coming from me—and that indeed reporting the phone call would have made both my client and me look bad.

Rob said, "I could have asked you, but it wouldn't have been fair; figuring out what to do was up to me. Involving you would only have made you an accessory to a possible breach of ethics. Actually, a certain breach of ethics, except for the fact that the call was meant for me. Yes, you're my girlfriend, and yes, that's why I suppressed it; but no other defense lawyer in the world would be put in the position of appearing a horse's ass by my failure to take my own phone call."

I didn't say anything, trying to digest what he was saying.

"Rebecca, I'm sorry I asked you to take the call—it was unforgivably stupid."

"Oh, don't be silly. It seemed like the right thing to do at the time. Listen, thanks for doing what you did; I'm sure it was the right thing."

But I wasn't sure and neither was he. Maybe there just wasn't a right answer to the question.

Rob finished off my croissant. "I've got to run. Can I see you tomorrow?"

"How about tonight?"

"I have to work."

"Tomorrow then. I'll make something here."

"No. I want to take you out."

"I'd rather just wear jeans and put my feet up." Why stand on ceremony with a man you've been dating for more than a year?

"Okay, I'll cook."

"Wow. You're taking reconciliation to dizzying heights."

"I've been taking cooking classes."

"If you'd told me that, I would have called sooner."

"You love me for myself."

"That and your purple prose."

I had a morning court appearance and didn't get to the office till nearly noon. Imagine my surprise to find my secretary knitting; knitting something white and dainty and very small. Far too small for the hammy hands of a tall chap in a schlumpy outfit. He looked like someone playing dolls with his daughter. Daughter! What was I thinking of? And yet there was a fifty-fifty chance he was going to have one. I thought I'd better take time out and get used to the idea. I said, "Don't forget to purl."

"Pearl. That's it! We'll name her after Janis Joplin."

"What if it's a boy?"

"Jimi."

"Not Elvis?" I was sorry the instant I said it.

"Elvis. Better yet."

He was capable of going through with it. Even if Mickey managed a halfway-Jewish-sounding name that Mom and Dad could live with—like David, say—he'd probably call the kid El and we'd all end up doing it. Depressing, but that was the least of the Schwartz family problems-to-be. I was just going into a black reverie, imagining conversations with Mom that would spook a shrink, when Alan spoke again: "Your dad's on his way over. He wants to take you to lunch."

"He does? Great."

"I think it's time he knew about the baby."

Goose bumps started forming on my extremities. "What are you getting at?"

"How's this? He comes in, sees me knitting, and says, 'New hobby, Alan?' And I say, 'Not exactly, Mr. Schwartz. It's just that I don't know how Mickey and I are going to support little Pearl or Elvis on the pittance I make here, so I'm just trying to save a few precious pennies on bunting.' Then he says . . ."

"Very funny, Alan."

"Of course, if I were to get a raise it wouldn't be necessary."

I did owe him a raise. At least, most decent employees should get a raise after a year's faithful service. But Kruzick's work was distinctly slipshod and he was about as faithful as a tomcat—every time he had an audition for some amateur production he left Chris and me to fend for ourselves. I said, "Pearl can starve before I'll raise you a nickel."

"You'd starve your own niece?"

Dad's voice said, "But you don't have a niece. New hobby, Alan?"

"Dad! When did you come in?" I managed to speak before Kruzick could, but he gave me a now-or-never look and opened his mouth. Once again, I was too quick for him: "He's an expectant father in a play. I was helping him rehearse."

Dad chuckled. "He looks exactly the part, doesn't he? One

of those neurotic ones that worry all the time. I bet he'd make Mickey pack her suitcase about the third month."

I held my breath. "Oh, no, I wouldn't, Mr. Schwartz. I'm a regular cucumber. In fact, the only thing I'm really worried about is getting to the shul on time."

"Isn't that an odd place to have a baby?"

"Alan's playing an unmarried father, Dad." I didn't think Kruzick was really going to do anything rash—just torment me to the limit—but I was starting to sweat. This was entirely too close to the bone.

"A modern twist," said Dad.

Kruzick said, "She can't make up her mind to marry me."

"I think we better eat, Dad. I'm feeling faint."

"You don't look so good," said Kruzick.

Dad was still chuckling when we hit the pavement. "Alan sure gets into his roles, doesn't he?"

"Great little actor."

"I could really see him as a father."

Dad opened the door of Sam's Grill, ushered me in, and held up two fingers to let the maître d' know the size of our party. "I need a drink," I said.

"Worried about your case, Beck?"

I nodded, pulling a serious face and making a mental note to nag Mickey into telling Mom and Dad to get the tsuris over with. "Dad, I need your help."

He gave me one of the sparkly smiles that had won the hearts of juries by the dozen. "I'll do anything I can. I wanted to see you today to let you know that."

"Will you be co-counsel?"

"I thought you'd never ask."

Dad loved a good fight, but he hated to lose. If he was willing to be co-counsel, maybe that meant something. "Do you think we have a chance?"

He gave me one of the glasses of white wine the bartender had just handed to him. "Want me to be honest with you?"

"I'm not sure."

"Well, I'm going to be."

"I'm ready."

"Frankly, no. We haven't a chance."

"Then why do you want a piece of it?"

"Because it's too much for you."

"Too much for me!"

"Now, calm down. I don't mean you can't handle it—the legal aspects of it, I mean. You can handle it as well as I can."

"That's not true and you know it. You're one of the best criminal lawyers in the country. I'm not quite in that exalted class."

"Very well, then. You can handle it as well as any lawyer in the city except me."

We both laughed, but I was feeling tense. "What did you mean when you said it was too much for me?"

"I meant emotionally. I'm sorry, Beck, but I don't see a way to win this thing. You're not ready to lose a case like this; it could break your confidence as a trial lawyer. If you lose, I don't want you going down alone. I want you to see that no one could have won."

"You're treating me like a child."

"I was afraid you'd feel that way. But it isn't that. I'd do the same for any talented young lawyer."

"You would?"

"I have. Remember Jude Morgan? The Oliver George case? Jude had sort of been my protégé for a while. When that case came up I didn't think he could win it. So I offered my services."

The maître d' came along and showed us to our table. As we were settling ourselves, I pondered what Dad was saying. "You mean," I said, "you decided to take the fall for him?"

"Exactly that. I could afford to do it without losing faith in myself; he wasn't ready for that big a defeat." Dad buttered a piece of sourdough, contriving to get his tie in the way so that it ended up with a tiny grease spot on it; poor grooming was his trademark.

"But you won that case."

"So we did," he admitted modestly. "But you know what? It was Jude's work that really did it; in the end, it turned out he didn't really need me at all. When we started working, though, I didn't have any more hope for it than I have for your case."

"I'm feeling a little better."

"Shall we work on a change of venue?"

"That'll be a start, anyway. But I can't help thinking the only real answer is to find the real Trapper."

"You know how your mother hates it when you play detective."

"Oh, stop." I brought him up to date on Les.

Dad attacked his petrale, brow furrowed. Finally, he said, "Why don't you call his mother back? Maybe she'll give you the names of friends who might know where he is."

"Okay. But I get the feeling she's tried everything she knows to find him."

"Can you think of anyone at all who might know him?"

"Only Miranda Warning—I mean, Waring. But she's as elusive as he is."

"A couple of needles in haystacks."

"I've got a feeling it might be the same haystack—maybe the Tenderloin. But you might as well try to find someone in Chinatown."

"Why don't you advertise?"

"What?" A bite of fish fell off my fork. I had the sort of feeling you'd get if you said, "My shoes keep falling off," and someone answered, "Try tying them."

"Place a classified ad," said Dad, as if I hadn't caught on. "Maybe offer a reward."

He'd certainly been right—obviously I needed an experienced co-counsel. Probably the day would come when my car wouldn't start and I'd need advice to turn on the ignition.

I hurried back to the office to call the *Chronicle* before the 2:00 P.M. deadline, composing the ad in my mind: "$100 reward for information about the whereabouts of Les Mathison or Miranda Waring." No. Fifty dollars ought to do it.

After I'd made the deadline, I called Les's mother; she couldn't give me any names, but promised once again to send me a religious tract.

The ad ran the next morning, and I got ready for work with all the hope in the world. Which was quickly dispelled by the time I hit the streets. They were all but deserted. Once again fear stalked, in the wake of the Bonanza Inn bombing. I thought of going back for my car, but decided against it—it was a lovely morning and I wasn't going to be bullied. Still, I can't say I enjoyed the walk; in spite of myself, I had sweaty palms by the time I got to the office. The rest of me was slightly damp, too—I'd run the last couple of blocks.

Kruzick was just making a pot of his execrable coffee. I said, "Any calls?"

"No. Expecting any?"

I told him about the ad. And the rest of the day, every hour on the hour, he amused himself by reporting sweetly that no one had called about it. So I was feeling fairly depressed at quitting time, as I took off my workaday heels and put on Nikes for the walk home—upset that the ad hadn't worked and decidedly not looking forward to the walk.

The day that had started out so beautifully had turned nasty with evening fog. The sidewalks were nearly empty, and once again the streets were jammed with traffic. Damn the Trapper! I walked fast, nervous but eager as well—I had an evening with Rob and a home-cooked meal to look forward to.

I tried to cheer myself up—and get my mind off the Trapper with thoughts of Rob. I wondered what he'd make me for dinner. He might have learned some new tricks in his cooking class, but I was betting they were new tricks with chicken; he never made anything else. Basil was in season, though—maybe he'd make a pasta with pesto sauce. As I turned into Green Street, I hardly noticed that I was now off the beaten track—not only weren't there any pedestrians, there wasn't even any auto traffic. I'd succeeded in distracting myself rather thoroughly. Even so, I thought to look behind me once or twice, just in case. But I guess, in retrospect, I should have tried the trick they teach you in rape-prevention lectures—walking in the middle of the street. Someone was waiting for me, hiding in a doorway; someone wearing tennis shoes. I never heard a thing; I just felt a sudden, awful pain at the back of my head, followed by the certain feeling that I was going to throw up, followed by nothing at all, not even a sense of losing my balance.

14

I was literally lying in the gutter when some kind soul found me—or more accurately, a little knot of kind souls, ringing my battered body and looking concerned. I think I can best express the unutterable pain of the headache I had if I say I wasn't the least bit upset that my panty hose were no doubt destroyed or my lavender raw-silk suit would have to be cleaned, and I never even considered the probability that my clothing might have been immodestly rearranged by my fall.

"Are you all right?" asked an unfamiliar male voice.

"I'm not sure," I said, and my rescuers fairly heaved a collective sigh of relief, reassured, I guess, that I still had the power of speech. Some of them drifted off to their various chicken or pesto dinners.

"Can you walk?"

But that didn't seem to me to be the first order of business. Someone hit me," I said.

"You were mugged?"

I nodded. The kind souls began to whisper and fret; we like to think Telegraph Hill is as safe as Our Town.

"But here's your briefcase. And you're lying on your purse."

I sat up to retrieve the purse, sending new waves of pain down my neck and shoulders. Looking in, I saw what I thought I'd see—my wallet, still holding the twenty dollars I'd just gotten from an automatic teller machine.

"You're sure someone hit you?"

With supreme prudence, I touched the back of my head and felt a doorknob. "Feel this."

But the stranger stepped back; the AIDS scare had made folks in these parts unduly fastidious. "Maybe you got that when you fell."

You can't imagine what a frustrating feeling it is to get mugged and then have people argue with you about it. I'm sorry to say there was an unfortunate whine to my voice: "Didn't anyone see him?"

Blank looks all around. And finally: "Who?"

"The guy who hit me?"

No response at all. I had a sudden urge to regain my dignity—anger was doing wonders for my headache. I needed to get out of that gutter, and fast. I pushed up into a crouch, ready to stand—and promptly toppled back. It took four brave people, unafraid of exotic diseases carried on the skin of strangers, to get me upright, and even then I still felt dizzy. A kind woman about my age helped me up the hill to my apartment; I didn't have to lean on her exactly, but it was good to know she was there just in case. We walked very slowly, she carrying my briefcase.

Rob had already arrived, parked, and fetched up at my doorstep with a bag of groceries, a six-pack of beer, and a wok which he was wearing on his head. God knows what my escort thought. I sent her away: "There's my boyfriend. I'll be all right now." She looked decidedly skeptical.

"Confucius say she who keep cook waiting get knuckle sandwich for dinner."

"I've already had one."

"Wha?" Usually Rob is more articulate than this, but he was reacting not only to what I said but, by now, to my general bedragglement and decelerated gait.

"I got mugged."

Still not putting things together, he searched my face for bruises.

"Okay, maybe it wasn't really a knuckle sandwich; more like a deluxe club—prompt delivery at the rear."

He blinked, but caught on in a split second that no one would mug a person by smacking her bottom: "Back of the head?"

I nodded, realizing for the first time how much I wanted to cry.

Having finally got the lay of the land, Rob went quickly into action. He dumped his six-pack and his bag of groceries on the sidewalk, covered the distance between us in two swift paces, and took me in his arms. Very tender and comforting; exactly the thing to do if he'd only remembered to remove the wok. This time I saw the blow coming, but I wasn't fast enough to dodge it. The most sickening clang rang through the streets as metal hit forehead. It hurt like the most ingenious torture of hell, but I was sort of grateful it happened: If a person got mugged and then got argued with about it and then her boyfriend mugged her again with a free-swinging wok on his head, surely she was entitled to cry. The tears started to form into great luxurious drops, and I let them slide impenitently into the open.

Despite Rob's exotic cooking skills, hot and sour soup was about all I could manage, but I was glad to have it and gladder still to have Rob with me that night. He was the one person in the world I could talk to about my worst fear—that Les had seen the ad and responded to it. At least he hadn't followed me all the way home, so he didn't yet know where I lived. But he knew far too much about the route I took to and from work.

"Maybe," said Rob, "you can get police protection."

"Are you crazy? Even regular people on the street didn't want to believe someone really hit me. Martinez would probably accuse me of sapping myself."

"You've got to get it on the record."

I sighed and picked up the phone. A mere forty-five minutes later a pair of polite young cops turned up, took the report, acted properly concerned, and said they'd be sure to tell Martinez all about it. It was almost enough to restore my faith in the police department, but as long as Martinez worked there I'd have to consider it only a cut above the *Ton-Ton Macoute*.

After the nice cops left, Rob and I settled down to the serious business of reconciliation, but I'm afraid there was a small hitch—I had to tell him I had a headache.

Dad called early the next morning: "Any response from the ad?"

"Not yet, but it's going to run a week. I still have high hopes."

"I'm starting to have second thoughts. I don't think you should have used your name."

"But if I hadn't, Les could find out who placed the ad just by calling the phone number."

"You could have used a box number."

"I thought of that, but anyone likely to know Les or Miranda might not be able to write."

"Maybe we should have used my number."

"Don't worry, Dad, I can take care of myself." I spoke with fingers crossed.

After I'd hung up, Kruzick came in: "Somebody finally answered your ad."

"No!"

"Two somebodies. One left a message, one wouldn't."

"Men or women?"

"Women." He handed over a message slip: The caller was Barbara Fuller.

I dialed. "Ms. Fuller, this is Rebecca Schwartz returning your call."

"Who? Leath, stop that. Gina!"

"You called about my ad."

"Oh, yes. Gina, nooo! I thought I might be able to help about Les Mathison. You're not the only one who's looking for him, you know. Someone came by the house the other day."

"The house?"

"Leath, leave your sister alone! He used to live upstairs from me."

"I see. The person who came by—was it a woman? Late twenties, dark, about five feet five?"

"Uh-huh. A little on the chunky side."

"Do you live on Twelfth Avenue, by any chance?"

"Ouch. Gina—you don't pull your mother's hair!"

I hung up without waiting for an answer—I didn't need my ears assaulted and I could call back if there wasn't a Fuller on Twelfth Avenue at Les's address. Chunky-schmunky. "Alan, what about the other woman?"

"She said she'd call back about noon."

"Damn!" I'd have to cancel my lunch date.

"Don't take it out on me; this isn't Babylon, you know."

Hardly. If it were, I could kill Alan for relaying bad news, but I was afraid I'd go through quite a few replacements as well. Could it be I was a pessimist? No. Absolutely not. If I erred, it was surely on the side of optimism—I actually expected that woman to call back at noon.

By two o'clock my stomach was doing a fair imitation of a pride of lions. "Alan, could you do me a favor?"

"Yes, ma'am, Miz Boss—I'll get y'all a hamburger *toute de suite*. There's nothing I loves more than fetchin' and carryin'."

"How'd you know what I wanted?"

"Your tum growlin' like a ol' houn' dog."

"Know what, Alan?"

"Yes'm. I ain't never caught a rabbit and I ain't no friend of yours."

"Quite correct. And one other thing."

"I know, I know. Never use y'all in the singular—Miz Chris done filled me in."

I reached for my wallet, but my hand closed on one of the frothing blood capsules Rob and I had bought at the Pier 39 magic shop. It burst. As I drew a gory hand out of my bag, Kruzick drew back: "Stigmata! Lord help me, I ain't gon' study war no more."

One day, I thought, I was really going to have to clean out my purse. But for the moment I was glad I had a little bag of tissues in it. Kruzick calmed down as I fossicked for them: "You aren't really hurt, are you? I mean, that's gotta be nail polish, right?"

Nail polish! I'd worn it twice in my life—at my senior prom, and once when I had interesting occasion to impersonate a hooker. "Look, Alan—how about if I pay you later?"

"Why not just give me a raise and we'll call it even?"

I made one more dive into the purse: "Here's five bucks. Keep the change."

"Maybe I can find a *cheap* burger somewhere."

Being hungry makes me mean and so do Kruzick's adorable little *bits*; at the moment I was feeling quite as murderous as the Trapper himself. It was a fine time for the phone to ring and of course it did. "It's about your ad." A woman's voice.

"I've been waiting for your call." Perhaps I spoke a bit testily; at any rate, I got a defensive response.

"I been at the doctor's. My leg's actin' up again, and with the diabetes I'm in there two, three times a week. Sometimes more."

"I'm sorry to hear that." I waited, but she seemed to have forgotten what she called about. "You saw my ad?"

"I can tell you what you want to know."

"Wonderful."

"Come on over and bring the hundred dollars."

"I beg your pardon?"

"I said come on over. You deaf?"

"What was that about a hundred dollars?"

"You want to know about Miranda and Les, don't you?"

"Yes."

"The way I read your ad, you're offering fifty for Les and another fifty for Miranda."

I was so taken aback by the matter-of-fact way she peddled information, so much like the way Kruzick and company had played poker on Easter eve, I couldn't think of a thing to say. I was thinking: "See your Les and raise you one Miranda."

"I got gallstones, you know. My leg's been actin' up lately, and ever since that attack last winter, I ain't been the same. Even close to it. Doctor said he never saw nothin' like it."

I didn't care if it kept me from catching the Trapper, I wasn't going to ask about her attack. Instead, I said, "Of course. If you can tell me what I need to know, I'll be glad to pay you a hundred dollars. If you'll give me your address, I'll come over in an hour or so."

"Doctor says I got to get some rest. I told him, 'Don't you worry. You know I'll be in bed by three o'clock.' He said I got to have two hours rest every afternoon, but I got to be up at five to fix supper for my son. He works nights, you know, so I always got to make sure I do that. I got no choice but to be in bed by three."

My watch said 2:25; that meant good-bye to my burger. It also meant there wasn't time to get someone to go with me, in case I needed a witness, but she left me no choice. "Okay. What's your name and address?"

"Nola Pritchett; the Bonaventure Arms on Eddy Street." The address she gave me was one of the seediest in the Tenderloin; my confidence wasn't vastly increased when she said, "Come alone."

"May I ask why?"

"Three people in my building right now got AIDS, a couple got TB, and I don't even know how many's walkin' around with hepatitis. Strangers carry germs, so I don't like 'em comin' in and out, know what I mean?"

It was just as well about the burger. I was fast losing my appetite. Mrs. Pritchett certainly didn't sound dangerous, but just in case, I wrote a memo explaining where to look for me before I went out to find a taxi. I'd walked to work but I'd cut into Mrs. Pritchett's naptime if I tried to hoof it to the Bonaventure Arms; or considering the neighborhood, I might not even get there. I mentally slapped my wrist for thinking that last thought. The Tenderloin was unwholesome, certainly, but maybe less so of late, as families of Asian refugees moved in because of the rock-bottom rents. It was not the kind of place where a Marin County native was completely comfortable, but plenty of hookers ranged about unmolested at all hours of the day and night; not to mention the unsuspecting tourists who booked rooms at the Hilton, not knowing the neighborhood wasn't exactly Beekman Place West.

There were plenty of junkies, crazies, and small-time thugs roaming the Tenderloin's streets and juicing it up in its sleazy bars, but its true chambers of horrors were the filthy flophouses where who knew how many had serum hepatitis, and where crime—robbery and up—was as much a way of life as pasta in North Beach. The Bonaventure Arms was one of the vilest. The stink of vomit, urine, and rot was instantly evident, followed by equal assaults on the eyes—forty or fifty years of dust and piled-up crud on walls, floors, stairs, windows, and worse yet, what fragments there were of carpets. Specimens of Tenderloin humanity seemed almost to be blinking in the half-light, as if they'd been languishing like the Prisoner of Zenda. Surely Mrs. Pritchett's ailments could only get worse in this atmosphere.

I still stand by that opinion, but after learning that she owned the building and managed it—if you could call it that— I found my sympathy stretched to the thickness of poor-grade plastic wrap. Her own chambers, while larger, I surmised, than most in the building, surely couldn't have been much better than the hole that made Calcutta famous. "I hope you can stand the mess," she said by way of greeting. "I haven't felt much like tidying up lately." By "lately" she had to have meant in the last ten years, as I actually saw a ten-year-old newspaper among the others piled on her floor. Every surface was crammed with litter and bottles and pill vials, all covered not with dust, but with accumulated gunk, reminding me of spices I bought for dishes I cooked once a year or so; whenever I needed saffron, say, or sage, I'd pull the bottle off my spice rack and find it sticking to my fingers. I had the feeling anything I picked up in Mrs. Pritchett's living room wouldn't be easy to put down again.

My hostess cleared a place for me on the tattered sofa and took a seat herself in an armchair that would have made Goodwill turn up its nose—not because it was old and sprung, but because there were stains on it in places where one would have to be an acrobat to get in position for landing a spill. Mrs. Pritchett barely fit into it; she was shaped like a fluffed-up pillow, and she was the color of one you might find in a hospital—dead white.

Her hair, also, was white and tightly permed, but scrupulously clean. Her apricot dress, which was meant to have a waist but didn't, looked fine as well. One of her stockings, however, looked like a cat's cradle, revealing random longish leg hairs and stark white patches of skin. It had been stretched to its limit, I imagined, by legs the shape and thickness of Doric columns. I thought a lot of her health problems might be traced to her weight, but in one sense the extra fat had served her well—her face was unwrinkled and rather pretty. It was also nicely made up (though a bit heavy on the blusher). She was an odd combination of fastidiousness and utter decay.

The apartment was not only a monument to Fibber McGee, it was made doubly oppressive by heavy drapes drawn over all the windows. I was sure if you patted one gently you'd raise enough dust for a desert khamsin. Yet, as my eyes became adjusted to the dark, I could see vestiges of

Mrs. Pritchett's tidy side. A religious statue of a madonna and child stood on a starched doily, the colors of the statue glowing unnaturally in that room, unencumbered by the gunk of the bottles and vials. While a filthy pink bedspread had been thrown over the sofa—apparently to improve it—Mrs. Pritchett's chair had pinned to it three old-fashioned antimacassars, only one of which was slightly stained and none of which had the grayish look of months or years without laundering.

I sat on the very edge of the sofa, hoping she wouldn't notice and be offended. "You know both Les and Miranda, I gather." As I said it, I had the unpleasant notion that they might live in the building—might even be there right now. I began to think I shouldn't have come alone.

"They used to live here."

I breathed easier. "Together?"

"Separate floors. Though she spent a lot of time in his room, if you know what I mean. But it didn't mean no more than a hill o' beans to him."

"What didn't?"

"She didn't. Her bein' there. Now she—she was in love with him. If a woman who spends three quarters of her time staggerin' from drink can love anybody."

"But he didn't reciprocate."

"If that means did he have any feelin' for her, I guess not. Not too much, anyway. Had a pet name for her, though."

"He did?"

"Miranda Warning. And she called him Les Ismore."

"Izzmore?"

She chuckled. "I didn't get it either at first. Meant Les is more—kind of cute, huh?"

So cute I would have been touched at the thought of two derelicts who still had enough spark to make puns if one of them hadn't been a multiple murderer. "It sounds like they were pretty tight."

"Uh-uh. Not so long as one of 'em was him. He wasn't tight with nobody."

"A loner?"

"That ain't the half of it. Mean bastard."

"Mean how?"

"Oh—just sullen. He'd as soon snap at you as say hello. Sometimes wouldn't speak at all." She shifted in her chair, grimaced, and bent down to rub her leg. "Ow. Hope it ain't the phlebitis comin' back."

"Did you ever think he might be homosexual?"

"Him?" She hooted. "Not likely. Why'd you ask?"

I'd asked because if he were the Trapper, Miranda had followed him to the Yellow Parrot, but really the question was just for form's sake. I thought he'd picked a gay man as a victim because he'd make an easy first target—drinking, maybe drunk, and eager to trust. "I just wondered," I said. "Because he didn't respond to Miranda, I guess."

She gave another little hoot. "You ever seen Miranda? I ain't sayin' she wouldn't be right pretty if she'd fix herself up, but she was usually too drunk to comb her hair. That ain't all, though. He just didn't have it in him. Real grim—seemed kind of preoccupied, like he was some executive instead of an unemployed laborer."

"Like he had work to do?"

"Yep. Didn't, though. Took odd jobs, but spent most of his time in his room—or sometimes Miranda's. But mostly his."

"Did they leave together?"

"That's what I don't know."

"You don't know?"

"Both of 'em just disappeared. Didn't say they were going, just left. That's why I have to collect the rent in advance. If I didn't, see, half the bums in the place'd stick me for it."

"You own the building?"

"It was my Daddy's. It ain't much, but it's all he left me. He left home when I was eight or nine, didn't hear a word out of him till one day some lawyer called—forty years later it was—said my daddy'd left me a buildin' in San Francisco. I come all the way from North Ca'lina for this." She looked disgusted.

"We was always dirt poor, so at least it was somethin'. He owned other buildin's, though, the old buzzard. But he got married again, left 'em to his second family."

I was gettin' interested in spite of myself: "He was a bigamist?"

"Damn sure was."

"You didn't contest the will?"

She shrugged. "Didn't know how."

With an effort, I got back to the matter at hand. "When did Les and Miranda leave?"

"Don't know exactly. Could have been gone for a week or so, maybe more, by the time I realized nobody was livin' in Les's. So I checked Miranda's—she was gone, too. That's how come I don't know if they left together. Maybe he left first and she went to try and find him. Ain't no way to tell."

"When was it?"

She jumped. "Ow." This time she rubbed her arm. "Got shootin' pains. I got to get me some rest."

I was starting to think she wasn't going to be able to tell me what I needed to know. If she didn't, I certainly wasn't going to give her the money; but I wanted all the information I could get. I repeated my question: "Can you remember when you noticed they were missing?"

Her bland face got cagey. "Why do you want to know all this stuff, anyway?"

"I think they might have information about a case I'm working on."

"What kind of case?"

"I'm afraid I can't say. I just need to talk to them."

"You got the money?"

"Yes. Do you know where they are?"

"I'm pretty sure."

"A hundred dollars is a lot of money for pretty sure."

She pouted. "I got to buy me some med'cine."

We finally struck a deal: fifty bucks for the tips on each one whereabouts, and the other fifty if the tips panned out.

"I know where Les is from." She looked as self-satisfied as a sitting hen. "He's got family there."

I was disappointed in spite of myself. "You think he went to Turlock?"

"Oh. You already know."

"I know where he's from. Why do you think he went there?"

"Just a hunch." But she didn't have a poker face; she knew I wasn't going to go for it. She kind of crumpled around the eyes and then said, "I think I'm gonna have an attack. Could you get me a glass of water, please?"

I would gladly have paid fifty dollars just to avoid going into her kitchen.

"How about Miranda?"

"She'll be with him."

"I'll tell you what, Mrs. Pritchett. I'll give you thirty-five dollars if you can remember when you first noticed Miranda and Les were missing."

"I just don't know how I'm gon' pay for my med'cine. The doctor said I couldn't afford another attack; said if it happened again, might be the last time."

"Fifty, then."

She cheered up. "That'll be just fine."

"It's coming back to you?"

"Did I say I forgot? I couldn't of forgot. 'Cause I was just back from Mass, wearin' my new Easter dress, and Juney Carmichael, she comes in, says, 'Oh, Miz Pritchett, what a pretty dress,' and then she says, 'There's a terrible stink comin' out of Les's room.'"

"It was Easter, then?"

"No, the Sunday after. See, I was took so bad on Easter, I couldn't hardly hold my head up, much less get up and go to Mass."

"What did you find when you went in?"

"Nothin'. Just some garbage—leftover pizza and a carton of milk and such. That's what was makin' the stink."

"And Miranda's room?"

"Funny thing. She didn't take nothin' with her. Didn't have very much—just a old sleepin' bag and some clothes. I give 'em to Juney."

"Can I talk to Juney?"

"She died of an overdose last week." Mrs. Pritchett crossed herself.

I decided to walk back for the air, which gave me time to turn the whole conversation over in my mind. But there wasn't much of substance. The only things I'd really learned were that Les and Miranda knew each other, and that they'd probably disappeared sometime during the week after Sanchez was killed. That helped to confirm what I already knew—that Les was the Trapper. But I wasn't at all sure that was worth fifty dollars.

When I got back to the office, I found a cold burger on my desk and a note from Kruzick: "Had to go home. Mickey had a miscarriage."

15

Without even taking time to dump the burger, I dashed out to get a cab, this time to go to North Beach for my car. I never thought of calling to ask if I should come—I knew my duty as a sister. But when I got to Mickey and Alan's I had to ring the bell several times before getting an answer. Mickey finally came to the door, looking very drawn and red around the eyes. "Oh, Rebecca."

I hugged her. "I'm so sorry."

"I'm okay. Come in."

"Shouldn't you be in bed?"

"I'm fine now. It happened this morning—I didn't want to make a big deal about it."

As we went in, I could smell spaghetti cooking—one of Mickey's favorite childhood foods, and still her preference over any fancy pasta the food mavens came up with. It made me shake with hunger. "Alan's cooking," said Mickey. "It's how he shows affection." Without asking me to sit down, she continued walking toward the kitchen, expecting me, apparently, to follow. I did, hoping I didn't faint before we got there.

Though Mickey's red face meant she'd been crying, she was now quite composed, if sad and subdued. Kruzick, on the other hand, sobbed as he stirred, big sloppy tears splashing onto his T-shirt. Instantly, I realized Mickey hadn't meant me to follow; she was simply so distracted she'd forgotten to tell me not to.

Not seeming to notice me at all, Kruzick put his arms around Mickey, held her like a child hanging on to its teddy bear, and said thank God she was all right, he didn't know what he'd do if he lost her, and more, I suppose, in that vein, but I wouldn't know because I backed out discreetly.

For a few uncomfortable minutes I waited, but Mickey didn't join me. Finally I left a note saying I'd been in the neighborhood and had just dropped in to be sure she was all right, but really couldn't stay, I was awfully sorry.

I stopped for a burger on Geary Boulevard and found I had more than that to chew over. For the first time I was starting to see what Mickey saw in Kruzick, and that was such an unaccustomed sensation I felt giddy. Underneath all that showy schmuckiness, he actually had a human feeling or two. I might be wrong, but I'd gotten the preposterous idea he really loved her. When I thought about it, the evidence had been there all the time—he didn't cheat on her; he wanted to marry her; in his own weird way, he was even there when she needed him. Which was more, I thought, than could sometimes be said of Rob. With the utmost chagrin, I realized that I was slightly jealous, actually jealous of someone who called Alan Kruzick sweetheart. I nearly choked on my burger.

And then, after another couple of bites, I developed a human feeling or two of my own—equally foreign ones. I started to be happy for Mickey; and to develop the slightest little shreds of affection for Kruzick himself. Unbelievable but there it was. I was ashamed to think it had taken a miscarriage to come to this.

When I got home, there was a call from Mickey. Returning it, I found her still slightly depressed, but philosophical: "I think I wasn't ready to have a baby. I mean if I wasn't ready for marriage, what was I thinking?"

"I sort of wondered that myself."

"But you know what? There's a good side to all of this."

"Don't tell me. It's brought you and Alan closer together."

"You think that's a stupid cliché."

"Actually," I said, "I don't. I'm glad." I never had more trouble getting two words out, but I meant them.

Dad and I made a deal: With his advice, I'd prepare Lou's case, and he'd help me try it. The change of venue was easy—there wasn't a judge in San Francisco who could be convinced he'd get a fair trial there. The case was put on the calendar in San Jose.

During pretrial skirmishing, I got to know the enemy a little—and she was me. Or so much like me it was eerie. Deputy District Attorney Liz Hughes was trying the case for the people. Liz was about my height—though maybe a little thinner—only a couple of years older, and a fellow graduate of Boalt Hall of Law. She dressed conservatively, but behaved in any way at all that might help her win her case. (Any ethical way, that is—I didn't know a thing against Liz, so far as her integrity went, and neither did anyone else.) But she'd cajole, bully, lose her temper, possibly even cry to sway judge or jury. Any lawyer might, of course, but Liz put so much energy into her court appearances she was downright colorful. I'm not at all sure that could fairly be said about me, but I will say there was one person who said it, regularly and ruefully—my mother. So in certain ways I identified with Liz.

But I was also a little awed and intimidated by her—much more so than if she'd been a man my age. She had a reputation as a hotshot, and her record supported it—since she'd been in homicide, she'd never failed to get a conviction. That had a depressing effect, but Dad told me a tale that came out of the sixties, when so-called political trials were crowding the calendars.

Members of a certain radical group, who'd allegedly engaged in a shootout with police, came to one of Dad's celebrated colleagues. "We need a lawyer like Perry Mason," they said. "You good as Perry?"

"I'm better," said the distinguished counselor. "His clients were innocent."

No doubt the defendants in Liz's other cases had been guilty. But I was only momentarily cheered. No matter how much I believed my client innocent, I knew Liz had the better case.

I ended up hiring an investigator, after all. He went up to Turlock and ascertained that Les's mom wasn't lying—Les wasn't there and nobody'd seen him in what Chris would call a month of pigballs. He combed the Tenderloin for Les and Miranda, drinking in sleazy bars and even offering bribes, for all I knew. And he got nothing. Dad and I asked for continuance after continuance, but finally there was no longer any point to it. After ten months, the case came to trial.

I should explain something. Lou was on trial for two murders only—that of Jack Sanchez, the gay man on the cross, and of Brewster Baskett, the old man who'd died of poisoning at Full Fathom Five. The police had no physical evidence in the cable car case, and none except the explosives manual to connect him with the elevator crash—since there was no note in either incident, they didn't feel they could sell either one to a jury.

But they had something very good indeed in the Sanchez murder—the gun that had killed him, found in my client's room. It was probably enough to tie the two fairly circumstantial cases together. And Liz had another ace up her sleeve, one she timed for maximum flustering effect. During the break right after jury selection, a D.A.'s investigator handed me a subpoena ordering me to take the stand against my own client.

If Lou hadn't been my client, I might have expected to be a witness, but under the circumstances, I couldn't possibly testify. It was a blatant conflict of interest. Surely no judge would permit it (except one, I worried, emotionally overcome by the horror of a serial killing). We had a judge with a far-flung reputation for being hard on defendants. But I felt confident he would see reason. Right was on my side.

"Requiring me to testify," I argued, "stands in complete contradiction of the ethical rules promulgated by the State Bar of California. When I became a lawyer, I took an oath to zealously represent my client to the best of my ability, and testifying for the prosecution would be in unthinkable violation of that oath." I lowered my voice here: "Futhermore, Judge, more important than all that legal gobbledegook, think about it. _How would it look to the jury?_" I put all the passion I had into the last seven words.

Liz was ready, of course. She argued that I hadn't yet met my client at the time I discovered the body, and that therefore there was no actual conflict of interest; that I was only there to testify to the crime scene, that it would be different if my client had been seen running from that scene, and also that, if I felt the way I did, knowing I might be called, I should never have taken the case in the first place.

"Because the crime is so serious and the city of San Francisco has been so terrorized," began the judge, and I knew he was going to deny my motion to quash. I didn't listen. I ignored Liz's smug expression. I was already engaging in my favorite morale builder for such moments—drowning my sorrows in appellate remedies. Surely, I thought, if there were anything resembling justice in the world, a conviction would be overturned. It felt momentarily better to think that, but it wasn't currently the point—the point was to _avoid_ a conviction.

In her opening statement, Liz said she would prove beyond a reasonable doubt that Lou Zimbardo had killed Sanchez, a drunk and helpless tourist from Gallup, New Mexico, and had wantonly brought deadly quarantined mussels to Full Fathom Five, killing Brewster Baskett and causing ten other innocent people to fall ill. She said she would produce the gun with which Sanchez was killed, and a (now frozen) plastic bag of eastern mussels, which he had stolen when he substituted poisoned ones, arrogantly leaving them in the restaurant's bathroom.

In my own statement, I said I hoped the jury understood the burden of proof was on the prosecution and if any member of that jury had the slightest doubt that Lou Zimbardo was guilty, he would burn in hell if he voted to convict. (Actually, I didn't say "burn in hell," but I tried to imply it.) I noted that Lou didn't have to take the stand to answer the charges against him, and that he didn't have to put on a defense at all. Indeed, I remarked, if the case against my client proved as ridiculously weak as I suspected it would be, I most probably wouldn't put on a defense. I said I fervently hoped that each member of the jury understood that failure to put on a defense, far from being an admission of guilt, was a choice open to any defendant and should not be considered in their deliberations. The ball, I said, was entirely in the D.A.'s court.

Don't imagine that, after saying all that, I didn't feel like the biggest ass in northern California. Liz objected a couple of times, on grounds that I was arguing, and I didn't blame her. But having no defense, Dad and I had more or less decided not to present one. We were leaving our options open, waiting for Liz to leave us openings, and hoping for a sign from heaven before making up our minds for good; but for openers we couldn't do any better than that. I'm not proud of it, and probably wouldn't even mention it, but it's a matter of public record and can hardly be hidden.

Almost immediately, Liz lived up to her reputation for being colorful—the first witness she called was none other than counsel for the defense.

"Miss Schwartz, were you at Mount Davidson shortly before dawn on Easter morning?"

"Yes, I was."

"Will you tell the court what you were doing there?"

"I was with my friend Rob Burns. He was covering the Easter sunrise service for the *Chronicle*."

"I see. But weren't you there a little early?"

"We were."

"May I ask why?"

"Objection, Your Honor." Dad's voice sounded tired, as if he had lived long enough to hear hundreds of second-rate lawyers try to get away with irrelevant lines of questioning, and would probably die of boredom if it happened again. His voice fairly begged the judge to spare him such an undignified death, yet somehow simultaneously managed to suggest that he wasn't begging at all, that his objection was so obvious, so utterly right, that he need hardly bother voicing it. He was wearing a gray suit with more polyester than wool in it, a rumpled blue shirt, and a tie bearing three strategic grease spots. He hadn't had a haircut in weeks, and his pants were a little too short. Any juror who didn't love him would have to have a heart of strictly lapidary interest.

"Overruled."

"Did you tell the police you and your friend were sleeping in the van near the mountain so as not to be late for the service?"

"Objection!"

"Sustained. Strike the question, please."

But the jury couldn't strike the question from their minds. Liz had now established me as a loose woman who would sleep on the street with a man to whom she wasn't married. Bad enough in San Francisco, but this was more conservative San Jose—I began to have doubts about that change of venue.

At Liz's request, we approached the bench. "Your Honor," she said, "Miss Schwartz will testify that she heard certain noises which led her and her—friend—to investigate the site at the top of the mountain. In order for the jury to understand the nature and intensity of the noises, I need to establish where the witness was and what she was doing when she heard them."

"Miss Hughes, I'm going to ask you to abandon this line of questioning."

The jury murmured among themselves. The judge had saved me from testifying that I was attempting to pee in public when I heard the noises, but now imaginations were free to run rampant—the very proper all-white, middle-class jurors probably thought I'd been copulating in the van with my "friend."

"Did you in fact hear noises, Miss Schwartz?"

"Yes. A crash, and then a sound like a person saying 'oof.'" Mild laughter in the courtroom. The judge gaveled.

"And did you investigate?"

"Mr. Burns and I did, yes." Normally I hate the courtroom formality of referring to everyone by last names, but under the circumstances I felt it necessary to restore a little dignity to the Schwartz-Burns camp.

"Will you tell the court, please, what you found at the top of the mountain."

This was a tricky one. She now had me, counsel for the defense, in the unhappy position of having to describe the gory murder scene. I had to be truthful, yet hold back as much as I could. "I saw a man on the cross, apparently dead."

"Could you explain what you mean, please, by 'on the cross.'"

I was starting to sweat. "His wrists had been nailed to the cross."

"Could you demonstrate the position, please?"

Dad spoke: "Your Honor, I think everyone gets the idea." Mild laughter—release of tension. Good old Dad.

"No further questions, Your Honor."

On cross-examination, Dad tried to reestablish my good name in the minds of the jurors by having me tell about climbing the ladder, trying to find out if the man was dead: "What did you plan to do if he wasn't?"

"I didn't know. I just thought I ought to do something."

"And what in fact did you do?"

"I'm afraid I fell off the ladder." Laughter in the courtroom.

"How did you happen to fall off? Did something startle you?"

"Yes. A woman's voice said, 'Hold it right there.'

"'Hold it right there.' Was she a policewoman?"

"She said she was making a citizen's arrest. She had her hand in her pocket, as if she had a gun.

"And what did you do?"

"I held out my hand for the gun and said, 'Let's talk it over.'"

"Did she give you the gun?"

"No. She hit my hand with it—without taking it out of her pocket."

"And what did you do then?" Dad asked this question because we didn't want Liz asking it—it would look better if I admitted voluntarily that I'd hit Miranda.

I said: "I fought her for it."

"You fought her for it?"

He sounded absolutely amazed.

"Yes."

"Well! You *look* properly brought up." The courtroom broke up. Dad knew he'd get reprimanded, but he'd scored big with the jury. I was more or less respectable once again, and had a funny father who joked with me in public. As for Dad, he was the cutest thing since Sam Ervin, and every juror who'd resisted his charm so far was now deeply in love. It wouldn't win the case, but it couldn't hurt.

The judge, naturally, was fuming. After restoring order, he said, "Mr. Schwartz, I'll ask you please to remember that this is a murder trial in a court of law and not a forum for stand-up comedy."

"I apologize, Your Honor."

It would have been great to leave them laughing, but we still had to get Miranda out in the open. Rob hadn't ever been able to write a word about her, but he could if her story came out in the trial. Then maybe someone who knew her would see the story and phone us. It was a big if—I was horribly afraid she was dead—but we had to try. It wouldn't hurt to establish an element of mystery in the case as well, to send the jurors' imaginations in directions of reasonable doubt.

"Who won the fight?"

"No one. The Reverend Ovid Robinson, who was scheduled to give the sermon, turned up and broke it up."

"Well, I'm sure you *would* have won."

Dad was really pushing it. Again, the judge gaveled for order. "Mr. Schwartz, my patience is not on trial here. Please confine your paternal feelings to your home." He said that, but his face was all twisted up from trying not to smile.

"Did the woman tell you her name?"

"She told Mr. Burns—Rob."

"And did you hear her?"

"Yes. They talked for several minutes. She said she'd been with a man—apparently her boyfriend. She hid in his car, and he drove to the Yellow Parrot, a bar on Castro Street. He went in, but she remained in the car, drinking. Then she fell asleep. When she woke up, she was still in the car, but it was parked near Mount Davidson. She heard noise and came up the hill. She tried to arrest me because she thought I'd killed the man on the cross."

"And what did she say her name was?"

"She said it was Miranda Warning."

"No further questions," said Dad, and left them laughing after all.

Liz came back strong on redirect. In chambers, she fought to keep out the testimony about Miranda, but the judge felt it was relevant. Naturally, she was going to belittle the tiny seeds of doubt we hoped we were sowing.

"What happened to Ms.—uh—Warning?"

"She ran away before the police came."

"Why didn't you try to stop her?"

Dad objected in his world-weary voice.

"Very well. I'll rephrase the question. Did you try to stop her?"

"Of course. I chased her until Inspector Martinez threatened to blow my head off." Score one for me.

"I beg your pardon?"

"When the police came, Inspector Martinez couldn't see what was going on. He yelled, 'Freeze, or I'll blow your head off.'"

"And you froze."

"Yes. But Miranda—Miss Warning—got away."

"Tell me something about Miranda Warning. What did she look like?"

I could have tried to be cagey, but ultimately Liz would have got what she wanted. I spat it out: "She looked bedraggled and rather unhealthy. Her clothes were very poor. And she reeked of alcohol."

"Alcohol!"

"Yes."

"Did you get the impression she was a derelict?"

"Objection—counsel is calling for a conclusion."

"Sustained."

"No further questions."

I was shaking when I left the stand. Rob was to be the next witness and the plan had been that I'd cross-examine him, but Dad took one look at me and said he'd do it. Things had gone no worse than we expected, but then we'd expected the worst. The only good thing that had happened was that Dad had made the jury love him; but he always did that. On the down side: They probably weren't too fond of me even though I was the daughter of their hero, and I was sure they hated Miranda. I realized that when our turn came, we could call the Reverend Ovid Robinson to confirm my testimony, and we could have Lou testify that he had no girlfriend and no car, but there wasn't a chance in hell the jury'd believe him. Also, once we got him on the stand, if he made just the tiniest reference to having been in prison, if any little inkling of it slipped out, we were done for. My morning was off to a completely lousy start.

Liz called Rob. He told about chasing someone down the hill after we heard the ladder fall, and then admitted getting the first Trapper note when he wrote the story about Sanchez. Liz introduced the note as People's Exhibit A.

"After getting that note, Mr. Burns, did you then go to Pier 39?"

"Yes."

"Did anything unusual happen while you were there?" She really had us: first me describing the grisly sight of a man on the cross at Mount Davidson, and now Rob on the subject of mass poisoning at Pier 39.

"I heard sirens, and followed the noise to Full Fathom Five."

"And what did you see there?"

"I saw paramedics remove some people on stretchers."

"Could you see any of the people's faces?"

"Yes."

"Were any of them speaking, or making any kind of noise at all?"

"Some of them were trying to catch their breath."

"Would it be fair to say, from looking at their faces and hearing them trying to catch their breath, that these people were suffering horribly?"

"Objection!" Dad and I shouted together. I'd forgotten he was supposed to be taking over.

"Very well; I withdraw the question. Mr. Burns, did you later get another letter signed 'Tourist Trapper'?"

"It was just signed 'The Trapper.'"

"Is this it?" She produced Exhibit B.

"It seems to be."

"Will you read it for us, please?"

She was unbelievably tricky—you can't have a witness read something he didn't write. "Objection," I said, trying to sound as world-weary as Dad. "Hearsay."

"Sustained."

"Very well, Mr. Burns. Can you tell us in your own words what the note said?"

"It said the writer had had nothing but trouble since he'd come to San Francisco and the whole city was going to pay. Then I think it said something like, 'What would this crummy joint be without tourists? Too bad a few of them have to suffer for the sins of Sodom and Gomorrah.' And then it said that the people who stayed away would be better off in the long run, and that they'd thank him. And the last line was something about closing the city down."

"Would you like to look at the note to refresh your recollection?"

Rob flushed. He'd spoken almost in a monotone, keeping it as low-key as possible, and he'd paraphrased as well as he could. But of course he knew the note by heart. "No, thanks," he said. "I remember. The last line was, 'Watch me close this hellhole down.'"

A literal gasp went around the room. I'd heard about courtrooms being electrified, but I hadn't seen it before. Probably most of the jurors and spectators had read the note in the paper, but hearing those words like that gave you that same sickish feeling in the viscera as a fingernail on a blackboard.

"Was there a postscript?" asked Liz.

"Yes. The writer said he hoped the tourists liked the local mussels and noted that he had put what he called 'the good ones' in the cabinet in the men's room."

"And how was the note signed?"

"The Trapper." Rob's voice was very low.

Liz left it there. She'd played Rob like a violin—like a kazoo, really; it had taken no skill at all. She was just lucky the man who got the letters happened to be the defense lawyer's sweetie; coming from him, the Trapper's words packed about three times the normal wallop.

After that, Terry Yannarelli and the bartender from the Yellow Parrot testified that a man resembling Lou, about the same height and weight, at any rate, had left the bar with Sanchez. I made a big point of their being unable to give a positive I.D., but considering the fact that the Trapper had worn a beard, shades, and a pulled-down hat, they'd really gone about as far as they could go toward putting Lou away for the next five hundred years, give or take.

The afternoon testimony made my throat close. Martinez told the court he'd found Exhibit C, a nasty-looking .44 Magnum, in Lou's monk's cell of a room; and then a ballistics expert assured us all that the gun had killed Sanchez.

All day Lou sat quiet in the new suit we'd gotten him for the trial, looking stony and sullen and utterly unlike anyone for whom a juror would muster up a shred of sympathy.

When we left the courtroom, Art Zimbardo, sitting in one of the back rows, followed Dad and me with his amazing eyes, not speaking, just smoldering in that resentful, vulnerable way that got to me every time.

16

Rob had left shortly before the session was adjourned for the day—to write his story, I supposed. We'd been seeing each other three or four times a week. Tonight I was avidly looking forward to hashing over the day and, not to put too fine a point on it, to crying on his shoulder. But he wasn't home when I called and didn't return my call.

I had to get up at six o'clock to make it to San Jose on time, and I was bleary-eyed in the morning when I picked up my *Chronicle*. The headline woke me up: "Damaging Testimony in the Zimbardo Trial." Oddly, the by-line wasn't Rob's, but Charlie Fish's. I'd seen Charlie hanging around the day before, assigned to help Rob, I thought. Come to think of it, though, they hadn't sat together.

The story all but convicted my client, made both Dad and me look like asses, and portrayed Rob as practically an accessory to the Trapper's crimes. Some excerpts: "In a highly unusual move, Assistant District Attorney Liz Hughes called defense attorney Rebecca Schwartz as her first witness.

Schwartz, who, along with *Chronicle* reporter Rob Burns, discovered the body of the Tourist Trapper's first victim, showed no emotion as she told the court, 'Jack Sanchez's wrists had been nailed to the cross.'

"On cross-examination by her father, Isaac Schwartz, she disclosed that she exchanged blows with a woman who then appeared on the scene and tried to detain Miss Schwartz in what the woman said was a citizen's arrest for the murder of Sanchez. The Reverend Ovid Robinson of the Third Baptist Church, arriving to give the Easter sermon, broke up the fight, Miss Schwartz said.

"The defense attorney said the woman told her and Burns a story about being in a car with a man who drove to the Yellow Parrot bar (where the murderer apparently met Sanchez), falling asleep in the car, and waking up to find the car parked at the foot of Mount Davidson. Isaac Schwartz, who bantered with his daughter as he might at the dinner table, seemed to be trying to establish the mystery woman as a suspect in the Trapper killings.

"Hughes, on reexamination, followed a line of questioning apparently designed to portray the woman as a harmless derelict. 'She looked bedraggled,' the witness admitted, 'and rather unhealthy. Her clothes were very poor. And she reeked of alcohol.' Laughter broke out in the courtroom when it was learned that the woman, who fled before police arrived, gave her name as Miranda Warning, a term police use to describe the procedure advising a suspect of his rights.

"In other testimony, Burns, the man chosen by the Trapper as his link with the public, admitted receiving letters from the killer threatening to 'close this hellhole down' by randomly murdering tourists."

Fish didn't neglect the other witnesses, either, but the most damning part of the story was the last paragraph: "Outside the courtroom, Art Zimbardo, the defendant's brother, told the *Chronicle* that his brother chose Miss Schwartz as his lawyer as a result of Art's friendship with her and Burns."

I could see what had probably happened. Art had no doubt thought Fish was a friend of Rob's and hadn't realized he was being interviewed when Fish sauntered up and passed the time with him. But knowing that didn't keep me from wanting to kill the little dope—along with Charlie Fish.

The story was as good a reason as I'd ever seen for admonishing jurors not to read papers. I knew Fish was jealous of Rob and desperate to make his reputation, but I still didn't see how this could have happened. Where was Rob, anyhow? He didn't answer his phone, and it was too early to be on the road to San Jose.

He wasn't in the courtroom that morning, but there was a much worse problem—neither was Dad. Everybody but me seemed to know why—even Lou. He looked concerned this morning, not stony at all: "Have you heard anything about your dad?"

"No. Why?"

"You don't know about the crash on the bridge?"

Like the Rebecca in Fish's story, I showed no emotion as I spoke; but my hands were as cold as whatever nasty little thing was beating in Fish's chest: "What crash?"

"Eight or ten cars piled up; there's a huge tie-up."

I asked for a recess.

I knew I should call Mom; she might even be able to reassure me—maybe Dad had heard about the tie up on the radio and hadn't tried to take the Golden Gate Bridge. Most likely, he was still stuck on a bridge approach, probably walking around and schmoozing with the other trapped commuters. But there was always the chance he'd been in the wreck; Mom would think that, too, and we'd feed on each other's paranoia. The only thing I could do to keep myself from feeling utterly helpless was go to the bridge and find out for myself.

But traffic was backed up for miles on the San Francisco side as well as the Marin approach; I was stuck for forty-five minutes.

Cursing my own stupidity, I went back to my office, having lost the whole morning; it was now nearly 11:30. I was about to call Mom, bracing myself for gnashings and wringings, when the phone rang. It seemed to be a bad connection; the caller sounded as if he were whispering. I said: "Could you speak up a little? I can't hear you."

The whisper was very distinct now. *"This is The Trapper."*

I couldn't believe it. How dare the Trapper call me? And at a time like this!

"Why are you calling *me?*" I knew what I sounded like, and even as I talked to a serial killer, I mentally reminded myself that lawyers do not whine.

"Never mind that. I did the bridge."

"You did the bridge."

"The accident. On the Golden Gate Bridge."

"The bridge!" Now I was getting the hang of it. Of course; what could be more of a tourist attraction than the bridge?

I said, "Les, listen to me. I know who you are."

"You don't know who I am."

"You're Les Mathison from Turlock; you were in the 4-H Club."

"Pay attention. I drove north on the bridge and picked out a car going south to San Francisco—a green 1984 Mercedes. It was easy. I just threw a rock at the windshield. The driver lost control and hit his brakes. Cars started piling up in both lanes, but I was already clear. Tell Burns. And tell him I need a million dollars."

"A million dollars for what?"

"To make me stop."

"Les, I'm speaking as a lawyer; turn yourself in. You'll get off on diminished capacity; I promise—look at Dan White."

"Listen to me, Rebecca. I want a million dollars."

"But Rob hasn't got a million dollars."

"Just get this in the paper, that's all. I'll call back about how to get it to me." He hung up. Quickly, I dialed Rob's number. But I got only the egregious Charlie Fish. "Charlie!

Where's Rob?" I was horrified to hear that I had only half a voice.

"Who is this?"

"Rebecca Schwartz."

"Oh. Rob's not here. He's taken a week's leave of absence."

"What?" I was shocked into letting a human toad know my boyfriend hadn't even told me his plans.

"He didn't tell you? He got pulled off the story." If I ever heard triumph in a person's voice, I was hearing crowing now. I'd happily have belted him if he'd been in the same room. He continued in the same crowing tone: "The city editor said he had a conflict of interest. I can see his line of reasoning, can't you?"

"So you're on the story now?"

"Uh-huh."

"Well, there's been a development. The Trapper just called me. He said he caused the accident on the bridge."

"How do you know it was the Trapper?"

"I—uh—he told me how he did it."

"So?"

"So _what_, Charlie Fish? What do you mean, 'So'? I said a man just called me and said he's the Trapper. It's your story— don't you even care?"

"Anybody might have called you—or maybe nobody did. Or maybe you caused the bridge accident to make it look like your client's innocent and now you're claiming you got a call from the Trapper. It's happened before, I hear."

"You're being insulting."

"I'm just saying how am I supposed to believe you? Did you tape the conversation?"

"No, I—"

"Well, if you haven't got a tape, what have you got?"

I hung up on him. He was a warty little brat, but he had a point—how was I going to get anyone to believe me? And where the hell was Rob when I needed him? I dialed him at home and still got no answer. Then I went to see Liz Hughes, hoping like hell she hadn't left for lunch yet.

Her office, shared with another lawyer, was one of the closet-sized cubicles our public servants are forced to inhabit—if they were unionized, there'd be a strike over working conditions. It was hardly bigger than mine.

Liz was wearing a peach-colored wool suit with beige blouse. I was wearing the same suit in black, with a white blouse—I'd been so worried about Dad that morning I hadn't even noticed.

She gave me an ironic smile. "I like your outfit."

"Half price at Neiman-Marcus."

"Pretty classy. I got mine at the Emporium."

I couldn't believe it. We were talking about clothes. How to extricate myself from inanities and get down to business? But Liz did it. "You seem upset," she said.

I noticed she hadn't asked me to sit, but I felt too weak to stand any longer. I flopped into the one rigid wooden chair she had for visitors.

She said: "I hope your father's okay."

"My father." I'd forgotten about him. "I haven't heard yet. I had another kind of excitement. The Trapper called."

She raised an eyebrow.

"Someone called me and whispered. He said he caused the accident on the bridge."

"I guess you have to expect those kinds of calls." She was trying to be nice, but she wanted me in her office like she wanted a scorpion in her shoe.

"He said he threw a rock at someone's windshield." I explained exactly how he said he'd done it. She took careful notes, looking very efficient. "And then he said he wanted a million dollars to stop."

"Did he say how he wanted the money delivered."

"No. He said he'd call back." I wasn't about to tell her he'd told me to get it into the paper.

She smiled very politely. "It sounds like a nut call, don't you think?"

"Liz, he told me how he did it."

"It's already been on the radio."

I was speechless. And furious with Charlie Fish for not telling me. "I didn't know. But, listen, if that's how it happened, then _somebody_ did it—how do you know it wasn't my caller?"

She shrugged, and I could see by the way her shoulders strained against the light wool that she paid regular visits to a gym. She had time for a husband and two kids, too—Superwoman in a peach suit. "It might have been your caller. Don't you think you should file a police report?"

"I will, of course. But won't you at least entertain the notion that maybe you've got the wrong man?"

"That would be pretty hard on my morale."

"Liz, I know who the Trapper is."

"Rebecca, listen. This is an important case to both of us. We've both got to try it tomorrow. I don't mean to be rude, but if I listen to this I'm going to have to get up two hours early to meditate tomorrow: I really can't afford to have you throw off my equilibrium at this point."

"You think this is some kind of ploy?"

"I have no doubt you're sincere. But I'm equally convinced we have the right man. That's the way it has to be or I wouldn't be trying the case."

If I were Superwoman, I'd have rudely stayed exactly where I was, pouring out the whole story—to throw her precious equilibrium off, if for no other reason. But there was something about the imperious way she spoke that stopped me cold. I wasn't a little bit intimidated, I was out of my depth. I'm ashamed to say I let her get away with it.

Filing the police report was no picnic, either. I thought I could just go down to the first floor of the Hall of Justice and tell my story at Southern Station. But the young patrolman I talked to would have none of it. He excused himself for a moment—to make a phone call, it turned out. In a few moments, we were joined by none other than San Francisco's most active human stumbling block to metropolitan justice.

"Inspector Martinez," said the cop, "handles all the Trapper reports." The next half hour was the least bit dispiriting—like the North Pole is slightly chilly. By the time I got back to the office, I was wondering how hemlock would taste. But then Dad called. "Sorry I didn't make it to court this morning."

"Dad! I forgot all about you."

"I knew you could handle things."

"No, I don't mean that—I got a recess. But everything's gone wrong. How long were you tied up on the bridge?"

"Oh, a couple of hours. It wasn't too hard—I found some nice people with a deck of cards."

"What was the damage?"

"You have no faith in your old man—I won ten dollars."

"I mean on the bridge."

"You haven't heard? My, you must have been busy."

"You could say that."

"Well, it was a miracle. A lot of cars smashed, but no one badly hurt. Did you hear how it happened?"

"I heard it firsthand—the Trapper called me."

"Called *you*—how about Rob?"

"He got pulled off the story, took a week's leave from work, and doesn't answer his phone. Even I can't get him."

"You're having quite a day."

"You don't know the half of it—I went to see Liz Hughes."

"Ah! A bold move."

"I think she thinks I'm nuts."

"That's okay. Let her underestimate you."

"She wouldn't talk to me—she said it might upset her 'equilibrium.'"

"I'm sure it did."

"What?"

"Well, you talked to her a little, didn't you?"

"Yes."

"So you probably upset her a little."

"Dad, you're a cockeyed optimist."

But talking to him cheered me up. Until Mom called. "Rebecca, this is too hard on your father."

"What is?"

"He was on the bridge for hours this morning. And where were you, darling? I called and called."

"Oh? Alan didn't tell me."

"I told him not to. I knew you were too busy to talk to your mother."

"How could I call you back if I didn't know you were calling?"

"I thought you might have called on your own—you knew I'd be worried about your father."

"Oh, I was, Mom, I was. I just wasn't in the office, that's all. I went to the bridge to find him."

"Well, darling, that wasn't very smart. You could have got stuck in traffic yourself."

"I did."

"Too bad you didn't call—I'd have told you not to go."

"I'm sure you would, Mom."

"Darling, I'm pleading with you; I'm begging you. Your father's not as young as he used to be. This case he doesn't need—and neither do you."

"You want us to withdraw?"

"Just set your father free."

I almost laughed—perhaps I was at last developing maturity. I'd always admired Chris's affectionately amused attitude toward Mom, but I didn't have enough distance to ape it. This, however, was hilarious—if there was anything that kept Dad young, it was a good scrap, a game that looked as if it couldn't be won. Ultimately, Mom had just given me reason to cheer up again—even if Lou went to the Green Room, Dad would probably live ten years longer as a result of working on the case. I said: "Okay, Mom. He's been looking a little peaked to me, too. I'll tell him he's fired."

"But you'll hurt his feelings."

"If it has to be done, it has to be done."

"I don't think you can handle the case alone." That could have hurt *my* feelings, but I knew by now that it was no reflection of Mom's regard for my ability; she just liked to find things to be nervous about.

"I probably can't, Mom, but if Dad's health is at stake—"

"Maybe he shouldn't leave you alone—" I knew she was genuinely torn. What was the bigger worry—the specter of Dad wearing himself out or me disgracing the family by going down in flames alone? I could see endless teasing possibilities—I could have kept her going for twenty minutes or so—but I was sure Liz Hughes would never tease her mother and I was currently taking Superwoman lessons. I said, "I'll think about it very, very carefully, Mom. I'm sure one of us will come up with a solution." Actually, I was sure she'd go back and forth, back and forth, undecided about the lesser of the evils, until the case was safely over; she thrived on indecision, so I knew I'd made her happy.

Hanging up, I called Rob again. Again no answer. I knew from experience that Rob could take care of himself; but there was a serial killer on the loose—one who knew Rob, who might have followed him from the *Chronicle* to—where? Some dark cul-de-sac. The Trapper had said "never mind" why he hadn't called Rob. Suddenly the words took on a new and ominous meaning. Maybe it was pure fear—like my mother's—or maybe it was that combined with the events of the day. I don't know. But suddenly I was sobbing in a most un-Superwomanly fashion. And in walked Jeff Simon.

17

"**Y**ou poor bubbe." He came around the desk and patted me. I was too humiliated to do anything but continue sobbing. "You're getting killed in court."

He maneuvered me into first a standing position and then a hug, so that I was quite literally giving his three-piece suit a saltwater bath. "Your nice clothes."

While it wasn't unpleasant to be held, I felt that using Jeff's shoulder wasn't ethical under the circumstances. I tried to get away, but apparently he'd decided to sacrifice haberdashery for gallantry. "Don't worry about the suit. I've got a great cleaner in L.A. that doesn't charge any more than the monthly payment on a Porsche."

"This is only making me feel worse."

"From the newspaper story I thought you'd be suicidal."

"What newspaper story?"

"In the *L.A. Times*."

"Oh, no!" I hadn't even seen that one.

"You must feel really ganged up on. And knowing your

client's guilty has to be about as galling as anything I can imagine. Having to defend scum like that! You're too fine a person for it, Rebecca."

In normal circumstances, I would have been furious with him, but I was so worked up about Rob I was quickly forgetting my embarrassment and also the fact that Jeff—as Jeff—was there at all. He could have been my shrink or my mom or a Phidian sculpture or an eight-foot poster of Boy George and all I'd have been aware of was a sounding board. "I'm so worried about Rob."

"Rob! You mean that newspaper hack?"

"Oh, Jeff—I'm afraid the Trapper's killed him."

"But your client's the Trapper. Isn't he?"

"Of course not. Les Mathison is. He just called and said something awful."

"Let me get this straight. The Trapper isn't your client, but he happens to be a friend of yours, anyway?"

"No. But I found out who he is and he called me. And Rob's disappeared."

"I'm sure you know that most missing persons are walk-aways."

"Oh, Jeff. What if he's hurt?" I really meant "dead," but I couldn't bring myself to say the word.

"I thought you'd be upset about your case."

"Jeff, aren't you listening? The Trapper might have killed Rob."

"I was going to surprise you. I flew to San Jose, but court wasn't in session and I had to rent a car to get up here."

"I'm sorry."

"Sorry! Not half as sorry as I am." He stepped back from me. "I thought you'd be glad to see me."

"I'm sorry." I hadn't the wit not to repeat myself. "I guess the timing wasn't right."

"With everyone against you like this, and such a weak case and all—and that D.A.'s really doing a terrific job—"

"Shut up!" I'm afraid I spoke a little more loudly than

necessary. But by now I'd begun to notice him as Jeff again and the fury I hadn't felt before had worked its way to the surface—that and a new batch.

"Rebecca, there's no need to raise your voice. I assure you my intentions were perfectly benign."

I said again, "I'm sorry." Back in the same old rut.

"I'm sure you're not really a bad person—even an ungrateful person—just the sort who cracks under pressure. Maybe you're not as strong as I thought you were. So I misjudged you—it's my loss. I thought you were somebody I could really have a relationship with. All this time I've been thinking about you—I couldn't get you out of my mind. I should have known when I heard you were defending this guy that I'd gotten stars in my eyes. That should have been a clue."

"A clue to what?"

"Even before that—when I found out you were dating that newspaper guy—I should have realized that underneath the Superwoman image you're really just another California loser."

"What did you say?"

"Listen, don't take it personally. It's this state—it does something to people. Even Jews. You can't help what you are."

"Being a loser, you mean."

He shrugged.

"But I gave some other impression before."

"You seemed sort of competent—on the surface."

"Did you say I had a Superwoman image?"

"Not Superwoman, exactly. Just sort of superficially—"

"Oh, never mind."

"Sorry things turned out this way."

He left, imagining, I suppose, that he'd leveled me. But in a small way he'd made my day, as we say in California. I couldn't get him to repeat the remark that was balm to my battered ears, but I like to think that the things people really mean come out under duress. I might not be Liz Hughes, but maybe I could fool some of the people some of the time.

"Rebecca! Have you heard from Dad?" Mickey had come barreling in while I was congratulating myself. "Where's Alan?"

"Alan's still at lunch, I think, but it's nearly two. He ought to be back in a few minutes. And I just talked to Dad. Why— what's up?"

"You haven't heard about the bridge?"

"Mickey, you must be the only person in all of San Francisco who doesn't listen to a news broadcast at least once a hour."

"I was just on my way to a late lunch when I heard some people talking about it. I heard twenty people were killed."

"No one was killed;. Daddy was hardly inconvenienced— he played poker on the freeway."

"Oh. Well. I didn't really think anything was wrong."

"You know what I did when I heard? Tried to drive to the accident."

She sighed. "We're our mother's daughters."

"Not really. Mom said she would strongly have advised me not to go there."

Mickey laughed. "As long as I'm here, have you had lunch yet?"

"I'm starving."

A heaping spinach salad—one with lots of bacon—fixed me up. "I just got told I'm a loser by a guy who flew up from L.A. so I could cry on his shoulder."

"And did you?"

"He's going to have a great-granddaddy of a cleaning bill— as Chris would say."

"Whizbang."

"What?"

"She'd really say 'great-granddaddy of a whizbang.'"

"So how're you feeling?"

"Fine. How about you?"

"Awful. Rob's disappeared." I told her the whole story.

"The Trapper didn't get him," she said. "Rob doesn't know any more than you do. Why not kill you, too?"

"He tried. I got mugged a while back." And I told her that story.

She said, "Pretty inept for a multiple murderer."

"Sometimes he's not really all that slick. He caused the bridge pileup by throwing a rock."

"Simple. But undeniably effective. I think he does fine when he puts his mind to it. So he must not have really wanted to kill you. Or else you were mugged by a common thug."

"Maybe. But about Rob. You think Les really has no motive for killing him?"

"Oh, he might. But he always moves fast—does the job, then claims credit. Or 'responsibility' as the newspapers say. He called you and didn't say a word about Rob; ergo, he didn't kill him."

I didn't think it was quite that simple. The Trapper *might* have killed Rob. Still, Mickey had put the thing in perspective. He hadn't necessarily done it. I felt better. "So if he isn't dead, where is he?"

"Same place he always is when he disappears—on a story."

"But he's on leave."

"It doesn't mean he's off the story."

The ramifications of that sent me into a new depression. When I got back, there was a glass bowl on Kruzick's desk. In the bowl was a large, nasty-looking rock, smeared with ketchup. Kruzick had affixed a typewritten label to the bowl: "Exhibit Z."

"I found the weapon," said my faithful amanuensis.

"Not funny, Alan. Distinctly not funny."

"Hey, listen. The 'Z' isn't for Zimbardo. Honest. Chosen at random, you know what I mean?"

"I'm not in the mood, Alan."

"Just trying to help. But listen, I've got another idea—in

case you lose. I mean, you and I know that's impossible, of course, but just in the slight eventuality. You could become a best-selling author. In fact, maybe you and Lou could collaborate. How's this: *The Tourist Trapper's Guide to Scenic San Francisco*. Can't miss. It could have, maybe, a little pop-up cable car, and when you open the book to the right page, not only does the cable car pop up, but little paper dolls spill out of it, you know? And then there's the spin-offs. We could sell vials labeled 'Paralytic Shellfish Toxin,' and maybe some 'Relics of the True Cross of Mount Davidson.'"

"Alan, you're fired."

"Hey, boss, you're young yet. By real loose standards, I mean. It's never too late to start a new career."

I ignored him, stalking in a dignified manner into my office and deeply regretting having thought well of him for half an hour several months ago.

"You're going to need a business manager."

I slammed my door.

18

ad was already in court when I arrived the next day, wearing a tie with only one spot on it and looking ready for anything. I hoped he was—today Liz was scheduled to present the most damaging part of her case. The first witness was a man named George Henderson, manager of Full Fathom Five.

"Mr. Henderson," said Liz, "have you ever seen the defendant before?"

"Yes. He worked in the kitchen at the restaurant for three days last April."

"Did anything out of the ordinary happen during those three days?"

"On the third day, we inadvertently served quarantined mussels to some of our customers. Eleven people became ill, and of those, one died."

"Had you bought any local mussels during the previous few days?"

"I hadn't bought any in a month because of the quarantine. We're very careful to use only eastern mussels if there's any danger at all. In fact, we don't even buy many of those when there's a quarantine because fewer people order them then."

"When did you last see Mr. Zimbardo?"

"He was there the night of the tragedy. But I don't remember seeing him after people started getting sick."

"He left the restaurant?"

"Yes."

"Did any of the other employees leave the restaurant?"

"No. They helped me take care of people until the paramedics came. Some of them helped calm people down. I don't even think any customers left—everyone was kind of—uh—paralyzed."

A nervous titter rippled throughout the courtroom.

"Did Mr. Zimbardo have access to the refrigerator where the mussels were kept?"

"Yes."

"No further questions."

"Mr. Henderson," I asked, "did anyone else have access to that refrigerator?"

"All the employees did."

"How do the kitchen employees dress?"

"In white. With white hats."

"Do you ever find it difficult to tell them apart—at a distance, say?"

Henderson's hands twitched. "Not particularly."

"From the back?"

"They look fairly similar from the back."

"If someone had come into the kitchen dressed as an employee on the night of the shellfish poisonings, is it possible he or she wouldn't have been noticed?"

"I don't think so."

"Were you very busy that night?"

"Extremely."

"So an imposter might have gone unnoticed?"

"I don't see how."

"Mr. Henderson, do you pride yourself on fine service at your restaurant?"

"Yes, we do."

"Would you say that most of your employees are very wrapped up in their jobs?"

"They wouldn't last a week if they weren't."

I sat down, but Liz got up again: "Did you see a stranger in the kitchen the night of the poisonings?"

"No, I didn't."

"Did any of your employees report seeing one?"

"No, they didn't."

"Thank you, sir."

I said to Dad, "Pretty bad, wasn't it?"

"It could have been worse." He paused. "And it's going to be."

The next scheduled witness was the medical examiner, then some doctors who'd taken care of the victims, and after that the big guns—an expert on paralytic shellfish poisoning, one of the surviving victims, and Mrs. Baskett, the wife of the man who died. "You take everybody but the last two," said Dad. "I'll do the victims."

The coroner's man and the doctors were fairly technical, but the expert was another matter altogether. Dr. Dan Ervin was a physician who worked for the State Department of Health Services, a distinguished white-haired chap who looked as if he ought to smoke a pipe.

For about ten minutes, Liz led him through the steps of his career, establishing his expertise on the subject of mussel neurotoxin. Then she got down to it: "Dr. Ervin, what causes paralytic shellfish poisoning?"

"The substance is called saxitoxin. It's produced by a kind of plankton—a dinoflagellate that goes under the name of *Gonyaulax catenella*."

"Do shellfish feed on the plankton?"

"Yes. Mussels are filter feeders; they concentrate what is in the water in their digestive systems."

"They're not selective about what they eat?"

"No. If the plankton is in what we call a 'bloom' stage, there'll be a lot of plankton in their systems. If the level of toxin is eighty micrograms, then it has reached the alert standard." Ervin crossed his legs and laid an elegant hand on the top knee. "But that's well below the level at which people get sick; they develop real symptoms at a thousand micrograms. When it gets into the multithousands, then people begin to get seriously sick. Last spring we measured twenty thousand micrograms at Drake's Estero—just north of Stinson Beach."

Liz was quiet for a moment, letting it sink in. Finally she said, "Twenty thousand micrograms!"

The doctor nodded. Liz said: "If one mussel in a given area had that much toxin in it, would it follow that most of the others in the area would?"

"It would vary with the size of the mussel, of course."

"But if you gathered mussels at Drake's Estero last spring, you'd have been almost certain to gather—"

"—a very deadly harvest," finished the doctor.

"Do the effects vary with each individual who eats mussels contaminated with the toxin?"

"Yes. They vary with the number of mussels eaten, the size of the mussels, the concentration of the toxin, and the individual's tolerance. People who eat a lot of shellfish tend to have more tolerance."

"Such as Bay Area natives."

"Possibly."

"Would you say that tourists would be particularly vulnerable to the effects of the toxin?"

"Undoubtedly, if they came from inland areas. Unless, of course, they had their mussels flown in from one of the coasts, as restaurants do. But a tourist like that probably wouldn't be at Pier 39." He got a laugh on that one.

"Dr. Ervin, why is it that the mussels are only dangerous at certain times?"

"We don't know, really. Our educated guess is that environmental factors come together to produce favorable growing conditions for the plankton. Sunny periods with calm seas, for instance, may be healthy for them. But no one knows for sure. So far we've had no luck in trying to predict the contamination, except from May 1 to October 31; that's the normal quarantine."

"Is it unusual to have a mussel quarantine in April?"

"It's not common but it happens. It's not impossible we might even have a quarantine in January. It's simply related to how much of the plankton is available."

Liz sat down abruptly. I got up with a sigh, ready to play one of the games lawyers play. She hadn't asked a word about the symptoms, so that the drama could come from the victims, the doctor who'd attended them, and the people who'd watched them get sick. It was up to me to take the sting out of the testimony to come. "Dr. Ervin," I began, "is the shellfish neurotoxin a fast-acting poison?"

"Very fast. It acts within minutes."

"How does the poison work?"

"It acts on the human central nervous system, eventually causing a respiratory paralysis that makes it impossible to get air into the body."

I took him through the poison's progress, symptom by symptom, and then asked, "Is there an antidote for it?"

"Not an antidote. But there is a cure."

"And what is the cure?"

"An iron lung." Damn him, he got another laugh. He had an ironic delivery that could turn the simplest statement into black humor.

"Is the paralysis reversible?"

"Yes. If you can keep a victim breathing, he'll probably be all right."

"You've studied the cases from Full Fathom Five?"

"Certainly."

"And is that what happened?"

"In six of the eleven cases, yes. Mr. Baskett didn't respond to treatment. But six people were easily revived, and four had eaten only one or two or three of the mussels—they had seen other people get sick, had begun having symptoms themselves, and had stopped eating. They were not seriously ill."

"Thank you, Doctor."

When the judge called the morning recess, I headed for the ladies' room to wash my sweaty hands. The previous two had been damaging enough, but Liz's next miracle was twenty-three-year-old Alice Jones, the very picture of Pepsi-generation wholesomeness. She had light brown hair, blue eyes, and a slight Oklahoma twang. She'd been in San Francisco on her honeymoon when she'd found herself in a restaurant suddenly transformed into a Bosch landscape; I was awfully glad I didn't have to cross-examine her.

Liz went through the honeymoon business (establishing that though the witness had ordered mussels, her new husband had had a perfectly harmless fillet of sole), and then asked Alice if she'd seen anything unusual that night.

"My mussels had just come," said Alice, "and Bob and I were talking about what color to paint the house. I ate one and then stopped for a minute to listen to Bob; he had some art courses in school and knows a lot about color. Bob wanted to paint the trim terra-cotta and cobalt blue. I wasn't sure exactly what color that was—the blue, that is—and it kind of gave me the creeps. Cobalt, I mean—it's sort of dangerous or something"—she looked confused—"at least I thought so. My fingers started to tingle. I thought it was my imagination at first; but Tom took both my hands and held them—kissed them, you know. Then he said, 'Your mussels are getting cold.' So I picked up my fork, but I dropped it—I didn't know why, I just couldn't seem to hold it. I was going to ask the waiter for another, but then someone got up and started walking—toward the men's room, I guess—and he was staggering; we thought he was drunk. He fell down and some people went to help him, and then I heard a scream—"

Liz asked, "Was it a woman who screamed?"

"Yes. I looked and saw she was flinging her hands about, as if she were shaking water off them—" Here, Alice demonstrated. "She was yelling something about electricity. I got real scared then, because that was the way my fingers felt— like I'd gotten a shock, or maybe hit my crazy bone. I started to feel sick."

"What did you do then?"

"I told Bob I was going to throw up. I knew I ought to go to the ladies' room, but I was too scared to move. The woman at the next table, who'd just been sitting there up till then, all of a sudden fell out of her chair."

"In a faint?"

"Oh, no, it wasn't like that. She moved her chair back and tried to get out of it, but— I don't know, it just seemed as if she'd lost her balance or something. She kind of fell over on her side. Bob went to help her, but she couldn't seem to get her feet under her. She couldn't get up at all, so finally her husband and Bob helped her lie down."

"Let's reiterate a minute," said Liz. "At this point, a man and a woman had collapsed and another woman was screaming about electric shock. You yourself were experiencing tingling and loss of coordination—"

"And nausea," said Alice.

"And nausea. How would you describe the overall scene in the restaurant at that point?"

I half expected to hear her intone, "Fear stalked Full Fathom Five!"

But she said, "It was real quiet. Then this young man on the other side said something about poison in a loud voice and it seemed as if everyone started talking at once. It got loud as anything." She paused, looking very white. "I was really scared—and feeling terribly sick. I tried to get up, but I couldn't. Bob helped me lie down on the floor, and after that, people started running around like crazy. People in white jackets—from the kitchen, I guess—were trying to help the sick people. A man who said he was a doctor came and started to take my pulse, but then he heard someone sort of trying to catch their breath—I mean, we both heard it—and he left me. After that, Bob held my hand and kept saying to take it easy, that they'd called some ambulances. And I just kind of closed my eyes. I didn't want to see any more."

"What happened after that?"

"The next thing I remember, they put me on a stretcher and took me to the hospital."

"Thank you, Mrs. Jones."

It was Dad's turn. He said, "Not a very good way to spend your honeymoon." He smiled at Alice and she smiled back. "No," she said. The color started coming back to her face.

"I think you're a very brave woman."

"You wouldn't if you'd been there that night." Dad had her chatting like an old friend.

"Did you have difficulty breathing?"

"No. I was lucky, I guess."

"Did you ever throw up?"

"No—I just felt as if I were going to."

"It must seem kind of like a bad dream in retrospect."

She looked at Dad as if he were the only person in th world who really understood her. "Sometimes I can hardl believe it really happened."

"Tell me, Mrs. Jones—have you ever had the flu?"

"Oh, sure. It gets me about two or three times a year.

"Would you describe the way you felt at the restaurant something like having the flu?"

"Oh, not at all. Like I said, I was lucky—it only lasted little while, and sometimes I can't even remember it too wel But of course if I'd eaten more mussels—"

"Are you absolutely sure you had paralytic shellfish po soning?"

"Well, sure—everybody else did."

"Did they do any tests at the hospital?"

"Oh, no. They were real busy with everybody else; I was the lightest case, so they hardly bothered with me at all."

"They didn't do tests to make sure you had it?"

"I don't think they really needed to."

"You're from Oklahoma, aren't you?"

"Yes."

"And you were willing to come all this way to testify?"

"Bob and I thought it was important."

"Do you by any chance have a lawsuit pending against the restaurant?"

"I don't see— Why do you want to know?"

She looked at Liz, then at the judge, who said, "Answer the question, please."

"Yes," said Alice, now slightly less the helpless victim.

"No further questions," said Dad. He hadn't demolished her, but he'd taken some of the shine off.

Next up was Hallie Baskett, wife of Brewster Baskett, the man who died at Full Fathom Five. She gave her age as seventy-two, but she looked ten years younger, with excellent color and a good, stout, small-town woman's figure. She looked so strong I figured she could probably have ordered mussels that night with impunity—but she'd had prawns.

"Was this your first visit to San Francisco?" asked Liz. "Last spring?"

"Yes. Our son and his family moved here six months before, so we decided to visit. It was like a dream come true."

"How's that?"

"We'd always wanted to come here." A brief sadness crossed her face, but she didn't cry; instead, she set her lips in a hard, unattractive line, not nearly as good for Liz's purposes as tears would have been.

"Had your husband been ill for a few days before you went to the restaurant?"

"Yes. He caught the flu—from the fog, I guess. But he said he wasn't going to leave without eating at a fish restaurant."

"I know this is hard for you, Mrs. Baskett, but can you tell me what happened the night you went to Full Fathom Five?"

"Well, Brewster had to have mussels. Never had had them and said he was damned if he was going to go to his grave without trying them." Her voice was getting a little unreliable. "Said he'd have ordered cockles, too, if they'd been on the menu." She reached in her purse for a handkerchief, dabbed at her eyes, then looked bravely back at Liz. "Well, he thought they were the greatest thing since sliced bread. Tried to get me to try one, and our son and daughter-in-law, too. But we wouldn't do it. I said, '"Everybody to their own taste," said the old lady as she kissed the cow.' Ugly things." She made a face. "Brewster always was a fast eater. He ate all of 'em before I'd hardly started my prawns."

"Did he complain of tingling or numbness in his mouth or his fingers?"

"Nope. Just sat there looking like the cat that swallowed the canary. He liked doing adventuresome things, you know—things people his age don't usually do. I could tell he was real proud of himself. Then I noticed his breathin' started sounding funny—real gaspy. I said, 'Brewster, what is it? That flu's got you again?' But he didn't answer; just sort of toppled over on the floor." Her words had come out in a great burst, and now her sobs did. Liz asked if she wanted a recess, but she shook her head.

In a moment, she said, "I'm a lifelong Presbyterian and know what happened was God's will. I don't want you to think I'm a crybaby."

"Can you tell the jury what happened to your husband after he fell on the floor?"

"He couldn't catch his breath. Just struggled and struggled to breathe. And I couldn't do nothin' to help him. Then the ambulance came, but he was quietened down by them; I don't know but that he was already dead." Her voice was firm again, the voice of a woman doing what she knew she had to do.

Taking a leaf from Dad's book, Liz said, "I think you're very brave, Mrs. Baskett. I have no more questions."

But Dad wasn't about to be outdone. He said, "I think you're very brave, too. You must miss your husband a lot."

"It's the Lord's will," she said. She looked straight at Lou. "I don't bear no one any ill feeling."

"Thank you, Mrs. Baskett," said Dad, having, through some magic he did with those blue eyes of his, evoked what amounted to a plea of leniency from the state's star witness. But leniency would be poor comfort to an innocent man. Even Dad's good work with Hallie Baskett and Alice Jones wouldn't offset the horror of their testimony. We were still getting killed.

Liz rose and said, "The prosecution rests." The ball was in our court.

19

I couldn't bring myself to go home. My apartment is uncluttered because I relax better when my surroundings are simple. My office is exactly the opposite: It's busy, and I catch its mood. So I went there and sat staring out the window, trying to think of something— anything, no matter how outlandish—that would help me salvage the case.

About nine o'clock, Chris came in. I heard her go into her office and rummage in her desk. Then she came into mine with a bottle of bourbon in one hand and two coffee mugs in the other. She knows I don't drink bourbon, but she poured two stiff ones, straight up, into the mugs and thrust one at me.

I started to shake my head, but she took my hand and curled the fingers around the mug handle. "Auntie says drink."

I lifted the mug and sipped. For once, the bourbon didn't taste too bad.

"Old Weller," said Chris. "I do my best thinking on it,

which doesn't happen often because it costs too much, but this is a clear emergency."

I took another sip. "Makes you want to holler 'hidey-ho.'"

"Sip slowly, now. The point is not to drown sorrows, but to plot strategy."

"Does that mean you've got an idea?"

"Not yet. But I feel one coming on. We're desperate, right?"

"What do you mean, 'we'?"

"We're partners, aren't we?"

"Yes, but—"

"I mean we. Now. Are we desperate?"

"Unquestionably."

Chris touched a long elegant finger to her long, aristocratic schnoz. Which meant she was feeling creative. I felt better already.

She said, "So desperate measures are called for."

"If I could think of any, I'd have already taken them. The only possible way out is to find Les. Or at least Miranda. And we've already tried everything."

"Everything normal people would try. But don't forget—we are two desperate women, solely responsible for saving an innocent man from a cruelly unjust fate."

"I think you've had enough Old Weller."

She took a mammoth gulp. "Nonsense. We've got to loosen up our minds and make them do somersaults. We can't think like lawyers. We've got to have innocence. We've got to be two kids who haven't yet learned the word 'impossible.'"

I sighed and sipped. "Okay. Let's go over what we've already done. First Rob, a trained reporter, went to the Tenderloin to find Miranda. He got mugged. Next we hired a pro to find her. He struck out. So what's left?"

Chris's nostrils quivered, as they did when she was upset. She was silent and so was I, which made the sudden ringing of the telephone all the more strident. Chris looked at her watch. "Nearly ten o'clock—who'd call this late?"

"Probably a wrong number."

"Maybe it's your dad—he might have had an idea."

Sighing, I picked up the phone. Rob said, "Rebecca. Thank God."

"Rob! You're alive."

"For heaven's sake. You sound like your mother. Listen, I've found Miranda."

"You're kidding!"

"You know what I did? I got this idea—I got mugged the first time I went to the Tenderloin, and our private eye couldn't get anywhere, so I decided to make a last-ditch effort. I mean things were going so badly and I felt so helpless. I decided to dress like a bum and kind of move into the Tenderloin, live there for a few days. I checked into a flophouse and started hanging out in bars. I wasn't picking up anything, so I just started exploring—you know, dirty-book shops and whatever there was. Anyway, I finally found Miranda working in this place where you can talk to a naked woman for a buck. I followed her to her hotel—I'm calling from there now—but this guy went in there with her and I had to wait for him to leave. Which took five hours."

"What did you get out of her?"

"Nothing yet. She's dead drunk—passed out and I can't wake her up. I need your help."

"Where are you?"

He didn't answer at first. Then he said, "Omigod. Oh, Jesus—" The phone went dead.

Chris shoved some more Old Weller at me, which I drank while I stammered out what Rob had told me.

She said, "The guy must have come back."

I nodded. "He could be slashing Rob's throat right now—Jesus! Maybe it's Les."

"I think we have to call the cops. This is pretty bad, Rebecca." Her voice was frighteningly serious.

"What's the point? If we can't tell them where to go, they can't go."

"Wait a minute. I've got the glimmerings of an idea. Let's do what Rob did—go to the Tenderloin."

"Like this?" I gestured at our business suits. "We'd get killed."

"I mean let's do it like Rob did—we can dress like bag ladies."

"There's no time. Les could be killing him now."

"Well, what do you suggest, then? Finish off the bottle and let him tackle Les alone?"

That did it. Chris doesn't often speak sharply; the fact that she did then woke me up. She was right; if Rob was alive, it was up to us to find him—the cops wouldn't have a chance even if they were willing to try. "Not bag ladies," I said. "Too hard to pull off."

"Whores?"

"Just burnouts. We can pose as friends of Miranda's." But I looked at Chris's fancy haircut and felt my nerve slipping.

She caught me at it: "Don't worry about the hair. I've got some platinum spray I used last Halloween. Not only transforms the hair into instant shredded wheat, also turns the complexion a splendid chartreuse."

We went first to Merrill's to buy some cheap cosmetics, made a stop for some Thunderbird, got some burgers and fries, picked up some clothes at my house, then headed for Chris's, home of the platinum spray.

We wet our hair to destroy all semblance of style, put a little cold cream on it to make it look dirty, and then turned Chris blonde. The platinum, as she'd promised, brought out yellow tones in her pink and white skin you couldn't have imagined. By the time we applied some truly revolting foundation, the combination of her natural skinniness and artificial jaundice made her look as if she'd be dead of cirrhosis within a month. A little black eyebrow pencil on her light brown brows and fuchsia lipstick completed the picture.

I looked more or less a fright in red lipstick and dead-white foundation, but still rather like a nice Jewish girl with awfu taste. Chris held up the spray can, but I stopped her: "I have to be in court tomorrow."

"It washes out—see?" She pointed to instructions on the can.

"Okay. Leave lots of dark roots." She sprayed and in minutes my mother wouldn't have known me. Would have disowned me at any rate.

Our clothes were easy—beat-up jeans and T-shirts; America is still in some ways a Democratic country.

Since we might need money and—God forbid—I.D.s, Chris put hers in my old black Sportsac, the more disreputable of our two bags; we could trade off carrying it.

The final touch was the Thunderbird, which we put in Chris's plant mister and sprayed all over each other—hair, neck, arms, T-shirts, everywhere as if it were the latest designer delight, guaranteed to liquefy strong men. When I thought about it, the Thunderbird would do that, too—but women and children weren't safe, either.

Finally, we each helped ourselves to a stick of chewing gum. Then, at 11:30, we hit the streets. Once on them, though, a logical question occurred. "Where," I asked the author of the outing, "do we start?"

"Believe it or not, I've got an idea. What's the one thing we know about whizbang's habits?"

"Miranda's? That she drinks too much."

"Right. Probably Thunderbird—or beer. Actually, we know she drinks beer—that's what she had when Sanchez was killed. She has to get it from some place, doesn't she?"

"Liquor stores! And corner markets."

"Right again."

"Let's start near the Bonaventure Arms."

There was a market right across the street. We decided I'd go in and do the talking, with Chris outside as backup, in case I needed rescuing. An old black woman who looked as if she could hold her own with the neighborhood thugs sat behind the counter on a high wooden stool. I said: "You seen Miranda around?"

"Don't know no Miranda."

"She used to live across the street. Medium height. Skinny. Brown hair."

"Could be anybody. Do you want anything?"

"Oh. Yeah." I found a Diet Coke and paid for it. Then I cracked it open and began to sip.

"That's all you want?"

"Miranda's my best friend." I reached in the Sportsac for a five-dollar bill. "She hasn't been around lately. I'm a little worried about her." I handed over the five.

She took it, folded it, and placed it safely in her pocket. "Honey, you wasting your money. I wouldn't remember no white girl. All look alike to me."

"All look alike? You think I look like, say, Dolly Parton?"

"Dolly Parton?" She laughed. "Dolly Parton? You ain't even in the same class."

"So we don't all look alike."

"Sure you do. Just some's ugly and some's halfway fit to look at."

"Wait a minute. I didn't pay five dollars to be insulted."

She laughed again, evilly. "Sure you did, honey. You're a loser, just like everybody else comes in here."

I left, internally questioning the wisdom of our brilliant disguises. "Any luck?" asked Chris.

"She didn't like my demographics. On the other hand, she was a greedy old trout—if she'd had any information, I think she'd have sold it. Here's the thing—assuming Miranda's alive and trying to stay out of the line of fire, she wouldn't go to her old haunts."

"True. Let's branch out."

Chris did the talking next time. While I was standing outside, a kid who looked about twelve sauntered by, casually grabbed the Sportsac, and tugged. With his free hand he hit me in the stomach. I shoved him in the chest, learning in the process he was a she and well over twelve. The effect of the blow was to dislodge the bag, still firmly in the girl's hand, and give her a slight advantage. She tugged again, pulling me over on top of her. We were rolling on the sidewalk before Chris could catch on and race out the door. A crowd started to gather. Chris shouted at the kid: "Jackie, you let go of that lady's bag right now. If I've told you once, I've told you a hundred times—" As she spoke she picked the kid up by the arm and began to shake her loose. "Now get on home!"

The kid took off as if pursued by a SWAT team; I had a feeling Chris had unwittingly done a fair imitation of the girl's mother. Amid good-natured chuckles, the crowd dispersed.

"Nice neighborhood," I said.

"I'm starting to like it." Chris was so pleased with herself she was practically ready to move in.

As for me, I wasn't sure I could take the excitement. And I was nearly crazy with worry. But we were left almost completely alone for the next hour or so—unless you count the man who propositioned Chris with a handful of hundred-dollar bills. Or the store owner who mistook me for a customer who owed him sixty dollars. That was no fun; after about fifteen minutes of shouting—fifteen minutes we couldn't afford—Chris finally sighed and said, "Tell him the truth."

It was a crowded store so I spoke in a whisper: "I don't even live in the neighborhood. Here's my driver's license."

The guy didn't take the hint. "Rebecca Schwartz," he shouted. "Oh sure. Anyone can pick a pocket. Or write a bad check, either. Sure you're Rebecca Schwartz of Green Street. Yeah, and I'm Perry Mason."

I was astounded, and not a little appalled that he was shouting my name up and down Leavenworth Street. "You know who I am." Still whispering.

Now he whispered, too. "Yeah. I know who you are. You're Marilyn Martin who hasn't been in here for four months and for good reason. You picked the wrong pocket, you know that? Because Rebecca Schwartz happens to be somebody I just read about in the *Chronicle*. She's going to be mighty interested to know who has her license. I'm calling her first thing in the morning. I'm calling the cops right now."

Chris shouted, "Run, Rebecca!" and blocked his way.

"Get her!" the guy yelled. I ran out of the store and halfway down the block, but not a single person followed. I figured the guy wasn't too popular even in his own neighborhood. I waited for Chris, wondering if our cover was blown. But Les no doubt had about as many friends as the store owner; unless he'd actually been in the store, we were probably all right.

By now, though, it was 1:15. The bars would close at 2:00 and so would everything else. After that, there'd be nothing to do—no way to help Rob, no hope. I was frankly terrified; we still had ten or twelve more stores to cover.

A lot of store owners were Chinese who pretended they couldn't speak English when asked anything other than a price; but they probably wouldn't have known Miranda anyway—or any of their customers. The great majority were Arabs. Arabs owned corner groceries all over the city and were usually extremely solicitous. But they treated Chris and me, in our burnout suits, like warty toads. The only people who were nice to us were old people so lonely they'd even pass the time of day with the likes of us—and young guys who wanted to flirt. It was one of these who finally said at 1:52 A.M., "Miranda? Sure. Comes in all the time. I know why you ain't seen her around, too."

"Why?"

"She's with Mean-Mouth now. Treats all his girls like prisoners. I mean, live and let live, you know? But Mean-Mouth's something else."

"He's a pimp?"

"You ain't heard of him?"

I shook my head.

"Yeah. He's a pimp. Never has more than two girls at a time; but, man, do they work."

"Poor Miranda."

"Lotta turnover. Sooner or later they all run away or he stops 'em runnin' away—if you know what I mean. Something tells me Miranda's going to be mighty glad to see you."

"Where do I find her?"

"Right across the street." He pointed out a run-down flophouse about on a par with the Bonaventure Arms. "But I wouldn't go in unarmed."

"You wouldn't know Mean-Mouth's other name, would you?"

"Nope. Nobody does. But you ain't thinking of asking for him by name, are you? Take my advice and don't."

We went outside and conferred. Clearly, we needed reinforcements. We could have called the cops then—and in retrospect, certainly should have—but we decided not to until we knew whether Rob was really in the building. Our judgment, frankly, was somewhat impaired by excess adrenaline.

We crossed the street and went into the flophouse. There was no lobby—nothing but a filthy corridor with a lot of forbidding doors on it. We walked up and down the corridor until we saw one partly open. I knocked, Chris standing slightly out of the way to back me up. "Yeah? Come in." A gruff voice.

Stepping in somewhat gingerly, I saw that it belonged to an unshaven black man, probably about three hundred pounds, lying on a bed in his underwear. He was sipping a beer and poring, by the light from an unshaded bulb, over a racing form. "Are you Mean-Mouth?"

"Look what the Good Lord's done and sent me. Come in, sweet thing."

"I'm looking for Mean-Mouth."

"I'll tell you where he is if you'll give old Ralph a little sugar."

"I'll give you ten dollars." I took out a ten-dollar bill and moved in close enough to make the offer seem serious.

"Ten dollars and a little lovin'."

"Twenty dollars." I produced another ten.

"What you want with Mean-Mouth?"

"I owe him some money."

Old Ralph guffawed. "You payin' *me* to find Mean-Mouth so *you* can pay *him*? Sweet thing, you a cop?"

"Do I smell like a cop?"

"Come closer and I'll tell you."

"Do you want the twenty or not?"

"Yeah. I'll take the twenty." He did, starting something like an earthquake in the bed just by sitting up.

"I'll give you another ten to tell me what he looks like."

"I thought you knew him."

I sighed. "Okay, I'm a cop."

"You ain't no cop."

"Okay, I'm not. Another ten or not?"

"Twenty."

"First tell me where he lives."

"Third floor, fourth door on the left. Okay?"

I handed over another twenty.

"Mean-Mouth looks like me."

"Are you related or something?"

"Brothers, in a manner of speaking. Mean-Mouth's th biggest, blackest, meanest dude I ever saw in my life."

We made Chris the lookout. Here was the plan: I'd go u and explore while Chris stood on the second floor. If I got i trouble, I'd whistle and she'd scream, run for help, whatev seemed appropriate. If Mean-Mouth came up the stairs, she whistle. Not a bad plan at all. If I got assaulted, then we certainly call the police. And hope they got there befo Mean-Mouth turned me into fertilizer.

I found the right door and knocked. No answer. I knock again and heard a noise from inside. Something lik "MMmmf." I heard it in stereo—a male "mmf" and a fema one.

I said, "Is anyone home, please?"

The male noises got louder. I opened the door to full light—and the sight of my sweetie in a double bed with Miranda. They were fully clothed, tied to the bed, and gagged. Quickly, I removed Rob's gag: "You recognized my voice."

"Voice! I recognized your knock." He looked at me in a way he never had before. I liked to think that sometimes he looked as if he loved me, even admired me for my mind. But this look had a new respect in it; and gratitude as well. It came to me that I was rescuing him—and that if I weren't, he had a good chance of dying. On impulse, I bent to kiss him. "Watch out," he whispered.

I turned around quickly, heard footsteps, saw a man come into view. With relief, I noted that it wasn't a giant black dude, but a scrawny, wiry white one—not Mean-Mouth at all. So why was Rob shouting another warning? "It's Mean Mouth!"

It hit me suddenly: I'd been had. Old Ralph's description was his idea of a joke; if ever anyone didn't look an iota like him, it was Mean-Mouth. But Ralph, I suspected, had been accurate in one particular—if Mean Mouth wasn't the meanest dude in the Tenderloin, you couldn't tell it by his face. He had no lips to speak of and no chin—just a nasty little point bereft of jaws for backup. His eyes were so small you couldn't tell what color they were. His nose would have been normal except that it was red—like the rest of his face.

I froze, as one does in a nightmare. Mean-Mouth came in quickly, slammed the door, reached in his pocket, and pulled out a switchblade.

When he pulled the knife, my mental processes thawed like the snowpack at Tahoe. If I hadn't been able to think before, suddenly I couldn't stop. It occurred to me to tell Rob I loved him before I died. Then it occurred to me to save my breath. Then I remembered to whistle—and then to do it again and still again—but with the door closed I didn't think his could hear me.

Several possible plans of action came crowding in at once, including the notion of jumping out the window.

But it was closed and besides, the bed *was* between me and it.

One plan stood out from all the others; but there were serious flaws in it. And yet—was it really impossible? If I could time things right, maybe not.

Mean-Mouth stepped toward me. As he did I dropped and rolled under the bed.

"Come out or I cut him." I imagined Mean-Mouth holding the knife at Rob's throat, and it was far from a pretty picture, but I could bear it—the thing just didn't have the impact it would have if I'd actually been watching. I took time to fumble in the Sportsac for the two things I needed, put one between two fingers so it couldn't be seen, and put the other in my jeans pocket.

Then I rolled out from under the bed on Miranda's side. She stared at me with terrified eyes. I didn't dare look at Rob. Mean-Mouth said, "Come over here." Which was exactly what I wanted to hear. I walked around the bed, making as wide a circle as I could so that, when I reached the foot, I was also near the wall with the door—and the light switch.

With my left hand I turned the light off, at the same time reaching in my pocket with my right. I pulled out the switchblade comb Rob and I had bought at the magic shop, brandished it, and pressed the button, praying there wasn't enough light to give me away. Mean-Mouth tensed and moved toward me. It looked as if I'd gotten away with it—so far. I backed away from Mean-Mouth, crouching a bit and trying to look fierce.

Rob spoke quietly: "Circle, Rebecca. Keep moving on his left side—stay away from the hand with the knife."

I started circling and so did Mean-Mouth, throwing his knife back and forth between his left and right hands. I didn't know if the gesture was meant to intimidate, or if it served some other purpose, but it did succeed in making my scar prickle. I had the sudden sinking feeling that I wasn't going to pull this off.

"If he comes at you, parry with your left hand."

What the hell did parry mean? I decided that asking would also create a poor psychological effect. I kept circling.

Mean-Mouth struck. Instinctively, I blocked him with my left arm. "Good," said Rob, but it wasn't that good. I had a nasty cut on my arm. I wondered if I'd need stitches, and if the cut would leave a scar, which was probably all to the good—it kept me from realizing I might be too dead to care sometime in the next five minutes.

I didn't have the nerve to strike at Mean-Mouth. If I tried—especially if I tried for the only part of his anatomy that was vulnerable to a comb—he'd get me in the ribs or the back. So I kept circling, hoping for an opening. I had another worry, too. My eyes were getting accustomed to the dark, which meant that his probably were, too. Any second he might figure out that I had no weapon at all.

Could I trip him? I couldn't see a way. But I had to get him off-balance. I figured I had exactly one ploy available—the realization made me wonder why I hadn't thought of it before. I was in a hotel full of people and I was being attacked. I could yell for help. But then I had second thoughts. If I yelled, Chris would probably come running, and I was afraid that, unarmed, she'd get hurt.

My left arm was bleeding badly and beginning to hurt. So when Mean-Mouth struck again, I stepped back instead of parrying. In retrospect I shudder to think how my survivors would have felt if I'd caught the blow—there was so much force behind it that, deprived of his target, Mean-Mouth tumbled. It was the opening I'd been waiting for. I squeezed the thing between my fingers—one of the blood capsules from the magic store—and used the comb to jab him in the eye as hard as I could. With a sound like "arrrr," he fell back.

I covered his face with my hand, leaving him with

simulated blood all over it. Then, as his left hand went to his eye, I jumped up on the bed, stepping on Miranda's leg, but remaining somehow upright, and shouted my own "arrr." Without a word or a sound—but also without dropping the knife—Mean-Mouth ran from the room. I hoped Chris was in the clear, but didn't dare yell for fear she'd step into the open just as he reached the second floor.

Instead, I chased him. Down the corridor, down the stairs to the second floor. But I stopped there. "Chris?" She stepped from the shadows. There wasn't a sound from anywhere in the flophouse. I supposed the denizens laid low when they heard a fight.

"Omigod," said Chris, looking at my arm, and then, seeing my face, "Jesus! Lie down."

I didn't have to be told. I'd suddenly started feeling very queasy indeed. I started to sink, looking forward to passing out, but remembered that Mean-Mouth would soon figure out he wasn't badly injured. I sat instead of lying, put my head between my knees, and closed my eyes. The last thing I saw was Chris pulling off her T-shirt. She was starting to wrap it around my left arm when I heard an army coming up the stairs. The cops, I thought, not knowing how they'd got the word, but grateful, anyhow. I opened my eyes. Old Ralph from downstairs, now wearing a pair of pants, was charging toward us. "Sweet thing, you all right?"

"You almost got me killed, you elephant."

"That ain't no way to talk, sweet thing. I s'pose I did wrong to tease you, but I figured you'd find out what Mean-Mouth looked like when you found him."

Chris said, "That was Mean-Mouth? The guy you were chasing?"

I nodded. She spoke to me, but looked straight at Ralph: "I could have warned you if I'd known what he looked like."

"Yeah," said Ralph. "We were just discussing that."

I said, "Rob and Miranda are tied up upstairs. We've got to get them out of here before he comes back."

Ralph said, "I'll take care of Mean-Mouth. I guess I owe you that."

"That," I said, "and twenty bucks."

He didn't respond, just settled his blubber on the stairs.

By now, I had a fresh surge of adrenaline; I went back upstairs with Chris. Ungagged, Miranda said, "There's a knife under the mattress." After I'd assured Rob I wasn't badly hurt and he'd congratulated me on the rescue, Chris and I cut their ropes with Miranda's knife and the four of us got the hell out, silently. We were back on the second floor in about forty-five seconds, Chris wearing Rob's jacket over her bra, Rob and me dragging Miranda.

Ralph was still standing guard—or rather sitting it—but he heaved himself to his feet to see us out. "No sign of him," he said. "But you be careful, hear?"

"Thanks for the help."

"I left the second twenty in my room. You come back and get it, okay?"

"Oh, never mind." I figured I owed it to him for sentry duty but I was too peeved to be gracious about it.

I guess Miranda had been conscious for most of the excitement—she'd certainly seemed fully awake when she told us where to find the knife—but now she could barely stand. Rob and I had her propped between us, and every now and then she'd manage a step or two, but we had to carry her, more or less, to the Volvo. Once in it, we assessed my wound, which had stopped bleeding and was already starting to close. So I declined medical assistance in favor of a thrilling morning at home. Spent, Chris declined any more thrills, so we dropped her at her place. Then the rest of us headed for Green Street, Rob occasionally reaching over to touch my knee, Miranda snoring in the back seat.

We settled her on one of the white sofas while I made coffee and pasta and Rob took a shower. It was 3:00 A.M. when he joined me in the kitchen and tucked into some fettucine carbonara—his first decent meal in days.

Then I went to wash the Thunderbird off. Standing under the shower, I had a momentary feeling everything was going to be all right. But moments later, when I looked in the mirror, I knew it wouldn't. The makers of the platinum spray were charlatans and liars—my client had worse than a fool for a lawyer. He had a green-haired one.

20

I now had less than six hours to figure out what Miranda knew and get to court. But where to start?

"What choice have we got?" said Rob. "Let's let her sleep for a while."

So we set the alarm for 6:00 and went to bed. At 5:30, Miranda staggered into the bedroom: "What the hell is this? Who're you?"

Rob said: "I found you at your hotel last night. Don't you remember?"

She shook her head.

"I couldn't wake you up, but your friend came in drunk and jumped to conclusions. God knows what he was planning to do with us."

"Oh, yeah. Then the next thing I remember, this lady was there." She was quiet a moment, remembering. "What the hell's this all about?"

"Why don't you take a shower?" I said. "We'll get dressed and tell you about it."

She nodded and staggered out. In a moment, we heard the shower running. Rob put on some clothes he'd left at my house, and after getting into a robe, I went out to the kitchen to put on more coffee. While Rob made toast, I found some clothes for Miranda and knocked on the bathroom door. No answer. I knocked louder and yelled. Still no answer. I tried the door, but found it locked.

Rob said, "Let's try a credit card." I don't know where he learned to do it, but somehow he made it work. Miranda was naked on the bathroom floor, out cold once again. The bathroom was so steamy we could hardly see. Rob bowed out, gentleman-fashion, while I turned off the shower and bent over Miranda. I shook her and her eyelids fluttered, then opened: "Who the hell are you?"

"I found you last night. Remember?"

"Oh, yeah." She shut her eyes again.

"Miranda. Miranda, wake up."

"How do you know my name?"

"You told me. Your friends call you Miranda Warning."

This time the eyes flipped wide open, and she sat up, flinging an arm that hit mine, right where Mean-Mouth had cut it. "Ouch."

"What the hell is this?"

"If you'll come into the kithen, I'll tell you."

"I feel awful. Me and Mean-Mouth tied one on last night."

"Let me get you a robe." I was afraid to leave her, thinking she might pass out again, but she was washing her face when I returned. She said: "Is your hair supposed to be that color?"

Rob called, "Your phone's ringing."

Six A.M. and the phone was ringing. What was going on? I raced to the kitchen and picked it up. "Rebecca," said Mom. "Are you all right, darling?"

My mind raced. This time, surely, I hadn't done anything my mother could have read about in the paper. Maybe she was just getting in the habit of greeting me that way. I gave her my usual answer: "Sure, Mom. Why wouldn't I be?"

"No reason, dear. I just wanted to make sure before I told you what I have to tell you. I just want you to know your dad's going to be okay; it's nothing to worry about, he's going to be fine."

My heart nearly pounded out of my chest. "Something's wrong with Dad?"

"Darling, he's fine, really. But I had to take him to the hospital last night."

"Mom, what is it? What's going on?"

Miranda walked into the living room and sacked out on one of the couches. Mom said: "Remember how I begged you not to let him get involved in this?"

"For heaven's sake, Mom, what's happened?"

"He had a little spell in Israel. I never knew what it was, exactly—he just said he didn't feel well and wanted to come home. We didn't want to worry you, darling, so we didn't tell you."

"Mom, what *is* this?"

As if reading my mind, Mom said, "Don't worry, darling, it's not a brain tumor. They think it's something you can have surgery for. Last night"—she sounded as if she were about to cry—"right after dinner, suddenly he couldn't talk. He couldn't say a word, Rebecca."

"My God."

"He's okay this morning, darling. Really. But they have to do more tests." She was starting to sob. "He wants to know if you can make it on your own today."

"Sure, Mom. I'll be fine." Sure I would; with green hair, a sick father, and an incoherent witness. Maybe I could get a recess. "Tell Dad I'll call him as soon as I can." I rang off quickly, not wanting to absorb any of Mom's fear—I had enough of my own.

I said: "Dad's not going to make it to court today."

"Is he all right?" asked Rob.

"They're doing tests." I was trying not to cry. "What shall we do about Miranda?"

Picking up my need not to talk about Dad, he said, "Make her drink this." He poured out a mug of coffee and took it over to her. She sat up and sipped.

"We've met you before," I said. "On Easter. At Mount Davidson."

"You chased me!"

"Well, you punched me."

Unexpectedly, she laughed. "I did? I'd sort of forgotten."

"Listen, a lot of things have happened since then. Remember the man on the cross?"

She looked panicked. "Yeah. I dream about that all the time." She dropped her coffee mug, spilling coffee all over my white rug, and started sobbing—great, wrenching sobs. "I'm getting out of here." She got up and tried to run, but stumbled instead, falling back down on the couch. "What are you trying to do with me?"

"I'm the lawyer for a man accused of killing the man on the cross. Only he didn't kill him. I want to know what you know about what happened there. You might be able to save my client's life."

She stopped sobbing and sniffed. "I don't know nothing."

"Do you know a man named Les Mathison?"

Again she looked panicked—trapped, surrounded by enemies. I needed to put her at ease. "Let's try some more coffee," I said gently, and Rob brought some. "We're not going to hurt you. We just want to know what you know."

"Why should I tell you?"

"Maybe," I said, grasping at any straw that fluttered by, "you need to get it off your chest. Maybe it would help stop your dreams."

She looked up from her cup, and for the first time I saw hope on her face. "It would?"

"I don't know. It might."

"Do you have something I could put in this?"

"Cream and sugar? Sorry, I thought—"

"Some booze."

"I'm sorry. I don't have any."

"I need some."

Suddenly, I felt terribly sorry for her. Out of the blue, I blurted, "Miranda, do you really want to be an alcoholic?"

She shook her head slowly. "No." It was almost a whisper. She looked around the room. "I've never been in a place like this. We were always poor when I was a kid. I left home because it was awful—and you know where I wound up. I'd like to live in a nice place. A clean place. I'm sorry I mugged you."

"You mugged me? You're the one who mugged me?"

"I saw your ad and I got nervous."

"Wait a minute. You knew all the time who we were and what we wanted?"

"Not exactly. I was a little disoriented this morning—I am a lot of the time. But sometimes I can do things okay. Only I couldn't kill you."

"Kill me!"

"I meant to when I followed you. But I hit you once and that was all I could do. I can't do that stuff anymore."

"What stuff?" I had a sudden wild thought that Miranda was the Trapper, momentarily forgetting that she was in no condition to have planned the crimes.

She shrugged, looking very sad. "Just live the way I've been living."

"Miranda, what happened that night? The Saturday night before Easter?"

"Les and I had a fight—" Rob came in and sat down as she began to talk, the words pouring out, finally, after so many months. What she told us might save Lou and it might not. I can't say I wasn't a little disappointed, but it was certainly better than anything I had so far. And there was still a crucial question she hadn't answered. "Where is Les now?" I asked.

"I don't know. When I left Mount Davidson, I didn't go back to the hotel. I figured he'd think it was because of the fight we had the night before—about how I thought he was seeing another woman. But that wasn't it. See, I figured he'd killed the guy."

"The man on the cross."

"Yeah. And I thought if he knew I suspected, he'd kill me, too. I'm a real bad drunk, remember—I never know what I might say if I get drunk enough. So I left and pretty soon I hooked up with Mean-Mouth and he put me to work in one of those naked-lady places—to meet johns. It wasn't really too bad." She folded her hands in her lap and looked down at them. When she raised her head, she looked like a small girl trying to explain that it was okay about the way her parents beat her. "I mean, it was the best I could do. I didn't know how to do nothin' else. I didn't think I could till now. But I can't live with those dreams. I gotta do something."

She'd strayed pretty far from the subject. I said, "Did you ever see Les again?"

She looked at her lap again, not at me. "No."

"You saw my ad—you must read the paper. Didn't you think Les might be the Trapper?"

"Yes."

"Why didn't you tell the police?"

Looking down, she said, "I don't know."

Rob said, "Rebecca, it's seven-fifteen."

"I've got to be in court by nine," I said. "Will you testify, Miranda? I'll get a recess and you can do it tomorrow."

Once again the panicked look. "No. Today."

I was so shocked that she'd agreed I barely heard the demand. "You'll do it?"

"Only if I can do it today. I can't go to sleep one more time before I do it."

"Because of the dreams?"

"Yes. See, I don't dream it the way it happened."

"No?"

"In the dreams it's me on the cross."

Trying to put aside my dismay at having to present my case with green hair, I dressed while Miranda showered. I found a black suit for her to wear, blow-dried her hair, and put some makeup on her. When I was done, she looked close to respectable, though my suit hung on her gaunt frame.

It was five after eight when we left, which meant I had to speed to get to San Jose. If the CHP had caught us, we'd have been dead, but we made it just under the wire. As we drove, I was concentrating so hard on getting there, I didn't talk much, but Rob and Miranda spoke briefly from time to time. Mostly, Miranda looked out the window, a look of utter despondency on her face. As we passed the airport, Rob said, "Why do you think you have the dreams?"

"Sometimes," said Miranda, "I think it's because I deserve to die."

After that no one said a word.

Liz tried everything she could to stop Miranda's testimony, saying Miranda was a drunk, she was unreliable, she was a surprise, and thus and therefore, but the fact remained that she was most certainly a witness at the scene of the crime. And I impressed on the judge that she was sober and reliable today, but might not be so tomorrow. It was 10:30 before we got out of chambers, and the spectators were restless. Looking white and waiflike, Miranda took the stand.

A ripple went through the courtroom when I stood up. You'd have thought no one in San Jose had ever seen green hair before.

"State your name, please."

"Miranda Waring." Gasps and whispers from the spectators.

"Occupation?"

"None."

"Ms. Waring, would you describe yourself as an alcoholic?"

"Yes, I would."

"Are you sober now?"

"Yes."

"Would you tell the court how you know me, please?"

"My boyfriend got mad and tied me up. I think he was going to kill me. You found me last night and stopped him."

"Objection!" cried Liz. "Irrelevant."

"Sustained."

"Very well. Ms. Waring, had you ever seen me before that?"

"Yes. Last Easter morning—at Mount Davidson. We got into a fight."

"Did you ever know a man named Les Mathison?"

"We used to live at the same hotel in the Tenderloin. I was in love with him."

"Was he in love with you?"

She looked unhappy. "We fought a lot."

"And did you fight on the Saturday night before Easter?"

"Yes."

"Will you tell the court what happened that night?"

"He said he had to go out. We got into it because I thought he was going to meet another woman. I was pretty drunk, so I got the idea I'd hide in his car to find out for sure."

"Why did you do that? Did you plan to confront the other woman?"

"I just did it because I was drunk." Miranda turned up her palms. Sober, she had a down-to-earth way about her. "I didn't think about confronting anybody. I don't think I was thinking at all. I just got a six-pack and got under a blanket on the floor of his car, in the back. He drove somewhere and parked. When he got out, I saw we were in the Castro District—you know, where all the gays are."

The spectators tittered, as if to say they might live in the boonies, but everyone knew the Castro.

"What did you do then?"

"I got out and followed him. He went to a place called the Yellow Parrot. A gay place."

"What did you think?"

"Objection!"

"Your Honor," I said, "I'm trying to establish the witness's state of mind."

"Overruled."

"Thank you. What did you think, Ms. Waring?"

"I thought he was gay. I thought, 'Well, this explains everything. No wonder he doesn't want me.'"

"Did you notice anything odd about his appearance?"

"He was wearing a fake beard and a cowboy hat."

"What did you do when he went into the bar?"

"I bought another six pack and went back to the car and drank some more. After a while, I heard Les get in with another man."

"Did you actually see Les?"

"Oh, yes. I was on the floor on the passenger's side. So I peeked out from under the blanket and saw him. I tried to see the other man, but I couldn't."

"What were they talking about?"

"Animals."

"Animals?"

"The other guy was talking about living on a ranch. Les had grown up on one, so they were talking about animals. It was real boring."

"Can you remember any more of what they were saying?"

"Uh-uh. I fell asleep. This real loud noise woke me up, like a gunshot. I was scared, but Les was still driving—"

"You heard the noise while the car was in motion?"

"Uh-huh. Like I said, Les was still driving, so I figured everything was okay."

"Did you think the noise came from inside the car?"

"Honey, I was skunk-drunk. I didn't think anything." It took the judge a good five minutes to quiet the courtroom.

"What happened next?"

"I don't know. I fell asleep. When I woke up, the car was parked at the foot of Mount Davidson. I was just beginning to come around when I heard a noise—a crash, kind of. I got out of the car and went to see what it was. When I got to the top of the hill, I saw that man on the cross—and you trying to climb up a ladder to get at him. I thought, 'This is a murder. I better make a citizen's arrest.'" Once again the courtroom broke up. Miranda's credibility was wearing thin.

"It didn't occur to you when you heard a noise like a gunshot that that might be a murder?"

She thought about it: "The honest truth is, I don't know. I think it went through my mind, but I was on a bender."

"You were more sober when you woke up?"

"Not so's you'd notice." She waited for the laughter to die down again. "But I was definitely more sober after you chased me down that hill, and the police fired at us."

"I think they were firing at *me*, actually." This time I got a laugh. "Where did you go after you ran down the hill?"

"I had just enough money to take a bus back home—I mean back to the Tenderloin. But I was afraid to go back to the hotel."

"You never went back?"

"No."

"Did you ever see Les again?"

She looked down at her lap, as she had when I'd asked the question before, and once again answered without meeting my eyes. "No."

Suddenly I didn't believe her.

21

Other things she'd said and the way she'd said them began to come back to me. Rob and I had had only about an hour with Miranda at my place, and there hadn't been any time to think, to reflect, to analyze. I felt the way I had the night before when Mean-Mouth walked in on me—suddenly unfrozen, thoughts coming in an avalanche. I had an inkling of what I was about to do and I was terrified. I was about to ignore the first rule of being a trial lawyer: Never ask a question you don't know the answer to. It was simply not done, and yet I couldn't stop myself. Once again I was a victim of adrenaline, perhaps; Kruzick says it happens to stage actors. If Dad had been there I would have had the sense to shut up, but on two hours of sleep, after everything I'd been through, I couldn't put on the brakes.

I started out with a safe question, one I'd asked before. "Why didn't you go to the police?"

Miranda fidgeted. "I guess"—pause—"I was afraid to."

"Afraid of what, Miranda?"

She looked down again. "I don't know."

"Were you afraid of Les?"

"Yes."

"Is that why you sleep with a knife under your mattress?"

I expected Liz to pop up with objections, but she sat as tensely as anyone else in the room. She probably guessed I was floundering and was letting me hang myself. Her silence unnerved me even more than my own audacity. I was starting to sweat.

I knew Miranda well enough to recognize her panicked look, and it flickered ever so briefly before she turned sullen. She said, "Honey, I live in the Tenderloin. Doors don't lock and people come through 'em." Her voice had turned tough, which scared me even more. She was probably turning the jury against her, if they didn't already hate her for being a drunk and a bum and a prostitute. Still, I couldn't stop myself

"Several months ago I placed an ad in the *Chronicle* seeking information about your whereabouts or Les's. Did you see that ad?"

"I saw it." Her face was stone.

"And as a result of seeing it, did you follow me from my office to North Beach?"

"I don't have to talk about that."

"Your Honor," I said, "bear with me." Amazingly, the judge nodded.

"Did you tell me this morning that you not only followed me but intended to kill me?"

"I was drunk."

"You were drunk this morning?"

"No. I was drunk when I followed you."

"Why did you want to kill me?"

"I don't know why—I was drunk, that's all." She was shrieking.

"You didn't want anyone looking for Les, did you? And that's why you didn't go to the police."

She spoke loudly and bitterly: "What would I care about Les? He was a killer."

All of a sudden Liz returned, as if from the dead. "Objection!"

"Sustained. Miss Schwartz, I think you'd better tell us what you're getting at."

"I'm trying," I said, "to establish why Ms. Waring has suddenly changed her mind and decided to testify."

"Very well. Ask your question."

I turned back to Miranda and saw that her face was on the verge of crumpling. I said very gently, "You didn't go to the police before. Why are you testifying today?"

What was left of her composure fell away like cellophane wrapping. "Because I can't get drunk enough anymore," she sobbed. "Every night I dream it's me up on that cross and every day I have to fight to keep from jumping off the bridge. I could have stopped him. I could have stopped him killing all those people!"

"You knew he was the Trapper, didn't you? He threatened to kill you if you went to the police."

"No! Not then—not after Easter. I thought it was him, but I wasn't sure. If I'd gone to the police they would have caught him."

"He told you later?"

"He found me last summer—at the place where I moved to." Her voice was quiet now, still sobby, but she wasn't shouting. "He busted in and said he missed me and wanted me back. He started grabbing at me and kissing me and saying he wanted me." She burst into full sobs. "So I went to bed with him. I mean, what could I do?" She looked up at me, pleading, and I wanted to pat her and say it would be all right. My heart went out to her, but at the same time there was a little piece of it that hoped the jurors were having the same reaction.

"We made love and were just lying there in bed, and he asked me if I'd ever heard of the Trapper. I said no, I hadn't, I didn't even know what he was talking about. But Les knew me; he knew I read the paper every day, even the ads, and he said, 'You know it's me, don't you?'"

The tension in the room was like the atmosphere before a thunderstorm—you could practically smell ozone and see heat lightning.

"We were just lying there on our pillows." She dabbed at her eyes, but her voice was steady. "And he said, 'Remember the last night you saw me? I killed the first one that night.' He said he wrote to this reporter—Mr. Burns—and then he poisoned some people in a restaurant and wrecked a cable car. I knew he did all that. But then he told me he made the elevator crash at the Bonanza Inn, just a few weeks before. I didn't know he did that, because I didn't see anything in the paper about a note or phone call or anything. He said he'd already wreaked vengeance on his enemy—those were the words he used, 'wreaked vengeance on my enemy'—but I didn't know who he meant. Maybe Mr. Zimbardo, but I don't know for sure. But he said he wasn't finished. He said San Francisco was still a hellhole and he was still going to close it down, and how he was going to get revenge was he was going to make the city pay him off. He said now he'd seen to it they'd try his 'enemy' and convict him, but he could keep killing because he could pretend to be a copycat of his own self. He said he could get away with it, because now he was asking for money, which the Trapper hadn't done before. So they'd still think his enemy was the Trapper and he was a Trapper copycat, but all the same, they'd still have to pay him off to get him to stop. He thought he was real clever. He said they didn't pay attention the first time—when he bombed the elevator—but he was going to keep on trapping tourists till they had to. He used those words, too—'trapping tourists.'

"I just lay there, you know, real scared and still. Then he told me how he finally got up the nerve to call Mr. Burns—instead of just writing notes—after he wrecked the cable car and Mr. Burns asked him my name." At the recollection, her face contorted. "See, Les always called me Miranda War ing—that was his nickname for me. And that day at Mount Davidson, that was the name I gave Mr. Burns. So when he said Mr. Burns had asked him that, I knew that was why he'd tracked me down. He thought I suspected he was the Trapper and I'd told Mr. Burns about it. He came there to kill me!" She screamed the last sentence.

"How did you know that?"

"He said it! He kept saying it over and over and over." She stopped for what seemed a long time and then began again, her voice dull. "But that was later. First he rolled over like he was going to kiss me, but he didn't—he started strangling me. Then he started saying, 'I'm going to kill you, I'm going to kill you,' over and over again. He put both hands around my neck, and I tried to pull them off, but I couldn't. But then I remembered the knife under the mattress."

I was so stunned I couldn't speak for a moment; my thoughts simply wouldn't arrange themselves into patterns I could recognize. Miranda looked straight at me, not down in her lap. "He hardly bled at all," she said. "We dumped the body in the woods. Mean-Mouth and me."

22

If I hadn't been in a half stupor, it would never have happened that way. The minute Miranda mentioned the knife, I would have smelled what was coming and asked the court to appoint a lawyer for her. The lawyer would have told her to take the Fifth and she would have. But as it happens, I wasn't the only one who was too slow to stop the confession. Both Liz and the judge had as much obligation as I did to see that she didn't incriminate herself. And neither of them thought quickly enough. The judge declared a mistrial.

As soon as I could get away, I went to Marin General, where I found Dad scheduled for surgery to clean out his left carotid artery. "Just like a rusty pipe, Beck," he said. "They tell me it happens all the time, to people of a certain age. You have a little arteriosclerosis, your artery goes narrow on you, and you don't get enough blood to the language center. So who needed me, anyway? Congratulations."

He and Mom had already heard some of the story on the radio, but I filled them in on the details and watched them react in their accustomed ways—Mom having a near breakdown because I'd taken such a chance, Dad chuckling because I'd pulled it off. They could both have been furious for all I cared—my client was free and my dad was going to be fine.

The thing Dad had was called a transient ischemic attack, or TIA to the docs. It had happened to him once before, in Israel, for about ten minutes. He couldn't speak and felt weak in his right arm and face. He got worried—thinking brain tumor thoughts—and got Mom to come home quickly without really explaining why. But then, when it didn't recur at first, he got the feeling it was only his imagination. With Mom's propensity for terror, I could understand why he'd kept it to himself.

I left feeling buoyant, but the mood lasted only as long as it took me to get to my car. Up till then, I'd had Lou on my mind, and Dad. With both worries removed, my mind switched to other things, and something began to nag at me. Something that still didn't fit. I drove around a long time, thinking about it, and finally I headed toward the Golden Gate Bridge, feeling perfectly miserable. I found Art Zimbardo at Full Fathom Five.

He should have looked like the happiest man in the world, but he didn't. His smoldering eyes seemed even bigger than usual, even darker, like a raccoon's. He looked as if he'd been losing sleep. He said, "I couldn't come to court today. I haven't even talked to Lou yet."

"But you've heard what happened?"

"Yes." He tried to smile. "You got him off."

If I had any doubts about the conclusion I'd come to, his odd, distant behavior was dispelling them. I said, "Can we go somewhere and talk?"

His face was sullen. "I'm working."

"Art, do you remember what I told Lou when you two first came to me? I said I had to advise him to turn himself in. I've come to tell you the same thing."

He turned around and walked back into the kitchen. I went outside the restaurant and stood blinking in the bright sun, not wanting to follow and create a scene, but not knowing what to do. I was still standing there when Art joined me, no longer wearing his waiter's jacket. He looked about fourteen, and miserable. "You knew it was me when I called, didn't you?"

I shook my head. "No. I figured it out after court today, when I found out Les had been dead for months the day someone threw that rock on the bridge. It might have been someone who was trying to cash in on the Trapper killings—Les had that idea himself—but that didn't really make any sense at that point, with Lou right on the verge of conviction. Everyone already thought the real Trapper was behind bars and on his way to staying there. Everyone except you and me and Chris and Rob. We all thought the real Trapper was still out there somewhere. And you had a strong enough motive to commit murder yourself to spring Lou. Once I thought it might be you, I started playing with the idea. Both Rob and I had talked to the real Trapper, and he hadn't whispered. But the person who called me did. So maybe it was someone whose voice I knew—once again, you. I was surprised I hadn't thought of it before. Throwing that rock wasn't nearly as sophisticated, as well planned, as the Trapper's other crimes. It was more like an act of desperation."

"I had to do something, Rebecca! I couldn't let him die. He was the only one who was nice to me when I was a kid. It just wasn't fair."

"What wasn't?"

"He saved my life once. Maybe more than once. We had a stepfather who beat us—beat me, mostly, because I was younger. He'd get drunk and lose control—you know what I mean?"

I nodded.

"Lou stepped in and stopped him once. I ended up in the hospital with a couple of broken ribs. Another time, Lou hit him—just hit him because he was beating on me. The old man took it out on Lou."

"So you tried to save Lou's life in return."

"I thought he deserved a chance. I didn't mean to hurt anybody."

"Tell me something. Why did you ask for the money?"

"I thought if Lou got loose, he and I could go somewhere. And be rich."

I was reminded of the time more than twenty years ago, when my mother was sick and my father away on business. I thought and thought of what I could do to make things better for her and finally came up with a plan that thrilled me: I cut every flower in her garden and got Mickey to help me arrange them artfully. Nothing I'd experienced before or since had dismayed me so much as the look on her face when we bore them triumphantly into her bedroom. I knew I was going to see the same look when I talked to Lou.

MORE MYSTERIOUS PLEASURES

HAROLD ADAMS

MURDER
Carl Wilcox debuts in a story of triple murder which exposes the underbelly of corruption in the town of Corden, shattering the respectability of its most dignified citizens.   **#501 $3.50**

THE NAKED LIAR
When a sexy young widow is framed for the murder of her husband, Carl Wilcox comes through to help her fight off cops and big-city goons.   **#420 $3.95**

THE FOURTH WIDOW
Ex-con/private eye Carl Wilcox is back, investigating the death of a "popular" widow in the Depression-era town of Corden, S.D.   **#502 $3.50**

EARL DERR BIGGERS

THE HOUSE WITHOUT A KEY
Charlie Chan debuts in the Honolulu investigation of an expatriate Bostonian's murder.   **#421 $3.95**

THE CHINESE PARROT
Charlie Chan works to find the key to murders seemingly without victims—but which have left a multitude of clues.   **#503 $3.95**

BEHIND THAT CURTAIN
Two murders sixteen years apart, one in London, one in San Francisco, each share a major clue in a pair of velvet Chinese slippers. Chan seeks the connection.   **#504 $3.95**

THE BLACK CAMEL
When movie goddess Sheila Fane is murdered in her Hawaiian pavilion, Chan discovers an interrelated crime in a murky Hollywood mystery from the past.   **#505 $3.95**

CHARLIE CHAN CARRIES ON
An elusive transcontinental killer dogs the heels of the Lofton Round the World Cruise. When the touring party reaches Honolulu, the murderer finally meets his match.   **#506 $3.95**

DONALD E. WESTLAKE
THE HOT ROCK
The unlucky master thief John Dortmunder debuts in this spectacular caper novel. How many times do you have to steal an emerald to make sure it *stays* stolen?   #539 $3.95

BANK SHOT
Dortmunder and company return. A bank is temporarily housed in a trailer, so why not just hook it up and make off with the whole shebang? Too bad nothing is ever that simple.   #540 $3.95

THE BUSY BODY
Aloysius Engel is a gangster, the Big Man's right hand. So when he's ordered to dig a suit loaded with drugs out of a fresh grave, how come the corpse it's wrapped around won't lie still?   #541 $3.95

THE SPY IN THE OINTMENT
Pacifist agitator J. Eugene Raxford is mistakenly listed as a terrorist by the FBI, which leads to his enforced recruitment to a group bent on world domination. Will very good Good triumph over absolutely villainous Evil?   #542 $3.95

GOD SAVE THE MARK
Fred Fitch is the sucker's sucker—con men line up to bilk him. But when he inherits $300,000 from a murdered uncle, he finds it necessary to dodge killers as well as hustlers.   #543 $3.95

TERI WHITE
TIGHTROPE
This second novel featuring L.A. cops Blue Maguire and Spaceman Kowalski takes them into the nooks and crannies of the city's Little Saigon.   #544 $3.95

COLLIN WILCOX
VICTIMS
Lt. Frank Hastings investigates the murder of a police colleague in the home of a powerful—and nasty—San Francisco attorney.
                                                      #413 $3.95

NIGHT GAMES
Lt. Frank Hastings of the San Francisco Police returns to investigate the at-home death of an unfaithful husband—whose affairs have led to his murder.   #545 $3.95